PENGUIN

SERVITUDE AND GRA

ALFRED VICTOR, COMTE DE VIGNY, was born at Loches in 1797 and brought up in Paris. He came from an ancient military family impoverished by the Revolution, and was ill at ease with his schoolfellows from the new Napoleonic aristocracy. In 1814 he received a commission in the restored royal bodyguard, and served in the army for the next thirteen years, though he was never to take part in a serious campaign. At the same time he mixed in Parisian society, as well as being acquainted with all the prominent literary figures of the day, and becoming intimate with Victor Hugo. *Poèmes* (1822) was followed by *Éloa* (1824), in which he envisages an Angel who sins through persisting in her compassion for a creation full of cruelty. He wrote some of his most famous poetry and part of his historical novel, *Cinq-Mars*, while stationed in the Pyrenees in 1824. The poems, which include his vision of Moses as the much overburdened servant of God, were later published in *Poèmes antiques et modernes* (1826). In 1825 he married the Englishwoman Lydia Bunbury, a marriage which was to be childless. In 1827 he retired from the army as a captain and settled in Paris. His reputation as the pessimistic intellectual of the Romantic movement grew. Dramatic success came with his translation of *Othello* in 1829, and continued with his own *La Maréchale d'Ancre*, a historical drama performed at the Comédie-Française in 1831. These were followed by a short, witty piece, *Quitte pour la Peur* (1833); then by *Chatterton* (1835), his masterpiece about the doomed young poet and forger – a romantic icon. Marie Dorval, with whom Vigny was having a stormy love affair, played the part of Kitty Bell. During this period he also published *Stello* (1832), which consists of three imaginative biographies dramatizing the suffering of oppressed poetic genius under different political regimes, and then *Servitude et grandeur militaires* (1835), which contains a comparable treatment of military life.

From the late 1830s until his death in 1863 much of Vigny's life was private and melancholy, a large portion of it spent away from Paris in Maine-Giraud. His mother, always very important to him, died after a long and painful illness in 1837 and, along with his continual money worries, his wife's invalidism required his constant and selfless care. He continued to write, mainly the journals published posthumously as *Journal d'un poète* in 1867, and his fine letters. The important small volume of poems, *Les Destinées*, was also published after his death, as was *Daphné*, a fragment of fiction about Julian the Apostate. He made a few dutiful but unsuccessful attempts to enter politics, and returned to Paris in 1853. However, he remained somewhat isolated from society, in spite of the compliments of Napoleon III and the fulfilment of his duties as a member of the Académie Française. His wife died in 1862 and he outlived her by only a few months.

ROGER GARD was educated at Abbotsholme School, Derbyshire, in the Royal Artillery and at Corpus Christi College, Cambridge. He is Emeritus Reader in English in the University of London. Among his previous publications are books on Henry James, Jane Austen and the teaching of fiction in schools. He has also edited Henry James's *A Landscape Painter and Other Tales*, *The Jolly Corner and Other Tales* and a selection of his literary criticism, *The Critical Muse*, for Penguin Classics.

ALFRED DE VIGNY

Servitude and Grandeur of Arms

Translated
with an Introduction and Notes by
ROGER GARD

PENGUIN BOOKS

TRANSLATOR'S DEDICATION

for Jack and Sydney

PENGUIN BOOKS

Published by the Penguin Group
Penguin Books Ltd, 27 Wrights Lane, London w8 5tz, England
Penguin Books USA Inc., 375 Hudson Street, New York, New York 10014, USA
Penguin Books Australia Ltd, Ringwood, Victoria, Australia
Penguin Books Canada Ltd, 10 Alcorn Avenue, Toronto, Ontario, Canada m4v 3b2
Penguin Books (NZ) Ltd, 182–190 Wairau Road, Auckland 10, New Zealand

Penguin Books Ltd, Registered Offices: Harmondsworth, Middlesex, England

First published 1835
Published in Penguin Classics 1996
1 3 5 7 9 10 8 6 4 2

Copyright © Roger Gard, 1996
All rights reserved

The moral right of the translator has been asserted

Set in 10.5/12.5 pt Monotype Fournier
Typeset by Rowland Phototypesetting Ltd, Bury St Edmunds, Suffolk
Printed in England by Clays Ltd, St Ives plc

CONTENTS

Memories of Military Servitude

BOOK I

BOOK 2

Memories of Military Grandeur

BOOK 3

Servitude and Grandeur of Arms[2] is, superficially considered, a book the least likely to appeal to a modern reader of English. It is written from a specific complicated political and military situation which awakens only vague and distant echoes outside France; and it recommends a personal ethic – that of Honour – which is ancient and aristocratic in origin, though general in application, and might well, by its directness, embarrass much of that liberal segment of the world that still reads books. For them anything that savours of a military élite is likely to be suspect. Also it is the work of a most sensitive poet, the fineness of whose prose is bound to be dimmed by translation.

Nevertheless, I shall show that these appearances are nothing compared with the pleasure and edification to be got from the work if a few background considerations are remembered, and a few simple points about its nature touched on and pointed up. For it is a most admirable book, and its admirers tend to turn into its lovers.

I

First, as is very clear from his frequent apostrophes to his former comrades, Vigny was addressing, besides the general public, a large professional standing army, or rather its officer corps, which was at a crisis in its sense of identity and purpose. France had long accepted such a force within itself, a standing army, whereas England, for example, had not – at least in theory.[3] But the Revolution's initially inspiring conscription of whole populations into the army, and the massive expansion of this by Napoleon into a nation permanently under arms, perpetually marching into Empire and into legendary triumphs, was followed by years of bitter war ending in the bloody and exhausting failure in 1812–15. The result was a sort of confused nostalgia for glory, behind a backwash of bewilderment and alienation. The unease of the legitimist Bourbon Restoration, at first imposed from without, was followed by the unease, and frequent civil disorders, of the constitutional monarchy established under Louis-Philippe after the revolution of 1830.

All this is implicit in *Servitude and Grandeur of Arms*, and much of it – from Vigny's autobiographical cameos in the first chapters onwards – very frequently explicit, as is the sense that foreign wars (what we now call Defence) and foreign conquest will, in 1835, no longer provide a respectable reason for existence. The French empire in Africa had yet to offer its temptations.

Within such a rhythm the younger Vigny had thrilled to the trumpet for the Bourbon campaign in Spain in 1823, only to be put to the ennui of garrison duties on the French side of the Pyrenees, and to be involved at Pau – and this is another important motive in his argument – with the suppression of a minor revolt, or riot, by his own countrymen. The resonant melancholy of his famous line, *Dieu! que le son du cor est triste au fond des bois!*[4] is perhaps, from our standpoint, the very best thing to accrue to France from that campaign.

And, like intelligent soldiers in every age since the first exploitation of gunpowder, Vigny tended to believe that war, and therefore the rationale for the canalized brutality and violence of an army, would soon be a thing of the past. Already, he thinks, war is comparatively civilized – even though armies are not. The progress of morals and technology would – surely? – render the huge assemblage of assassins, the dangerous and 'silent colossus' feared by its masters and professionally and spiritually cut off from the civil life of the nation, even more of an anachronism than it had become in 1815, and was certainly in 1835.

To this analysis is added, both in his discursive and polemical chapters and in the stories, a pervasive sense of the sheer dreariness and deprivation of peacetime army life and discipline. Distrusted and feared outside the ranks, within them the modern soldier is bored and ground down and stunted. His only remedies are comradeship and a grim abnegation and resignation. The only hope a renewed sense of honour.

In the end, therefore, the subject tends to become the question of how the thinking individual, rather than any organization, can act now – what attitude might be the most useful in an age which has grown too old for glory.

Such, it seems, is the drift of the argument; and where they are not specified in the text, the facts to support it can easily be read in history books. It was indeed a time when Europe was recoiling from its first experience of the corrupt terrors of total war. It was a time mesmerized by the ambiguous spectre of the shattering Napoleonic years – years when the whole resources and apparatus of France, military, economic, human, legal, social and even religious, had been compelled into the service of unlimited national expansion. It was a time instead, now, for commercial and industrial entrepreneurs. A time when the remnant of chivalric ideas, formerly settled into the conventions of the honourable eighteenth-century profession of arms, jostled along uneasily at the side of more democratic and humanitarian conceptions; and when the veterans of those years, used to glory, were enforcedly idle and frustrated in defeat.

This is the situation behind Vigny's writing; it is the world of Stendhal; its problems and disaffections dominated French literature for decades: and a regretfully complacent hindsight will find the larger predictions Vigny makes on its basis obviously falsified by subsequent and much more atrocious states and wars, by military degradations the pessimistic poet could hardly have dreamed of, and by military rulers who make Napoleon look polite, moderate and humane. Falsified also by a swiftly accelerating technology having – to put it mildly – done nothing to end war *per se*.

Nevertheless such hindsight might choose to pause: to shift its focus and address itself to the present – and to the future. It might consider that it is precisely now, as the third Christian millennium lumbers into view, and when a combination of factors, characterized by what is perhaps a moral stalemate, or at least stasis, coupled with devastatingly brilliant technology, have made it possible that the big wars are finally at an end; now, when every nation has its professional forces geared up to fight or co-operate in a proliferation of little wars all over the world (often bitter civil wars, grotesquely on television); when some of these forces are a menace to the state which employs them – although not in Western Europe; and now when the decline in quality of religion in the West is not just a threat to be divined and deplored by sensitive intellectuals like Vigny but a fact which has become a commonplace – it is precisely at this point, when the conditions recur, though in distorted and exaggerated form, that we might profitably look again at his analyses and at his proposed solution to problems which were his and are now our own.

These are matters for speculation.

2

But what is not speculation is the unusual art through which Vigny suggests, proposes, insinuates and dramatizes the argument about personal honour, and the curiously subtle nature of that argument. Before considering the nature and usefulness of his conception I shall look briefly at these.

It is easy, and legitimate, to state as I have done that Vigny argues for this view or that – but the reader will soon sense a quality in the work which militates against being quite content with such glib formulation. This is something like a quality of contradiction. And it is directly traceable in the first instance to the very peculiar form of his book. Form in its most obvious sense – the overt combination of discursive argument with a kind of fiction. I know of no other work of this kind. There are, of course, many very didactic fictions. The compelling and dramatic didacticism of *Servitude and Grandeur of Arms* is one of the numerous things about it that put one in mind of, though they scarcely resemble, Tolstoy. And there are even more numerous works of suggestive social criticism. (The two will always tend to shade together because even discursive argument must proceed by metaphors, growing into examples, growing into figures – like the image of the man in the iron mask deployed early on by Vigny.) Here, however, Vigny boldly cuts through any problems in their mutual relation by flatly laying them side by side.

But what is laid side by what side? Essays and . . . fiction? In the third tale, 'The Life and Death of Captain Renaud, or, The Malacca Cane', which is the longest and certainly the best, the fictional Captain Renaud produces what is in context a provokingly sophisticated piece of criticism:

We can only be taught by experience, and by the reasoning which comes from our own observations. Consider, since you are involved in it, the uselessness of literature. What does it accomplish? – who is changed by it? – and who, may I ask, ever understands it properly? You almost always achieve a success for the cause opposite to the one you plead. For example, the most beautiful epic poem possible about female virtue has been written about Clarissa – and what's the result? Readers take the opposite view and rave about Lovelace . . . Everything goes wrong when literature tries to teach. (Book 3, Chapter 6)

These remarks, apparently undermining the context that contains them, are only the most open manifestation of a pleasing but disturbing tendency in this book. Unlike Sterne, whose manner might be said to be influential here (or in the short humorous interjected chapter, 'A Sigh', in 'An Evening at Vincennes') but whose purpose is playfulness, Vigny is very much in earnest. So what is a serious character in a didactic story doing denying his own usefulness? The short answer must be that the remark further characterizes him as the sober practical hero he has become, and further ensures that the reader keeps a distance from simple identification. But on a longer look it also points to the danger of taking any of the arguments in the book as naive productions. Immediately, it may make one inquire how far the stories include fiction at all. Not only are the big figures – Napoleon and Collingwood – and the big events near or on the periphery – the battle of the Nile, the Royal Navy blockade, the Russian campaign – historical, but, as Vigny is often at pains to emphasize, so are many of the minor ones. Ernest d'Hanache was his friend until he was killed in the second Vendée, Le Kain did create the lead role in *Irène* in 1778, there was a great explosion at Vincennes in 1819 – and so on. Vigny insists more than once on the preternatural excellence of his memory for literal detail, on his ability to recall entire the true stories which he says are the main fruit of his regretted years in the army. And for confirmation – out of the artistic context – he wrote to Louise Lachaud in 1847 that she ought to know that in this book the 'I' is not just a narrator, but really I: ' *"je"*, *c'est la vérité* '.

Yet, on the other hand, does not that well-known remark itself suggest that other parts of the book are not necessarily veracious in the same way? And this doubt will quickly be supported and multiplied by all kinds of detailed arguments that can easily be made against simple factuality: that the relations of Pope and Emperor are presented as being in 1804 what they really were in 1809 and later, that it is unlikely that a passenger on Collingwood's flagship could remember phrases from letters to the Admiral's wife – and so on. There are many more. Furthermore, and more positively, there is a definite flavour of literary genre to the stories, especially the first two, which in part read far too much like a powerful melodrama of terror on the high seas, and a weaker piece of early nineteenth-century rococo pastoral fairy-tale, for one readily to believe that they are records of pure fact as opposed to fictions within strong literary conventions.[5] – The term 'faction' springs to mind, only to be dismissed for its vulgarity.

Really, the question of literary definition is of little importance, except to tease out and suggest the kind of mixed experience a reader may expect. Thus: *Servitude and Grandeur of Arms* is a series of arguments tending to a conclusion, cast in an autobiographical mode, and conducted in a series of short emotive discourses exemplified and bodied out by three long stories based on real events, each part of which tends to link and interact with the others.

That would do. It can be improved by arguing that with this method the grand generalizations of the framing theoretical chapters and remarks are illustrated and substantiated (one could not look for proof in such cases) by the accretive effect of the dramatic episodes. – And by re-marking that the structure thus incidentally pieces together, reaching backwards and forwards in time, forwards and backwards in apparently random tableaux – 1835, 1814, 1797, 1819, 1778, 1830, 1804, 1835 – a kind of history of France, or a history of what France may be thought to have felt like, for the previous sixty years; quite a dense picture in its impressionistic sidelit way – for *Servitude and Grandeur of Arms* is also one of those short works which has an effect of bulk quite disproportionate to its length.

But to return to the most interesting result of the method – the quality in the argument which this slight epistemological uncertainty promotes. I have said that it borders on contradiction. Actually it is more properly a delicate tissue of half-contradictions which add weight and conviction both to its general structure and its intimate texture. This is not confined to the stories. Vigny himself adverts us to a characteristic of his discursive prose in his first chapter:

I . . . feel able . . . to evoke that which is attractive in the savage life of arms, harsh though it is, because I have lived so long a time between the echo and the dream of battles.

Here are the beginnings of half-contradictions, mixed feelings, qualifications: and consider how, even in translation, nostalgia and love for arms breaks through one of those addresses properly devoted to deploring the military condition:

You will remember – you, my comrades – how we never ceased to read over the *Commentaries* of Caesar, Turenne, and Frederick II, and how unremittingly we devoured the lives of those generals of the Republic so cleanly seized by Glory: those candid and humble heroes like Marceau, Desaix and Kléber, youths of an antique virtue; and how, after having studied their combat manoeuvres and their campaigns, we fell into bitter distresses comparing our destiny to theirs, and reckoning that their elevation had been so high because they had found their feet immediately, at the age of twenty, on the highest step of that ladder of promotion, each rung of which cost us eight years' climbing. You, who I have so often seen suffering the boredom and disgust of military servitude – it is above all for you that I write this book . . . (Book 3, Chapter 1)

Like Byron, Vigny was a Romantic poet in possession of an exceptionally sharp and realistic intellect, and *Servitude and Grandeur of Arms* is full of these quick alternations from the glowing to the chill, or from the pleasantly collusive to the disastrous. This is true of the detail of the prose, the structure of the arguments, and of the flow of the stories.

It is not that these ruffles and stirs defeat themselves, as would logical contradictions, but that a tension is felt between the obvious meanings of the argument, or the drama, and its underlying impulses – a sort of unstressed dialectic. One interwoven strand impinges on another, disturbs, and therefore refines it. Complexity of feeling is a nearer description than contradiction. Sainte-Beuve, who was grudging in his estimate of his erstwhile friend, complained that in him 'imagination and intelligence are always at war'. To put it even more negatively one could say that if this is a moral tract there is too much freedom in the stories; if its main purpose is the stories then there is too much overt moralization. But it is not felt like that. On the contrary it is felt as a virtue; and a virtue that, by the sense of depth it conveys, builds up belief in the truth of the argument.

The quality is most resonantly present in the stories, where a strong nostalgic affection for the conditions of military life, and moreover some of its rigours – the Major's cramped but shipshape cabin in 'Laurette', Mathurin's absurdly taxing firing drill in 'An Evening at Vincennes', the grenadiers' rock-solid night-time discipline on the boulevards in 'The Malacca Cane' – is created within narratives which purport to show, indeed do show, the grim upshots of military life. More patent is that although quite a lot is said in the discursive parts about the violence of the soldiery and the brutalizing effects of their life, the men in the stories are all more or less sympathetic. I find only one episode savage, and that is primarily concerned with remorse. – The reader will soon be acquainted with developments in Vigny's rather lofty and critical, but deeply enthusiastic, self-figuration; with the bluff tough sea-captain cum infantry major, and his finer sentiments; Vigny's quizzical and melancholy friend Timoléon, who will never receive recognition; the cosy, obstinate, over-conscientious Mathurin; the stoical master of the seas, Admiral Collingwood; and the much enduring hero, Captain Renaud. – All of them, in various ways, figures of virtue, or *virtù*. Even Napoleon, the idol whose horns and feet of clay are so devastatingly revealed to the eavesdropping boy Renaud in his great interview with the Pope at Fontainebleau, and who becomes the subject of an early critical analysis of the *Führer prinzip*, tends to elicit a feeling different from what one might expect from his position in the argument. This portrait of him must be the finest in literature. It far outdoes the doctrinaire presentation in *War and Peace*. The Emperor lives through Renaud's reactions, but also – a little like Renaud's Lovelace – in spite of his judgements; and he is created in glimpses and side glances and implications as well as by direct accounts. His final appearance in the rain outside Rheims is a most poignant piece of understatement. In fact, so far is it from being the case that the overt polemical meaning is the only one playing on the reader, that it is hardly a surprise to learn that one of the Emperor's devastating opinions which shocks the young Renaud at Fontainebleau (that the world consists in those that have and those who take) may be found, much later, in Vigny's *Journal* for 1847.

A pattern of this nature might, incidentally, be half expected from a writer whose life was such a tissue of contrast – the royalist aristocrat raised under the Revolution and Empire, the delicate poet serving as a humdrum garrison officer, the celebrated Romantic also famous for his aloof decorum and 'English' manners (who was never, according to Alexandre Dumas, seen satisfying any bodily need), the devoted son and husband who was denied children and who engaged in a stormy liaison with one of the most flamboyant actresses of the day, Marie Dorval – the seeker after glory who was never granted a campaign . . . The engrossing half-contradictions of *Servitude and Grandeur of Arms* seem to find here their mirror.

Likewise it is appropriate that the general mode of narration is one of indirection. Unlike more straightforward talkers 'I' offers his impressions, 'I' frames the tales, but the tales are told by someone else. Or told even, in the best parts of 'The Malacca Cane', by someone within that first narrative – by Renaud *père*, by Napoleon's successive presentations of himself, and by Collingwood's musings. Or the tale is taken up by another person, as in the unnamed grenadier's account of his captain. This suggestive method has the effect of the truth being arrived at, and pieced together, rather than stated authoritatively by the writer of fiction. It is part of what I meant by calling the method impressionistic, and is perhaps especially appropriate to stories which run by the side of history. There is an obvious literary heir – Conrad's father had translated Vigny's famous play *Chatterton* (1830) into Polish, and Gide later wrote to the novelist that if he were to speak of his work in public it would be 'to Alfred de Vigny' and 'to him alone, that I would wish to establish your kinship'. Beside so much that is similar in their general natures – the aristocratic pessimism, the plangent tones, the hopeful disillusion, the stoicism, and the faith in a life of service – Vigny's way of approaching a subject, teasing it out and reflecting on it, would suggest Conrad to the reader of English literature. Here is the voice, confidential in the night, of a knowledgeable man of the world, a man of action, inquisitive, hardened yet sensitive:

'How strange it is,' he said, 'that I've never told anyone of all this, yet this evening I have the desire to do so. Bah! It doesn't matter! I'm pleased to confide in an old comrade. It'll be something for you to think about seriously when you've nothing better to do. It seems to me not unworthy of that. Maybe you'll think me feeble or completely mad; but it doesn't matter.'

This is not Marlow, but Renaud. It is no surprise that in *Lord Jim* the stoically heroic French officer whom Marlow consults about Jim's failure of nerve and duty should evince every lenient and sympathetic response, but then come to the end of them: 'But the honour – the honour, monsieur! . . . The honour . . . that is real – that is! . . .' – and then depart offering no extenuation.[6]

3

Which returns us to Vigny's ultimate subject. As I have said, the reason for considering his artistic methods is to see how to apprehend his general conceptions – to see how they live. And in this light the prime purpose of the stories is, in their differing ways, to make it easy for the reader to experience sympathetically what Vigny means by honour, and the grimmer related concepts of duty, abnegation and resignation; and to know as at first hand their austere reality and heat. Aristotle is supposed to have said that the difference between poetry and history is that

. . . it is not the poet's function to describe what has actually happened, but the kinds of thing that might happen, that is, could happen because they are, in the circumstances, either probable or necessary . . . For this reason poetry is something more philosophical and more worthy of serious attention than history; for while poetry is concerned with universal truths, history treats of particular facts. (*Poetics*, 9)

Later he talks of the engagement of the emotions in art. Perhaps this is why Vigny chose to stud and illustrate his discourses with stories, and why they are still interesting after so long.

But, finally, whether Vigny's idea of honour comes alive or not is up to the reader as an individual. It is impossible in this space to do more than throw out a few personal reactions.

Flaubert was depressed by *Servitude and Grandeur of Arms* because he thought he wanted to be what Vigny calls a *Séid* (see Book 3, Chapter 4) and valued the blind devotion to a man – Napoleon – more than 'the abstract, dry idea of duty, a concept I've never been able to grasp and which does not seem to me inherent in human entrails'.[7] But twentieth-century readers may be more careful of the great dictators, and the dryness will seem less dry if we respond to the array of human figures who, it seems to me, are so beautifully evoked by Vigny.

Can we really still take Honour seriously? They did in English schools when Dr Hawtrey of Eton set his pupils to read this book in the 1840s; they still did at the military academy of Saint-Cyr in 1994 – but can the modern civilian follow? – Especially in view of the monstrous crimes committed or permitted by some European armies in the twentieth century?

For me – in that 'universal shipwreck of beliefs' of which we have not ceased to be conscious – what is so attractive in Vigny's argument is that it turns out not really to depend on strictly military values or life at all. So fine and personal a sense of rightness, while living in and respecting a social structure, is likely to be proof against becoming its slave – let alone becoming part of a totalitarian ethos, which has been the terrible fate of so many other nineteenth-century ideologies conceived in good will. Nor does it depend, with scientific pretension, on rationalizing, Enlightenment ethics – you 'can be too sane to understand the modern world', as Orwell remarked. If Vigny is right, honour is innate. And it is generalizable.

Modern men – men of the hour in which I write – are sceptical and ironical about everything else besides. But each becomes serious the moment its name is mentioned. – And this is not a theory, but an observation. – The name of Honour moves something in a man which is integral to himself . . . (Book 3, Chapter 10)

No doubt it will be argued that the response is culturally conditioned, and no doubt it applies to women equally, but one's culture and point of view are inevitably one's own, and I find it hard to deny the pragmatic force of the observation. What else is so positive? So attractive? Vigny's honour is independent of religion, though related and not hostile to it – 'like a substitute not simply an auxiliary'.[8] Contemplating it, like contemplating the chivalric ideas which are its ancestors, can be disconcerting but elating. What, in the latter case, can respectably be denied to the doctrine that one should cultivate courtesy, hardihood, courage, generosity, frankness, prowess, loyalty, magnanimity? What but the difficulty of doing so. Yet Vigny has it that honour in his sense is natural, indeed inevitable. It is not a sloppy affair, an impossible ideal: he observes with characteristic psychological acuteness that

This strange, proud virtue is animated by a mysterious vitality, and it stands erect in the midst of all our vices, blending so well with them that it is fed by their energy. (ibid.)

Surely this is realistic as well as eloquent? And is it not time that we evolved something other than mundane hedonism to invigorate our lives – even if it might mean that we have to strive for taste enough to feel its beauty?

ROGER GARD

NOTE ON THE TEXT AND TRANSLATION

The text used is that of the Garnier Edition, edited by François Germain (Paris, 1965). This collates the eight versions of *Servitude et Grandeur Militaires* extant from Vigny's lifetime: the corrected manuscript; parts which appeared in the *Revue des Deux Mondes* from 1832; the first edition of 1835; then editions of 1836, 1838, 1842, 1852 and 1857. Professor Germain bases his text on the 1857 edition, with certain emendations from earlier texts, which he lists.

No attempt has been made to pretend that this is a book of modern English prose. It is my impression that one of the pleasures in reading the translation of a classic comes from hearing behind it the ghost of the original language. So, when given the choice, I have leant towards a fairly close rendering of syntax and vocabulary, while nevertheless, I hope, making the sense plain enough, and readable.

Memories of Military Servitude

Ave, Caesar, morituri te salutant[1]

BOOK I

I

Why I have assembled these recollections

If it is true that, as the Catholic poet says, there is no greater grief than recalling a happy time in times of misery,[1] it is true also that when the soul is calm and free it finds a sort of pleasure in conjuring up periods of pain or subjection. It is this melancholy feeling that inclines me to cast a rueful look back on certain years of my life, even though these years are recent ones, and that life still not very long.

I cannot resist recording how much I have witnessed of the obscure sufferings bravely born by a race of men who are always either despised in excess or honoured in excess, according to whether nations find them superfluous or indispensable.

But it is not this sentiment alone which impels me to write, for I hope also to be able to demonstrate – by retailing details of some of the customs I have seen with my own eyes – how much anachronism and barbarity still survives in the organization of even the most modern of standing armies, where the warrior is alienated from the citizen, and where he is miserable and ferocious because he feels his condition to be offensive and absurd. It is lamentable that whilst all around us changes, the state of armies alone stagnates. Christian law once transformed the savage practices of war; but in this respect the new standards it introduced have never been pushed far enough. Prior to it, the vanquished were massacred or enslaved for life, captured towns sacked, their inhabitants hunted down and scattered; so that every state, appalled, constantly held itself ready for desperate counter measures, and the defence was as terrible as the attack. Now conquered towns have nothing to fear but financial penalties. War has become civilized, but armies have not – for not only has their unthinking routine preserved all that is bad in them, but the ambitions or the fears of governments

3

have compounded the evil by separating them increasingly from the life of the nation and putting them into a state of servitude coarser and more indolent than ever. I have little faith in sudden reforms; but I do believe in gradual amelioration. When general attention is directed to a wound, healing will soon follow. Such healing undoubtedly presents a problem difficult for the legislator to resolve, but that makes it all the more necessary to draw attention to it here. I do this now; and, if our time is not destined to find a solution, at least I will have formulated the desire for one, and in doing so perhaps lessened its difficulties. If we are ever to arrive at the time when armies and war are no more, and the earth holds but one nation, agreed at last on its social forms – something which ought to have been accomplished long ago – we cannot sufficiently speed that day when armies become one with the nation.

I have no wish to excite interest in myself, and these memoirs will consist rather of the recollections of others than my own; nevertheless I have been galled by the peculiarities of army life sharply enough and for long enough to be qualified to speak about them. It is solely to establish this melancholy authority that I say a few words about myself.

I belong to that generation born with the century, and suckled on the dispatches of the Emperor, who saw a naked blade ever present before the eyes – but became ready to grasp it only at the very moment when France returned it to the scabbard of the Bourbons. Therefore, in this little tableau of an obscure part of my life, I have no wish to appear other than what I was: to my great regret, a spectator rather than an actor. The events I sought never turned out so important as they should have been. What could one do? A man cannot always command the role he would love to play, and the costume does not always arrive at the moment when we would wear it best. Now, as I write,[2] a man who has done twenty years' service will never have seen a pitched battle. I have few adventures to tell you, though I have heard many. I shall therefore speak of others rather than myself, except when forced to call upon myself as a witness. I have always been conscious of an aversion for taking the stage, being hampered by a certain shame at the moment of doing so. But when it comes to it, I can at least promise that I shall tell the truth. – In speaking of oneself, sincerity is

4

the superior counsel. I have not the knack of sporting peacock's feathers with good grace; fine as they are, I think one must prefer one's own. Nor am I so humble, I confess, as to think I should gain much by appropriating someone else's manner, or by striking a grandiose attitude, arranged with art but uneasily maintained – and then only to the detriment of healthy natural inclinations and that bent towards the truth which is born in all of us. – I wonder if there has not been in our day some abuse of such literary posturing; it seems to me the gloomy pout of Bonaparte and of Byron has distorted many an otherwise innocent countenance.

Life is too short to waste any precious part of it in deceit. Even if one were dealing with a boorish and gullible public! – but ours has so sharp and quick an eye that it would instantly catch the model from which one took this word or that gesture, that phrase or this favourite gambit – or simply this hair style or that cut of a coat. Having first blown aside the trappings of your little charade the public ends by despising the true face, when without all the pretence it might well have taken your natural self to its heart.

Therefore I shall not play the warrior, having seen so little of war. But I do claim the right to speak of the rigorous usages of life in the army, where I was spared nothing of the fatigues or the boredom, and where my mind was tempered to an unshakeable patience by the turning of my powers inward towards solitary meditation and study. I do feel able, too, to evoke that which is attractive in the savage life of arms, harsh though it is, because I have lived so long a time between the echo and the dream of battles. I would assuredly have wasted fourteen years of my life had I not laid up profit for the future by the exercise of attentive and untiring observation. I even owe to the army insights into human nature which one could never encounter except under a uniform. There are some discoveries impossible to arrive at except through that species of disgust which would be intolerable, were one not forced by honour to tolerate it.

I have always loved to listen, having acquired the taste early as a little boy at the wounded knee of my aged father. He nurtured me from the first on the stories of his campaigns, and upon his knees I found war seated at my side. He showed me war in his wounds, war in the

pedigrees and blazonry of his ancestors, war in the huge portraits of
them in armour that hung in an old château in the Beauce. I imagined
the nobility as a great family of hereditary soldiers, and thought of
nothing better but to grow tall enough to become a soldier myself.

My father recounted his long campaigns with the profound observa-
tion of a philosopher and the grace of a courtier. Through him I became
intimately acquainted with Louis XV and the great Frederick;[3] indeed
I can scarcely be sure that I was not alive in their day, so familiar did
I become with them from a wealth of stories about the Seven Years
War.[4]

For Frederick II my father had that kind of enlightened admiration
which appreciates high talents without being superstitiously overawed
by them. He impressed me from the first with the good sense of this
attitude, teaching me also that immoderate enthusiasm for their illustrious enemy had been the fault of the officers of his time; that they had
been already half conquered by it when Frederick, his powers enhanced
by French exaltation of them, advanced; that the frequent quarrels of
the three powers between themselves, and the disagreements of the
French generals, had contributed to the brilliant success of his arms,
but that his greatness had resided above all in a perfect knowledge of
himself, a just valuation of the elements of his own superiority, and the
capacity to carry off the honours of victory with the modesty of a wise
man. He sometimes seemed to think that Europe had treated him with
consideration. My father had seen this philosopher king at close quarters
on the field of battle, where his brother, the eldest of my seven uncles,
had been struck down by a cannon ball; he had been often received
with a positively French politeness by the King within the Prussian
tents, and had heard him speak of Voltaire and play on the flute after
winning a battle. I detail these things at length here, almost in spite of
myself, because this was the first portrait of a great man to be presented
to me, within my own family and from the life, and because my admiration for it was the first symptom of my futile passion for the life of
arms, the first cause of one of the most complete illusions of my life.
The portrait still glows in my memory in the most vivid colours – a
picture of a physical presence as much as anything else. The hat tilted
over the powdered brow, the stoop-shouldered way of riding, the great

6

eyes, the mouth both mocking and severe, the cane shaped like a crutch – nothing of all this was not familiar to me; and, after these stories, I could only observe with contempt that Bonaparte adopted a similar hat, snuffbox and mannerisms. He seemed to me at first a plagiarist; and who knows whether the great man was not in fact, in this respect, something of that? Who knows how to judge how much of the play actor enters into all men who are constantly on view to the public? And was not Frederick II the prototype of the great modern fighting tactician, military organizer and philosopher king? – Such were the first ideas that excited my mind as I participated in that past age, which was related to me with such verisimilitude, and so filled with salutary lessons. I can still hear my father's irritation at the bickerings between Soubise and M. de Clermont;[5] still hear his bitter indignation at the intrigues in the Œil de Bœuf[6] which led the French generals to fail in support of each other on the battlefield, preferring the defeat of the army to the triumph of a rival; and I am still moved by his old friendship for M. de Chevert and for M. d'Assas,[7] with the latter of whom he had been in camp on the night of his death. The eyes that had seen these men projected their image into mine, together with those of many other celebrated figures dead long before I was born. Family recitals have the especial excellence that they engrave themselves on the mind much more deeply than does the written word; they live with the life of their venerable narrator, and they project our existence back into the past just as a prophet's imagination can project it forward into the future.

Perhaps one day, for myself, I shall write down all the intimate details of my life, but now I wish to speak of one alone of the preoccupations of my mind. Sometimes a soul tormented by the past and expecting little of the future gives way easily to the temptation of amusing idle people by revealing the secrets of his family and the mysteries of his heart. I know that some writers have taken pleasure in exposing the innermost regions of their lives, and even their intimate consciousness, to all who care to look, opening up and flooding with sudden light a tumbled glut of personal memories and cherished faults. Among such are some of the best-written books in our language, and they will live amongst us like those wonderful self-portraits Raphael never stopped painting. Those who have represented themselves in this way, whether behind a disguise or barefaced, had a right to do so; in other cases I think that one should not make these confessions public before being old enough, famous enough, or repentant enough to merit an entire nation becoming interested in one's sins. Until then one can only pretend to be useful through one's ideas or one's actions.

As the Empire drew to an end I was a distracted schoolboy. War stirred throughout the school, the drum drowned out the master's lessons from my ears, and the mysterious voices of books spoke only in frigid and pedantic tones. To our eyes logarithms and figures of speech were merely steps by which to climb up to the star of the Legion of Honour[8] – which was to us children the most brilliant star in the heavens.

No subject of study could long hold the attention of heads made giddy by cannon fire and the bells of the *Te Deum*. When one of our brothers, a few months out of college, reappeared in hussar's uniform with his arm in a sling, we blushed to be at our books and hurled them at the heads of our masters. The masters themselves constantly read out to us the bulletins of the Grand Army, and our cries of '*Vive l'Empereur!*' cut through Tacitus and Plato. Our instructors were like heralds-at-arms, our classrooms like barracks, our recreations manoeuvres, and our examinations military reviews.

Then more than ever I conceived an inordinate passion for martial glory; a passion all the more unfortunate because this was precisely the time, as I have said, when France began to cure herself of it. But the storm still rumbled on, and neither the severity, the rigour and rude compulsion of my over-precocious studies, nor the bustle of the great world into which – in an effort to distract me from this determination – I was thrown while still adolescent, were able to remove my obsession.

Often and often have I smiled with pity at myself in contemplating how violently an idea sweeps us away, how it makes us its creature, and how long a time it takes to play itself out. Satiety itself has only allowed me occasionally to disobey this passion, not to destroy it in myself – and this very book shows how I still take pleasure in dallying with it, and that I am never far away from its resurgence. So very deep are the impressions of childhood, and so deeply graven on our hearts was the burning sign of the Roman Eagle!

It was not until much later that I realized that my military service was nothing but a long mistake, and that I had brought to the life of action an entirely contemplative nature. But I had followed the tide of the generation of the Empire, which was born with the century, and to which I belong.

War seemed to us so very natural a state for our country, that when, freed from the classroom, we poured ourselves into the army along the familiar course of the torrent of those days, we found ourselves unable to believe in a lasting calm of peace. It appeared to us that we risked nothing in our seeming idleness, since inaction was not a serious threat in France. This impression endured with us throughout the length of the Restoration. Each year brought hope of a war; and we dared not put down the sword, for fear lest the day of our resignation should be the eve of a campaign. So we trained and thus lost precious years, conjuring up the field of battle on the Champ-de-Mars,[9] and exhausting our formidable and futile energies with parade exercises and in personal feuds.

Overcome at last with the unforeseen boredom attendant on a life I had so ardently desired, I found it necessary to steal away in the nights from the vain exhaustions of the military day. Out of these nights, where I built in silence on that knowledge which I had gleaned from my noisy public studies, issued my poems and my books. Out of those days there remain to me memories, the salient points of which I will here organize around an idea. For, having abandoned the quest of glory through arms, either now or in the future, I searched for it in the reminiscences of my comrades. The little experience that came my own way makes only a frame for the resulting pictures of military life and of the customs of our armies – the features of which are so ill understood.

2

On the character of armies in general

The army is a nation within the nation; and this is a weakness of our times. In antiquity it was otherwise: then each citizen was a warrior, and each warrior a citizen; men at arms had a bearing no different from that of men of the city. Fear of the gods and of the laws, fidelity to the motherland, austerity of morals, and – most remarkably – a love of peace and order, were found even more in camps than in towns, because they were inhabited by the élite of the nation. For these intelligent armies the works of peace were even more redoubtable than those of war. It was by armies that the land was covered with monuments or furrowed with great roads; and the cement of the Roman aqueducts was kneaded – just as Rome herself was built – by the hands that defended her. The periods of quiet for those soldiers were as fruitful as those of our own are sterile and injurious. Citizens felt neither amazement at their valour nor contempt for their idleness, because the same blood that was in the veins of the nation circulated constantly in the veins of the army.

In the Middle Ages and later, up to the end of the reign of Louis XIV, the army still partook of the whole nation – if not through every soldier, at least through their commanders. A soldier was the noble's own man, recruited by him on his land, led to the army in his retinue, and dependent on him alone: and his lord, as a landowner, had his being at the very heart of the mother nation. Subject to the encompassing popular influence of the Church he could not do otherwise, during the Middle Ages, than devote his body and his belongings to his country. Often in conflict with the Crown, he was ceaselessly struggling against a hierarchy of powers which would have intruded excessive abasement into obedience, and, consequently, humiliation into the profession of arms. The regiment belonged to the colonel, the company to the captain, and both knew perfectly well how to lead their men away from the field if the orders they received as soldiers conflicted with their conscience as citizens. This independence of the army in France lasted up to the time of M. de Louvois,[10] who was the first to subject it to a bureaucracy, and convey it, bound hand and foot, into the hands of the sovereign power. He met with no little resistance, and the last defenders of the gallant freedom of military men were those tough and plainspoken gentlemen who would lead their band of dependants into the army only if they must go to war. And then, even though they had not passed the years dinning incessant arms drill into automatons, I observe that they and their men acquitted themselves pretty well on the battlefields under Turenne.[11] In particular they loathed uniform – which by making every-one look alike subdues the spirit to the insignia and not to the man. But they were well enough content to dress in scarlet on the day of battle, the better to be recognized by their own side, and the better to be picked out by the enemy. I love to recall, on the authority of Mirabeau,[12] the old marquis de Coëtquen, who, rather than appear in uniform at the King's review, let himself be broken by him at the head of his regiment: – 'Fortunately, Sire, the pieces still belong to me,' said he afterwards. To address Louis XIV like that was an achievement.

I am not ignorant of the thousand organizational defects that died out at the same time: but I would still say that their system possessed a quality superior to ours which allowed the warlike and patriotic fires of France to glow and blaze out with greater freedom. An army such as that was a very strong and complete suit of armour in which the motherland clothed the sovereign power; but, should that power try to use it against the motherland, all its pieces were able to take themselves off and away, one after the other.

The fate of a modern army is completely different, and the centraliz-ation of power has made it what it is. It is a body separated from the greater body of the nation – and it resembles the body of an infant in that its intelligence is retrograde, forbidden to grow up. As soon as it ceases to be at war a modern army becomes a sort of constabulary. It feels ashamed of itself, and knows neither what it should do, nor what it is; it constantly asks itself whether it is the slave of the state or its highest manifestation: it is a body that seeks everywhere for its soul and never finds it.

The enlisted man, the soldier, is a glorious pauper, both executioner and victim, a scapegoat daily sacrificed to his people and for his people – who amuse themselves with him. He is a martyr, at once ferocious and humble, thrown back and forth in the perpetual strife between government and nation.

How many times, when I have had to take an obscure but active part in our civil disturbances, have I felt my sensibilities outraged by this cruel condition of inferiority! How many times have I compared it to the condition of a gladiator. The public is an unconcerned Caesar, a sniggering Claudius, before whom the soldiers defile, chanting without end: *Those who are about to die salute you.*[13]

When a few workers, becoming the more miserable the more they increase their labour and output, begin to riot against their overseers; or when some manufacturer has the dream of adding a few hundred thousand a year to his income; or simply when some coming town, jealous of Paris, wishes to have its own three days of gunfire – then cries for help arise from each side. The government, whatever it is, replies sensibly enough: *The law doesn't allow me to judge between you; everybody has a case; as for me, all I can do is to send in my gladiators, who will kill you, and whom you will kill.* So they go, they kill, they are killed. Peace returns; people embrace and compliment each other, and hunters of small game congratulate themselves on their marksmanship in front of the officers and soldiers. The reckoning done, there remains a simple debit of a few dead; but soldiers are not included in this number, they do not count. One hardly worries about them. It is agreed that those who die in uniform have neither father, nor mother, nor wife, nor sweetheart to expire in tears at their loss. It is anonymous blood.

Sometimes, quite frequently now, the two opposing parties unite in order to heap hatred and contempt on the unfortunates who were condemned to conquer them.

So the impulse that will rule this book is that which made me begin it, the desire to avert from the soldier's head the curse that the citizen is all too apt to throw at him, and to call down upon the army the forgiveness of the nation. There is one thing that is nearly as fine as inspiration, and that is devotion: after the poet, the soldier. It is not his fault if he is condemned to the condition of a slave.

The army is blind and mute. It strikes down whatever is put in front of it. It has no desires, and acts by rote. It is a great machine which is set in motion, and kills. But it is also a machine that can suffer.

This is why I have always spoken of it with involuntary tenderness. We are now thrown into terrible times when, one after another, the towns of France have become battlefields – and for some time now we have had much to forgive the men who kill.

In looking closely at the life of these armed troops who are daily forced on us by successive governments, we shall certainly find it is true that – as I have said – a soldier's existence is (except for the death penalty) the saddest relic of barbarism that subsists among men; yet also that no body better deserves the concern and the affection of the nation than this family of victims who confer on it, sometimes, so much glory.

3

Of the servitude of the soldier and his individual character

The everyday words of our language sometimes have a perfect aptness of sense. To obey or command in an army really is to serve. We may lament this servitude, but we should admire its slaves. All of them accept their destiny in every consequence, and, especially in France, acquire extremely promptly the qualities demanded by the military condition. All the spontaneity natural to them melts away at a stroke, giving way to an indefinable state of dejection and dismay.

The life is dull, monotonous, hidebound. Its hours are as hollow and sombre as the drum beat that sounds their passing. Gait and demeanour are as uniform as dress. The vivacity of youth and the deliberation of maturity end by taking on an identical look, the look of the *forces*. The *forces* in which one *serves* are the mould into which a character is thrown – and there re-stamped to a common pattern, which is impressed on it for ever. The man disappears under the soldier.

Military discipline is weighty and unbending like the iron mask on the nameless prisoner, and gives every man of arms a uniform expression of rigidity.

Thus merely glancing at a corps of troops one notices that boredom and discontent are the typifying characteristics of the soldier's appearance. Fatigue adds its furrows, the sun its yellow stains, and a face at thirty is ploughed by premature age. Nevertheless a single idea common to them all frequently lends a majestic character to this forbidding mass of men, and this is the idea of *abnegation*. The abnegation of the warrior is a cross heavier than that of the martyr. To understand its grandeur and its weight it is necessary to have borne it a long time.

It must truly be that sacrifice is the finest thing on earth, since it manifests so much beauty through simple men, who usually have no

14

idea of their merits or of the meaning of their existence. It is this which ensures that out of a life of boredom and restriction there comes, as if by a miracle, a character formed by artifice, but generous, whose lineaments are as grand and fine as those on an antique medal.

The complete self-abnegation of which I speak, the continual and unconcerned expectation of death, the complete renunciation of the freedom to think and act, the impediments imposed on petty ambitions, and the impossibility of acquiring wealth – these produce virtues which are much less common amongst freer and more active classes of men.

In general the soldier's character is simple, good and patient; and one finds something childish in it, because regimental life somewhat resembles school life. The traits of roughness and melancholy which obscure it are imprinted by boredom, but above all by a permanently false position in regard to the nation, and by the necessarily factitious nature of authority.

If a man exercises absolute authority it constrains him to a perpetual reserve. He cannot unbend in front of his inferiors without allowing them a familiarity which will prejudice his power. He denies himself relaxation and friendly conversation from fear that some indiscretion about his life should be used against him, or some weakness set a bad example. I have known officers who shut themselves up into silence like a Trappist, and whose severe lips never ruffled their moustaches except to give passage to a command. Under the Empire this countenance was common to nearly all higher-ranking officers and generals. The example had been given by the master, the custom was rigorously preserved, and with good reason. For to the essential matter of avoiding familiarity was superadded the further need to conserve the dignity of veteran experience in the eyes of a much better instructed youth – those who were conveyed ceaselessly from the military schools, and who arrived bristling with science and the prizewinner's self-assurance, and whom only silence could discipline.

I have never loved young officers as a breed, even when I was one of them. An obscure instinct for truth told me that in all things theory counts for nothing compared with practice, and the grave and silent smile of veteran captains put me on my guard against all that trifling knowledge which can be acquired in a few days' reading. In the

regiments in which I served, I loved to listen to the old officers whose
bent backs still had the look of the back of a trooper loaded with a pack
full of clothes and a box full of cartridges. They told me well-worn tales
of Egypt, Italy and Russia, which taught me more than the Ordinance of
1789, the Army Regulations and all those interminable Instructions,
starting with those of Frederick the Great to his generals. By contrast
I found something wearisome in the confident conceit, idleness and
ignorance of the young officers of that time – eternal smokers and
players, concerned only with the exactitude of their turnout, connoisseurs of the cut of a coat, orators of the café and the billiard saloon.
Their conversation had nothing in it to distinguish it from that of
ordinary smart young men of the world, except that its banalities were
a little more gross. In order to derive some benefit from my surroundings
I lost no opportunity listening; and most often I awaited the hours
of the regular daily strolls when the older officers liked to mull over
their memories. For their part they had no objection at all to impressing
the individual stories of their lives on my mind, and – finding in me a
patience equal to their own and a silence as serious – they always
showed themselves prepared to confide in me. We often walked of an
evening in the fields, or in the woods around the garrison, or on the
sea-shore, and the overall prospect of the landscape or one of the details
of terrain would call forth inexhaustible memories: a naval battle, a
famous retreat, a fatal ambush, an infantry fight, a siege – and, running
through these, nostalgia for the dangerous past, respect for the memory
of a great general, or a naive recognition of some obscure name they
believed to be famous: and in everything a touching simplicity of heart
which filled mine with a kind of veneration for this manly character,
forged in continual adversity, and in the dubieties of a false and contrary
condition.

I have the – often painful – gift of a memory which time never alters:
my whole life, every day of it, is present to me as an ineffaceable picture.
The lines never become confused; the colours fade not at all. Some of
these are dark, and never lose their power to afflict me. But some flowers
are found there too, the petals of which are as fresh as on the day they
saw the light – especially when my eyes drop an involuntary tear and
bestow on them a heightened glory.

The most trifling conversations of my life are present to me the instant I invoke them, and if I wished to tell stories which had only artless truth to recommend them I would have too much to say; but, filled with a friendly pity for the misery of armies, I shall choose from my memories those which appear to me likely to provide a vestment suitable to my chosen theme, with a form worthy of enveloping it, and able to show just how many circumstances inimical to the development of character and intelligence derive from the gross servitude and the backward customs of standing armies.

Their crown is a crown of thorns, and, amongst its spikes, I can think of none more doleful than that of passive obedience. So this is the first whose sting I shall try to make felt by the reader. I shall treat of it to begin with because, in tracing through the course of my experience, it furnishes me with the first example of the cruel necessities of the army. When I delve back into my most distant memories there comes into my mind a story from the infancy of my army days which I will recount just as it was told to me – neither seeking out nor avoiding in the telling the minute details of the military life or character, both of which, I cannot often enough repeat, lag behind the general spirit and progress of the nation, and are, as a result, stamped always with a certain puerility.

4

Of an encounter I had one day on the high road

The high road to Artois and Flanders is long and melancholy. It runs in a straight line, without trees and without ditches, through a flat countryside perpetually full of yellow mud. In the month of March 1815 I travelled along this road and had an encounter I have never forgotten.

I was alone, I was on horseback, I had on a fine white cloak, a red tunic, a black helmet, pistols and a great sabre; it had been pelting with rain for four days and four nights, and I remember that I sang *Joconde*[14] at the top of my voice. I was so young! – In 1814 the Royal Household had been filled with children and dotards; the Empire seemed to have taken the men and killed them.

My comrades were ahead of me on the road, in the retinue of King Louis XVIII; I saw their white cloaks and red tunics far on the horizon to the north; Bonaparte's lancers, who watched and followed our retreat step by step, showed the tricoloured pennant on their lances from time to time on the opposite horizon. A cast shoe had delayed my horse: he was young and strong, and I spurred him on to rejoin my squadron; he broke into a full trot. I put my hand to my belt, which was well lined with gold; I heard the ring of my iron scabbard against the stirrup, and I felt very proud and perfectly happy.

Still it rained, and still I kept singing. But before very long I quietened down, tired with hearing nothing but my own voice, and became aware only of the rain and the hoofs of my horse splashing in the ruts. The paving of the road was faulty; we began to flounder and I had to slacken to a foot-pace. My top boots were coated outside with a thick crust of yellow mud, like ochre; inside they began to fill with rain; I looked at my brand new gold epaulettes, my comfort and my joy – they had been made all shaggy by the water, which upset me.

My horse lowered his head; I did the same: I began to reflect, and asked myself for the first time where I was going. I had absolutely no idea; but that did not preoccupy me long: I was certain that where my squadron was, so there too lay my duty. And since at heart I felt a profound and unalterable calm, I gave thanks to the ineffable sentiment of Duty – and I sought to understand it. Having witnessed at first hand the way in which unheard of fatigues were cheerfully borne by young heads and old alike, and the cavalier fashion in which an assured future was put at risk by so many successful and worldly men – and now partaking myself in the miraculous satisfaction given to every man by the conviction that he cannot evade even the slightest obligation due to honour – I realized that *abnegation* is something easier and more generally felt than one might think.

I asked myself whether the abnegation of self was not an instinct born within us; and then asked what was the true nature of this need to obey and to put one's will into the hands of others, as though it were something onerous and irksome; from whence came the secret happiness at being relieved of the burden, and why it was that human pride never rebels against this.

I saw well enough the mysterious instinct that binds peoples everywhere into corporations more powerful than the individual, like a fasces. But nowhere did I see so complete and so formidable a renunciation of actions, words and desires, almost even of thought, as in the armies. Everywhere else I saw the possibility of resistance, and its exercise – the citizen having, wherever he is, an observant and intelligent obedience which discriminates and can pull him up short. I saw too that even the tender submission of a woman ends when she is ordered to do wrong, and that the law will take up her defence. But military obedience, at once passive and active, receiving an order and carrying it out, striking with blind eyes, like Fate in the ancient world! I pondered the possible consequences of the soldier's abnegation, without mitigation, without recall, and leading sometimes to awful duties.

Such were my thoughts as I continued at the pace chosen by my horse, glancing at my watch, and seeing the road stretching away, always in a straight line, without a tree and without a house, and cutting the plain up to the horizon like a great yellow stripe on a grey cloth.

Sometimes this watery stripe would melt into the watery earth which surrounded it, and when a slightly less feeble daylight lit up the melancholy tract of land I envisaged myself as in the midst of a muddy sea, following a current of mire and chalk.

Gazing attentively along the yellow stripe of road, I noticed a small black spot which moved, about a quarter of a league away. I was pleased – here was someone else. I kept my eyes on it. I saw that like me the black spot was travelling in the direction of Lille, and that it went in zig-zag – which indicated difficult going. I increased my pace and gained ground on this object, which lengthened and grew bulkier to my sight. On firmer ground I got back to a trot, and I thought I could make out a sort of little black vehicle. I was hungry, and, hoping that it might be a sutler's cart, I imagined my poor horse to be a longboat, and made him row full speed ahead to reach this blessed isle in a sea which engulfed him sometimes up to his belly.

At a hundred paces I could clearly make out a little wagon of white wood, with three hoops over it covered with black oilcloth. It looked like a small cradle on two wheels. The wheels were embedded in mud up to their axle; and the little mule which drew it was being painfully led along by a man on foot holding its bridle. I approached and looked at him curiously.

He was a man of about fifty, big and strong, with white moustaches, his back bowed in the manner of infantry officers who have carried a pack. He was in uniform, and one could glimpse a battalion major's epaulette under his threadbare short blue cloak. He had a hard but kindly face, of which there are so many in the army. He gave me a sidelong look from under his large black brows, then smartly grabbed a gun from his cart, which he cocked as he stepped to the other side of his mule, using it as a rampart. Since I had seen his white cockade, I thought it enough to show him the sleeve of my red tunic,[15] and he put his gun back into the cart, saying:

'Ah! that's different, I took you for one of those clever lads who're running after us. Will you take a nip?'

'I'd be glad to,' said I coming up to him. 'It's twenty-four hours since I had anything to drink.'

From his neck hung a very finely carved coconut, made into a flask with a silver mouthpiece, of which he seemed rather proud. He handed it to me, and I drank some poor white wine with great pleasure; then I gave him back the nut.

'The King's health!' said he, drinking. 'He made me an officer of the Legion of Honour,[16] so it's only fair that I see him to the frontier. But then, as I've only my commission to live on, I shall take up my battalion again – it's my duty.'

Talking thus, almost as if to himself, he put his little mule into motion once more, remarking that we had no time to lose; and, since I agreed with him, I too started again on the road, a couple of paces behind. I continued to look at him, but asked no questions, never having cared for the idle prattle so common amongst us.

We proceeded without speaking for about a quarter of a league. As he then halted to rest his poor little mule, whose state it gave me pain to see, I stopped also and tried to squeeze the water out of my riding boots, which were like two cisterns in which I was bathing my legs.

'Your boots are starting to grip your feet,' he said.

'I haven't had them off for four nights,' I replied.

'Bah! in eight days you won't even notice them,' said he in his hoarse voice; 'but it's quite something to be on your own in the times we live in. Any idea what I've got in there?'

'No,' I replied.

'A woman.'

'Oh,' I said without too much astonishment, and calmly started again at a foot-pace. He followed.

'That rotten little barrow there didn't cost me much,' he resumed, 'nor did the mule. But it's all I need, though this road here is a *pigtail's ribbon*[17] too long.'

I said that he might ride on my horse when he was tired, and since I spoke seriously and simply about his equipage, about which he feared ridicule, he suddenly put himself at ease and coming closer to my stirrup, tapped me on the knee and said:

'Well, you're a good lad, even if you are in the Reds.'

In the bitter tone he used in referring thus to the four Red Companies

I sensed just how much envious prejudice the good living and easy promotions enjoyed by this corps of officers had caused within the army.

'However,' he added, 'I won't accept your offer because, me, I don't know how to ride and it's not my business.'

'But, Major, senior officers like you have to.'

'Bah! Once a year for an inspection, and then on a hired horse. Me, I've always been a sailor, and since then a foot soldier – I don't understand riding.'

He continued for twenty paces looking at me sideways from time to time as if expecting a question: and when no word came, he continued:

'You're not very curious, I must say! – it ought to astonish you, what I just said.'

'I'm not often astonished,' said I.

'Oh! well, if I were to tell you how I came to quit the sea, we'd see.'

'All right,' I took him up, 'why don't you try it? It'll warm you up, and make me forget that the rain is running down my back and not stopping till it reaches my heels.'

So the good major prepared to talk, solemnly, with a childlike pleasure. He readjusted the oilcloth covering the shako on his head, then gave that brisk shrug of the shoulders which is impossible to picture if one has not served in the infantry, the shrug which a foot soldier gives to his pack to hitch it up and lighten the weight for a moment – a ranker's habit that, after he becomes an officer, remains as a tic. After this convulsive movement he drank a little more from his coconut, gave the stomach of his little mule a kick of encouragement, and began.

5

The story of the red seal

'You ought to know first of all, my boy, that I was born in Brest; and because my father was in the Guards I started out as a boy soldier, earning my half-ration and half-pay from the age of nine. But I loved the sea, and one fine night when I was on leave in Brest I hid myself deep in the hold of a merchantman bound for the Indies; I wasn't discovered until we were right out at sea, and the captain preferred making me a ship's boy to throwing me in the water. By the time of the Revolution I'd made my way pretty well, and was in my turn captain of a trim little merchant ship, having scoured the seas for fifteen years. When the old Royal Naval Service – a fine old Service, by God! – found itself bled of officers all of a sudden, they took on captains from the Merchant Marine. I'd had a few brushes with pirates I can tell you about later, so they gave me command of a brig-of-war called the *Marat*.[18]

'On the 28th Fructidor 1797[19] I received an order to get under way for Cayenne. I had to take sixty soldiers there, together with a deportee who'd been left behind from out the hundred and ninety-three taken aboard the *Décade* a few days previously. My orders were to treat this individual with discretion, and the first letter from the Directory enclosed a second, sealed with three red seals, of which the middle one was enormous. I was forbidden to open this letter before reaching the first degree latitude north, between the twenty-seventh and twenty-eighth of longitude – which is to say, just before the Equator.

'This big letter had a very peculiar look. It was long, and sealed so tightly that I couldn't make out anything between the folds or through the cover. I'm not superstitious, but it frightened me, this letter. I put it in my cabin, under the glass of a nasty little English pendulum clock which hung on a nail over my bed. This bed was a real sailor's bed – you know the kind of thing. But, hold on, I'm not thinking what I'm saying! – you can't be more than sixteen and you'll never have seen one!

'A queen's chamber couldn't be more neatly arranged than is a sailor's cabin – and that's said with no wish to boast. Everything has its little place or its little nail to hang on. Nothing can move about. The ship can roll as much as it likes without upsetting anything. The furniture is made to fit the shape of the ship and the narrow cabins. My bed was a chest. When it was open I slept in it; when it was closed it was my sofa and I smoked my pipe there. Sometimes it was my table, and then one sat on two little casks that were provided. My flooring was waxed and polished like mahogany, and shone like a jewel – a real mirror! Oh! it was a fine little cabin! And the brig was quite something as well. We often had some high old times, and this voyage started off pretty agreeably too, if it hadn't been . . . But I mustn't anticipate.

'We had a fair wind nor'-nor'-west, and I was busy putting that letter under the glass of my clock, when my deportee came into my cabin. He was hand in hand with a pretty little girl of about seventeen years old. He told me that he was nineteen; a handsome lad, though rather pale, and too fair for a man. But nevertheless he was a man, and a man who conducted himself when occasion demanded better than a lot of his elders would have done – as you'll see. He held his young wife by the arm; she was as fresh and blithe as a child. They were like two turtle doves. Myself, it gave me pleasure to see them. I said to them:

' "Well, my children, you've come to visit the old captain! That's nice of you. I'm taking you quite far away; but so much the better, we'll have time to get to know one another. I'm grieved to receive Madam without my coat on, but it's that I'm nailing up this brute of a letter here. Perhaps you'd care to give me a bit of help?"

'They really were fine little folk. The little husband took the hammer, and the little wife the nails, and they passed them to me as I required; and she said, "To the right! to the left! Captain!", laughing away because the pitching of the ship made my clock swing about. I can hear it now, her little voice: "To the right! to the left! Captain!" She was making fun of me. – "Ah!" said I, "you wicked little thing! I'll get your husband to scold you, you'll see." Then she flung herself on his neck and kissed

24

him. They were really charming, and that was how we got to know each other. We soon became excellent friends.

'It was a good passage, too. The weather behaved as though it'd been made to order. Since I usually never had any but grim faces aboard, I made my two little lovers dine with me every day. It cheered me up. When we had eaten our biscuit and fish, the little wife and her husband would sit and gaze at one another as if they had never seen each other before. Then I would burst out laughing heartily, and tease them. They laughed with me. You would have laughed as well to have seen us, three imbeciles not knowing what was going on. It really was pleasant to see them in love like that! They found everything around them good; they found everything that one gave them good. Nevertheless they were on the same rations as the rest of us; I added only a little Swedish spirits when they dined with me – a little glass – to show the dignity of my rank. They slept in a hammock, rolling with the ship like these two pears I've got here in a moist handkerchief. They were lively and happy. I behaved as you do, and didn't ask any questions. What need had I to know their name and their business – me, their shipper? I was taking them across the sea, just as I'd take two birds of paradise.

'I ended up, after a month, looking upon them as my own children. At any time, when I called them, they'd come and sit with me. The young man would write at my table – that is to say on my bed; and when I asked him, he'd help me plot our position: he soon knew how to do it as well as I, so that I was astounded sometimes. The young woman would seat herself on a little cask and get on with her sewing.

'One day, while they were sitting like that, I said to them:

' "D'you realize, my little friends, that as we sit here we look like a family group? I don't want to question you, but you probably have no more money than you need, and you're too finely made, both of you, to ply the spade and pickaxe as deportees to Cayenne must do. I can tell you frankly, it's a villainous country – but I, an old sea-dog dried up with the sun, could live there like a lord. If you have, as it seems to me – without wanting to press you – some little bit of a liking for me, I'd willingly quit my old brig, which is a bit of a tub anyway nowadays, and settle down there with you – if it'd suit you. Myself, I haven't any more family than a stray dog, which grieves me. You would be a little company for me. I could help you in lots of ways; and I've got together a fair bundle of more or less honest loot, which we could live on, and which I'd leave to you when I come to turn up my eyes, as they say in polite circles."

'They sat staring at one another with complete astonishment, looking as if they couldn't believe I'd truly said this. And the little lass ran, as she always did, to throw herself on the neck of her husband, and then sat on his knee, all blushing and crying. He held her very tight in his arms, and I saw tears in his eyes too. He held out his hand to me and became even paler than usual. She whispered to him, her long fair hair falling over her shoulders; her chignon had come undone like a cable unwinding all of a sudden – for she was as lively as a fish. That hair! – if only you could have seen it! It was like gold. As they continued to whisper, the young man kissing her forehead from time to time and she weeping, I began to get impatient.

' "Well, how does it strike you?" I said to them at last.

' "But . . . but, Captain, you are very good," said the husband "but it's . . . you couldn't live with *deportees*, and . . ." He lowered his eyes.

' "Myself," said I, "I don't know what you've done to be deported, but you'll tell me that some day – or never, as you like. You don't have the look of a man with much of a burden on his conscience, and I'm pretty sure I've done worse than you have in my time! – come on, my poor innocents! Anyway, so long as you're my prisoners I shan't let you go, and you mustn't look for it; I'd sooner cut your throats like a brace of pigeons. But once these epaulettes are off, I'll not have to pay attention to the admiral – nor to anyone."

' "It's only that," replied he, sadly shaking his head, which was dark, though a little powdered as was still the custom in those days,[20] "it's that I believe it could be dangerous for you, Captain, to seem to know us. We laugh because we're young; we have a happy air because we love each other; but I have frightful moments when I think of the future, and I don't know what will become of my poor Laure."

'Again he clasped the head of the young woman to his breast.

' "That's really how I ought to speak to the Captain, isn't it, my girl, and wouldn't you have said the same thing?"

'I grasped my pipe and got up, because I began to feel my eyes

26

moisten a little, and that's not the kind of thing for me, not a bit.

'"Come! Come!" said I, "this'll all clear itself up eventually. If the tobacco inconveniences Madam, she should leave."

'She rose, her face burning and wet with tears, like a child who has been scolded.

'"But besides that," she said to me, looking up at my clock, "you two haven't thought of this – there's that letter!"

'When she said that I felt something indefinable strike me, and my hair prickled.

'"By God! I hadn't thought any more about that," said I. "Well, well, here's a pretty business! If we've passed first degree, latitude north, there's nothing for me to do but throw myself into the sea. – It must be my good fortune that this child here has reminded me of that brute of a letter!"

'I quickly consulted my sea chart, and when I saw that we still had at least a week, I was relieved in my mind, but not – without knowing why – not at heart.

'"It's just that the Directory don't fool around on questions of obedience!" I said. "Well, I'm fully up to date again now. The time has slipped past so fast that I'd forgotten about all that."

'Well, sir, there we stood, all three, with our noses in the air, looking at that letter as if it was going to speak to us. What struck me most was that the sun, shining through the deck hatch, lit up the glass of the clock so that the great red seal, with the smaller ones around it, seemed like the features of a face in the midst of a fire.

'To divert them I said, "Wouldn't you say its eyes are starting out of its head?"

'"Oh! my darling," said the young woman, "they look like spots of blood."

'"Oh! No, no!" said the young husband, taking her by the arm. "You deceive yourself, Laure; it looks more like an invitation to a wedding. Come now and rest yourself, come – why should that letter worry you?"

'They ran out as if pursued by a ghost, and went up to the deck. I stayed alone with that huge letter, and I recall that while smoking my pipe I stared at it constantly, as if its red eyes were fixed to mine, and were drawing them in like the eyes of a serpent. The great pale face, the third seal, bigger than the eyes, wide open and gaping wide like the jaws of a wolf . . . it put me in a foul temper; I took my coat and threw it over the clock, so that I could see neither the time, nor that swine of a letter.

'I went up to finish my pipe on deck. I stayed there until night-fall.

'We were now off the Cape Verde Islands. The *Marat* was gliding along, wind astern, at an easy ten knots. The night was the most beautiful I'd ever seen in the tropics. A moon as vast as the sun was rising on the horizon; the sea cut it in the middle, and itself became as white as a sheet of snow covered in tiny diamonds. Seated on my bench, smoking, I contemplated the scene. The officer on watch and the sailors were silent, gazing like me at the shadow of the brig on the water. I was pleased to hear nothing. I'm one who loves silence and order, myself, and I'd forbidden all noises and lights.[21] However, I did notice a small reddish line almost under my feet. I should've straightway been seized with anger – but, since it came from the cabin of my little deportees, I wished to see what was going on before upsetting myself. I'd only to bend forward a little to see through the big hatch, into their little room; so I peered in.

'The young woman was on her knees, saying her prayers, lit by a little lamp. She was in her shift, and from above I could see her bare shoulders, her little bare feet, and her long blonde hair all dishevelled. I thought to leave, but then I said to myself: "Dammit! an old soldier, what's it matter?" So I stayed to watch.

'Her husband was seated on a little trunk with his head in his hands, looking at her praying. She lifted her head up as if to heaven, and I could see her great blue eyes full of tears like a Magdalen. While she prayed he took the ends of her long tresses and silently kissed them. When she'd finished, she made the sign of the cross, smiling with the air of one who is about to go to heaven. I saw that like her he made the sign of the cross, but as though he were ashamed. – And, really, it is a bit odd in a man.

'She rose to her feet and kissed him, and lay down in the hammock first – he lifting her up into it without a word, as one would settle a child in a swing. It was stiflingly hot: she felt herself pleasantly rocked by the motion of the ship and seemed already to be falling asleep. Her little white feet were crossed and raised to the same level as her head, and her whole body wrapped in her long shift. What a little love she was!

'"My dear," said she, half asleep, "aren't you tired? It's very late, you know?"

'He still sat without speaking, his head in his hands. This upset her a little, the lovely creature, and she stuck her pretty head out of the hammock like a bird out of its nest, and looked at him, her lips parted but not venturing to say more.

'At last he said:

'"Oh! my dear Laure, the further we travel towards the Americas, the less I can prevent myself feeling sad. I don't know why, but it seems to me that the happiest time of our life will have been this crossing."

'"It seems like that to me too," she said. "I wish we didn't have to get there."

'He looked at her, clasping his hands with an ecstasy you won't be able to imagine.

'"And yet, my angel, you always weep when you pray to God," said he, "and this pains me greatly, because I know very well who you are thinking of, and I believe you regret what you have done."

'"Me, regret it!" said she with a hurt look – "me regret following you, my love! Do you believe that because I've belonged to you for so short a time I've loved you the less? Am I not a woman, and at seventeen doesn't one know a woman's duties? Didn't my mother and my sisters say it was my duty to follow you to Guiana? Didn't they say that there's nothing extraordinary in doing that? I'm only surprised that you should be so touched by it, my dear; for it's only natural. And now I don't understand how you can possibly think I regret anything when I'm with you to help you to live, or to die with you should you die."

'She said all this in a voice so sweet that it might have been music. I was much moved and said:

'"Good little wife, well done!"

'The young man began to sigh and tap his foot while kissing the pretty hand and the bare arm she extended to him.

' "Oh! Laurette, my Laurette!" said he, "when I think that if we'd delayed our marriage by four days they'd have arrested only me, and I'd have gone away quite alone, I can't forgive myself."

'Then the little beauty extended both her lovely white arms from out the hammock, bare to the shoulders, and stroked his forehead, his hair and his eyes, taking his head as though to carry it away and hide it in her breast. She smiled like a child, and said to him a lot of little wifely things, the like of which I'd never heard. She stopped his mouth with her fingers so that she alone might speak. Playing with her long hair and using it as a kerchief to dab his eyes for him, she said:

' "But tell me, isn't it much better for you to have with you a wife who loves you, my darling? For myself I'm very happy to go to Cayenne; I shall see the savages, and coconut trees like those Paul and Virginia[22] saw – will I not? We'll each plant one. We'll see who will be the best gardener. We'll build a little hut just for ourselves. I shall work all day and all night, if you like. I'm strong; see, look at my arm: – there, I can almost lift you up. Don't mock me; also I know how to embroider; won't there be a town somewhere out there where they'll need embroiderers? I'll give lessons in drawing and music too if anyone wants them – and if they can read, you will write, my dear."

'I remember that the poor boy became so desperate that he let out a great cry when she said this.

' "Write!" – he cried – "Write!"

'And he grasped his right hand in his left, gripping it at the wrist.

' "Ah! Write! – why did I ever learn to write! To write – it's the occupation of a madman! . . . – I believed in their liberty of the press! – Where were my wits? Oh! – and why do it at all? To print five or six little mediocre ideas, read only by those who already agree with them, thrown into the fire by those that hate them, and effective only in getting us persecuted! For myself that's that; but you, my lovely angel, who'd been a wife barely four days! – What had you done? I beg you to explain how I came to allow you to be so loving as to follow me here! Do you really know where you are, my poor little one? Or where you're going – do you know that? Soon, my child, you'll be sixteen hundred leagues from your mother and your sisters . . . and for me! All that for me!"

'She hid her head for a moment in the hammock; and from above I could make out that she wept; but down there he couldn't see her face, and when she raised it from above the cloth, she was smiling to cheer him.

'"Well, it's true that we're not rich at the moment," said she with a burst of laughter; "oh dear, look at my purse, I've only one solitary louis.[23] And you?"

'He too began to laugh like a child:

'"Good heavens, I did have an écu myself, but I gave it to the little boy who carried your trunk."

'"Ah! Bah! – what does it matter?" she said, snapping her little white fingers like castanets – "one's never happier than when one has nothing – and haven't I the two diamond rings my mother gave me, as a reserve? They are good anywhere and for anything, are they not? When you want we'll sell them. Besides, I believe that that good man of a Captain hasn't revealed all of his kind intentions for us, and that he knows very well what's in that letter. Surely it'll be a recommendation for us to the Governor of Cayenne."

'"Possibly," said he – "who knows?"

'"Well won't it be?" replied his little wife – "you're so good that I'm sure that the government has only exiled you for a short time, and isn't really angry with you."

'She had put this so sweetly! – calling me that good man of a Captain, that I was much touched and softened; and in my heart also I rejoiced that she'd perhaps guessed rightly about the sealed letter. They began to embrace again; I stamped briskly on the deck to make them stop.

I cried out to them:

'"Heigh there, my young friends! there's an order to extinguish all lights in the ship. Will you blow your lamp out, please."

'They blew out the lamp, and I heard them laugh as they chattered softly away in the dark, like schoolchildren. I resumed my solitary walk on deck, smoking my pipe. All the stars of the tropics were there in their place, each as large as a little moon. I contemplated them, breathing in the fresh sweet air.

'I told myself that certainly these excellent little folk had divined the truth, and I was cheered by this. It was a good bet that one of the five

Directors had thought again and recommended them to me; I wouldn't be able to explain why, myself, because I've never understood affairs of state; but anyway I believed it, and, without knowing why, I was pleased.

'I descended to my cabin, and went again to look at the letter under my old uniform. It had a different face; it seemed to me that it laughed, and its seals seemed rose-coloured. I no longer doubted its good will, and I made it a friendly little acknowledgement.

'But despite this I covered it again with my coat; it bothered me.

'For several days we didn't think of looking at it again, and we were happy; but then when we drew near to the first degree of latitude, we started to be silent with one another.

'One fine day I awoke rather amazed to feel no movement in the ship. To tell you the truth, I always sleep with one eye open, as the saying is, and, when I missed the usual rolling, I opened them both. We'd fallen into a flat calm, and it was just within one degree latitude north, at longitude twenty-seven degrees. I put my nose out on deck: the sea was as sleek as a bowl of oil; all the sails that had been set had fallen hanging around the masts like empty balloons. Looking across sideways at the letter, I said at once, "I'll have plenty of time to read you, to be sure!" I waited until the evening, at sunset. However, the moment had to come. I pulled the clock open, and quickly snatched out the sealed order. – And well! – my dear fellow, I held it in my hand for a quarter of an hour, because still I couldn't read it. At last I said: "This is too much!" and I broke open the three seals with a flick of my thumb. As to the great red seal, I ground it into dust. After having read, I rubbed my eyes, thinking myself mistaken.

'I re-read the whole letter through; I re-read it again; I started once more at the last line and worked back to the first. I couldn't believe it. My legs trembled a little under me, and I sat down; I felt a kind of twitching of the skin on my face; I rubbed my cheeks a little with rum, and put some in the hollows of my hands; I felt sorry for myself for having been so stupid. But this was over in a moment; and I went up to get some air.

'Laurette was so lovely that day that I didn't want to go near her. She had on a simple little white dress, her arms bare to the collar, and

32

her long hair falling around her as she always wore it. She was amusing herself by trailing her other dress in the sea on the end of a rope, and laughing as she tried to catch a type of seaweed, plants which resemble grapes and float on the surface of the water in the tropics.

'"Come on and see the grapes! come quickly!" she cried; and her lover leant against her, and bent down, and didn't look at the sea, for he was gazing at her with the tenderest air.

'I made a sign to the young fellow to come and talk to me on the quarterdeck. She turned round. I don't know what my face looked like, but she let go of her rope. She grasped him violently by the arm, and said to him:

'"Oh no! Don't go, he looks so pale."

'This might well have been so; there was certainly enough to make a man pale. However, he came up to me on the quarterdeck. She stared at us, leaning against the mainmast. We walked up and down for a long time without a word. I was smoking a cigar, which I found bitter, and I spat it into the sea. He followed me with his eye. I took him by the arm; I was choking, by God; on my word of honour, I was choking!

'"Look here!" I said to him at last, "tell me then, my young friend, tell me something of your story. What have you done to these dogs of lawyers who sit up there like five fragments of a king? It seems that they've a fearsome grudge against you! It's bizarre!"

'He shrugged his shoulders, bowing his head (with such a gentle air, the poor boy!) and replied:

'"Oh, my God, Captain, really not much! – indeed, three satirical couplets on the Directory, that's all."

'"It's not possible!" I said.

'"My God, yes! The couplets weren't even very good. I was arrested on the 15th Fructidor and taken to La Force;[24] I was tried on the 16th and at first condemned to death, but then to deportation as an act of clemency."

'"It's bizarre!" said I. "These comrades of Directors are touchy indeed: for that letter which you know about – it orders me to shoot you."

'He didn't reply, but smiled, making a pretty good show of it for a boy of nineteen. He looked only at his wife, and wiped his forehead, on which stood some drops of sweat. I had at least as much sweat on my own face, and other drops in my eyes.

'I started again:

'"It seems that those Citizens down there are unwilling to do your business on land; they think that here it won't show up so much. But for me it's unfortunate all right; because however fine a lad you may be, I can't get out of it. The sentence of death is there, properly drawn up, and the order of execution signed, initialled, sealed; nothing is missing."

'He bowed to me very politely, his colour rising.

'"I ask nothing of you, Captain," he said in a voice even softer than usual; "I should be grieved to hinder you doing your duty. I'd like only to speak with Laure a little, and ask you to protect her should she survive me, which I think unlikely."

'"Oh, as to that, most certainly, my boy," said I to him; "if it doesn't displease you, I'll take her to her family when I return to France, and I won't leave her until she no longer wishes to see me. But, in my view, you can flatter yourself that she won't recover from this blow, poor little girl!"

'He took both my hands, pressed them, and said:

'"My brave Captain, I see very well that you are suffering more than I am from what you have to do; but what else is there? I trust you to preserve for her the little which belongs to me, to protect her, to see that she receives anything her old mother will be able to leave her – you will, won't you? To guarantee her life, her honour – you'll do that? Also to see that her health is looked after. – Look," he added in even lower tones, "I must tell you that she is very delicate; often her chest is so afflicted that she faints several times a day; she must always be well wrapped up. In the end, you'll stand as much as possible in place of her father, her mother, and myself, won't you? If she's able to keep the rings given to her by her mother, it would please me very much. But if they have to be sold for her, then so be it. My poor Laurette! – see how lovely she is!"

'As this was beginning to become too emotional, it disturbed me, and I knit my brows; I had talked to him with a cheerful air so as not to weaken myself, but I couldn't keep it up: "Very well, that's enough,"

34

I said to him, "between decent men there's a lot that's understood. Go and speak to her; for we must get on with things."

'I clasped him warmly by the hand, and, since he didn't let go of mine, and looked at me with a singular air, added: – "Oh well, if I have one piece of advice to give you, it's not to tell her of this. We'll arrange the thing so that she won't expect it, and no more will you, you can be sure. I'll look after that."

'"Ah! that's different," said he, "I didn't know . . . that will be better, really. Otherwise, farewells! Farewells! – how they unnerve one."

'"Yes, yes," I said to him, "don't be like a child, that's the thing. Don't kiss her, my friend, if you can, don't kiss her, or you are lost."

'I gave him another firm handshake, and let him go. Oh! it was hard for me, all of it.

'It seemed that he kept the secret very well, by Heaven! – for they strolled, arm in arm, for a quarter of an hour, and then returned to the ship's side to pick up the rope and the dress, which one of my cabin boys had fished out.

'Night fell suddenly. It was the moment I'd resolved to take. – But that moment has endured until the present day for me, and I shall drag it around all my life, like a ball on a chain.'

Here the old Major was obliged to stop. I refrained from speaking so as not to interrupt his train of thought – and he resumed, striking his breast:

'I tell you, I still can't comprehend that moment. I felt rage grab me by the hair, but at the same time something obscure forced me to obey, and pushed me forward. I called my officers, and said to one of them: "Right, lower a boat . . . since we've now become executioners! Put that woman in it and take yourselves away from the ship until you hear musket shots. Then come back." – To obey a piece of paper! for it was only that in the end! There must have been something in the air which compelled me. I watched the young man from a distance . . . Oh! it was shocking to see! . . . kneeling before his Laurette and kissing her knees and her feet. Don't you find my situation appalling?

'I cried like a madman: – "Separate them . . . We're criminals, all of us! – Separate them . . . The poor Republic is a corpse! Directors,

Directory, they're its vermin! I quit the sea! I'm not afraid of all your lawyers; anyone can tell 'em what I say, what do I care?" – Ah! but I did care very much indeed, in truth! I'd like to have got hold of them, and I'd like to have shot all five of them – the cowards! Oh! I'd have done it; I care as little for life as does the rain that falls there, see . . . Much I care! . . . a life like mine . . . Ah, well, yes . . . poor life . . . go on!'

And the Major's voice faltered little by little and became as indistinct as his words; on he marched, biting his lips and knitting his brows in fierce and terrible abstraction. He made little convulsive movements and gave the mule blows with his scabbard as if he wanted to kill it. What amazed me was to see the sallow skin of his face become a deep red. He undid his coat and violently pulled it open across his chest, exposing it to wind and rain. We continued to march thus in profound silence. I realized that he was not going to say any more of his own accord, and that I must make up my mind to question him.

'I understand very well,' I said to him, as if he had finished his story, 'that after such a cruel event one would hold one's profession in horror.'

'Oh! the profession – are you mad?' he replied roughly, 'it's not the profession! A ship's captain is never obliged to be an executioner, unless there come along governments of assassins and thieves, who take advantage of a poor fellow's habit of obeying blindly, obeying inevitably, obeying like an unhappy mechanism, regardless of the feelings in his heart.'

At the same time he drew a red handkerchief from his pocket into which he wept like a child. I pulled up for a moment as if to adjust my stirrup, and, staying behind the cart, I continued for some time at the rear, feeling that he would be humiliated if I too obviously witnessed his copious tears.

I had judged rightly, for after about a quarter of an hour he came to join me at the rear of his wretched outfit and asked me if I had any razors in my portmanteau; to which I replied simply that, not yet having a beard, they would be completely useless to me. But he did not take this up – it was a pretext to talk of other things. I realized with pleasure though that he was coming back to his story, for he said to me suddenly:

'You've never seen a ship in your life, isn't that so?'

'I've only seen one at the Paris Panorama,'[25] said I, 'and I wouldn't rely too much on the maritime knowledge I got from that.'

'You wouldn't know, therefore, what a cathead is?'

'I've not the least idea,' I said.

'It's a kind of terrace of planks which comes out of the back of a ship, from which you throw the anchor into the sea. When you shoot a man, that's where you usually place him,' he added in a lower voice.

'Ah! I understand, because he'll fall into the sea.'

He did not reply, but started to describe the various sorts of ship's boats which a brig can carry, and their position in the vessel; and then, without ordering his thoughts, he continued his tale with that air of assumed indifference which is the unfailing result of long service – because in front of one's inferiors it is necessary to show scorn of danger, scorn of men, scorn of life, scorn of death and scorn of oneself; and under this tough casing is, nearly always, a deeply feeling nature. – The hardness of a warrior is like an iron mask on a noble face, like a stone dungeon which closes in a royal prisoner.

'Those craft hold six men,' he resumed, 'they jumped in and carried off Laure with them before she had time to cry out or to speak. Oh! that's a thing no honest man can console himself for, when he's to do with it. Try as you may, you never forget a thing like that! . . . Oh! this weather! – What the devil has made me tell this tale! When I tell it, I'm no longer able to stop, that's what's come of it. It's a story that makes me dizzy like Jurançon wine. – Oh! this weather! – My cloak is soaked through.

'I was talking to you, I think, still of that little Laurette! – the poor girl! – How many bunglers there are in the world! – my officer was stupid enough to steer the boat behind the brig. After all, it's true that one can't foresee everything. For myself, I'd counted on the darkness to hide the affair, and didn't think of the flare caused by twelve muskets firing at once. And, my God! from the boat she saw her husband pitch into the sea, shot.

'If there is a God above, he knows how what I'm about to tell you now came to pass; myself I don't know, but it was seen and heard just as I see and hear you. At the moment of the shots, she put her hand to her head as though a ball had hit her in the forehead, then she seated herself in the boat without swooning, without crying out, without speaking, and came back to the brig when and how she was asked to. I went to her, and spoke to her for a long time, the best I could. She seemed to listen to me and looked me in the face, rubbing her forehead. She understood nothing. Her forehead was red in an ashen face. She trembled in every limb as though frightened of everyone. That has stayed with her. She is still the same, the poor little thing! – idiot, imbecile, or mad, as you wish. Nothing has dragged a word from her, except when she asks that someone take away the thing she has in her head.

'From that time on I became as sorrowful as she, and I felt something within me which said: *Stay with her to the end of your days, and protect her.* That's what I've done. When I returned to France, I asked to transfer with my rank into the land forces, having been seized with hatred for that sea into which I had spilt innocent blood. I sought out Laure's family. Her mother was dead. Her sisters, to whom I brought her as a madwoman, wanted nothing to do with her and proposed that I should put her in Charenton.[26] I turned my back on them, and kept her with me.

'Ah, good Lord! – if you want to see her, comrade, it's up to you.' 'Is she in there?' I asked him. – 'Certainly! Hold on! Wait. – Whoa! Whoa! mule . . .'

6

How I continued on my way

And he halted his wretched mule – who seemed to me to be delighted that I had raised the question. At the same time he lifted up the oilcloth on the little cart as if to tidy up the straw which almost filled it, and I saw something truly distressing. Two blue eyes, I saw, of inordinate size and admirable shape emerging from a pale, long, emaciated face sunk in a mass of straight blonde hair. I saw, in truth, only those two eyes, which were all that remained of the poor woman, for the rest was dead. Her forehead was red; her white hollow cheeks were bluish at the cheekbones; and she was crouched so low in the midst of the straw that one could hardly see her knees, on which she was playing dominoes all by herself. She looked at us a moment, gave a long shudder, smiled at me slightly, and went back to playing. It seemed to me that she was trying to work out how her right hand could beat her left.

'You see, it's a month since she started that match,' said the battalion commander to me; 'tomorrow, perhaps, there'll be another game which'll last just as long. Peculiar, isn't it?'

At the same time he started to rearrange the oilskin on his shako, which the rain had upset somewhat.

'Poor Laurette!' said I. 'Surely you'll always lose!'

I brought my horse close to the cart, and held out my hand; automatically she gave me hers, with a smile of much sweetness. I noticed with wonder that she had two diamond rings on her long fingers; and I realized that these would be the ones from her mother – there still – and asked myself how they had survived such poverty. Not for the world would I have mentioned this to the old Major; but as he followed me with his eyes and saw mine fixed on Laure's fingers, he addressed me with a certain air of pride:

'Those are big enough diamonds, aren't they? They'd fetch their price if there was need for it, but I don't want to separate them from her, poor child. If one touches them she cries, and she doesn't take them off. The rest of the time she never complains, and she can do a bit of sewing from time to time. I've kept my word to her poor young husband, and, to tell you the truth, I've never repented it. I've never left her, and I've said everywhere that this is my daughter who is mad. People respect that. In the army everything gets arranged more smoothly than you'd believe up in Paris, you know! – She's been on all the Emperor's wars with me, and I've always made our way for us. I've always kept her warm. With a bit of straw and a small cart that's never impossible. She's always been neatly enough turned out, and me, being a battalion commander with good pay, with my Legion of Honour pension and the Napoleon's month allowance[27] – which was paid double at one time – me, I've always kept abreast of my affairs, and she hasn't hampered me. On the contrary, her childish ways sometimes made the officers of the 7th Light laugh.'

Then he went up to her and tapped her on the shoulder, as he might have done his little mule.

'Well, my daughter! what d'you say to giving a few words to the Lieutenant here; see now, give him a nod.'

She returned to her dominoes.

'Oh!' said he, 'it's that she's a little out of temper today because it's raining. But she never catches cold. Mad people are never ill, which is convenient around here. She went bareheaded at the Beresina[28] and all through the retreat from Moscow. – Go on, my girl, play always, that's good, don't bother yourself about us; do as you please, Laurette, go on.'

She took his hand which was resting on her shoulder, a big, dark, gnarled hand; then she lifted it timidly to her lips and kissed it as might a poor slave. At this kiss I felt a tightening of the heart, and turned my bridle violently.

'Shall we continue on our journey, Major?' I said. 'Night will fall before we reach Béthune.'

The Major carefully scraped off the yellow mud which clogged his boots with the end of his sabre; then he mounted the foot-board of his cart and rearranged the cloth hood of Laure's little cloak about her head. He took off his black silk cravat and put it round the neck of his daughter by adoption. After that he kicked the mule, made that shrug of his shoulders, and said: 'On your way, poor things!' – and off we went.

The rain still fell sadly; grey sky and grey earth extended endlessly; a kind of spiritless light, a pale sun, all watery, was sinking behind the great windmills, which were motionless. We fell again into profound silence.

I looked at my old Major: he marched along in great strides with ever sustained vigour, though his mule could hardly go on, and even my horse began to dip his head. The gallant fellow took off his shako from time to time to wipe his bald forehead and his few remaining grey hairs, or his thick eyebrows and white moustaches which were dripping with rain. He was not worrying about the effect his story would have had on me. He had shown himself neither better nor worse than he was. He had not deigned to show off himself at all. He was not thinking of himself – and at the end of a quarter of an hour he embarked, in the same tone, on a much longer story about a campaign of Marshal Masséna,[29] in which he had formed his battalion in square against some-body or other's cavalry. I did not listen, although he became very warm in demonstrating to me the superiority of the infantryman over the cavalryman.

Night fell, and we were not making good speed. The mud became thicker and deeper. – Nothing on the road, and nothing at the end of it. We halted ourselves at the foot of a dead tree, the only tree on the road. First he attended to his mule, as I to my horse. Next he looked into the cart, like a mother into her child's cradle. I heard what he said: – 'Come along, my girl, put this coat over your feet, and try to sleep. – Ah! that's good, there's not a drop of rain here. – Ah! dammit! she's broken my watch which I put round her neck! – Oh! my poor silver watch! – Come now, it doesn't matter; try to sleep, my child. You'll see, the fine weather will come soon. – It's strange! – she always has a fever; the mad are like that. Look, here's some chocolate for you, child.'

He leant the cart against the tree, and we seated ourselves under the wheels, as a shelter against the eternal downpour, sharing a little loaf of his and one of mine: a pathetic meal.

'It's a pity that we've nothing but this,' he said; 'but it's a lot better than the horsemeat we ate in Russia, cooked under embers and dressed with gunpowder instead of salt. That poor little woman, I really must give her the best of what I have. You see that I always leave her by herself. She can't abide a man near her since that business of the letter. I'm old, and she seems to think that I'm her father; even so she'd strangle me if I tried to kiss her even on the forehead. Their upbringing always leaves them something, that's how it seems, for I've never known her to forget to be as modest as a nun. – It's curious, eh?'

As he talked of her in this manner, we heard her sigh and say: '*Take away this bullet! Take away this bullet from me!*' I got up, but he made me sit again.

'Stay, stay,' he said, 'it's nothing. She says that all the time, because she always thinks she can feel a ball in her head. But this doesn't hinder her doing what one tells her, and always very gently.'

I was silent, listening sadly to him. I worked out that from 1797 to 1815, where we were, eighteen years had gone by in this way for this man. – I remained a long time next to him in silence, seeking to understand for myself such a character and such a destiny. Then, for no immediate reason, I shook his hand with great enthusiasm. He was astonished.

'You're an admirable man,' said I to him.

'Heigh! why all this?' he replied – 'is it because of this poor woman? You realize very well, my lad, that it's my duty. A long time ago I made an act of abnegation.'

And he spoke to me some more of Masséna.

The next day, at dawn, we arrived at Béthune, an ugly little fortified town, where one could say that the ramparts, in surrounding the houses, have pressed them one on top of the other. Everything was in confusion, for the alert had been sounded. The inhabitants had started to take down the white flags from their windows, and within doors to sew the tricolour. The drums beat the call to arms; the trumpets sounded out *to horse* by the order of His Grace, the duc de Berri. The long Picardy wagons carrying the Swiss Guard and its baggage, the cannons of the

Bodyguard being run onto the ramparts, the carriages of the princes, and the Red Companies forming up thronged the town. The sight of the King's Men-at-Arms and the Musketeers made me forget my old travelling companion. I joined my company, and lost the little cart and its poor inhabitants in the crowd. To my great regret, I had lost them for ever.

This was the first time in my life that I had made out the depths of the true heart of a soldier. This encounter revealed to me a side of man's nature which I had not known – of which the country knows little and which it treats so badly. From that moment I placed it high in my esteem. Since then I have often searched round me for some man comparable to him, capable of such complete and heedless abnegation of the self. And, during the fourteen years I have lived in the army, it was in it alone, and above all in the ranks of the poor and despised infantry, that I found again men of this antique character, men pushing the sentiment of duty to its final consequences, having no compunction about their obedience nor shame for their poverty, simple of manners and language, proud of the glory of their country and careless of their own, happily shut up in their obscurity, and sharing with the unfortunate the black bread they purchase with their blood.

I remained ignorant for a long time of what became of the poor battalion commander, the more so since he had not given me his name, nor had I asked it. One day in a café, however – I think in 1825 – an old infantry captain of the line to whom I had described him while waiting to go on parade, said to me:

'Oh! Good heavens, my dear fellow, I knew him, that poor devil! He was a good chap; he was *knocked over* by a cannon ball at Waterloo. He really did leave a kind of mad girl in the baggage train – whom we took to the infirmary at Amiens when we went to join the army of the Loire, and who died three days after, raving mad.'

'I can well believe it,' I said to him, 'she no longer had her foster-father!'

'Ah pooh! *Father!* what's that you're saying?' he said, with an air which he wanted to be knowing and lewd.

'I say that they're beating the call to arms,' I replied, leaving. And I too had made an act of abnegation.

43

BOOK 2

I

On responsibility

I remember still the consternation this story forced into my mind – perhaps it was the first stirring of my slow recovery from the disease of military ardour. Suddenly I felt humiliated that I should be running the risk of committing a crime, of finding in my hand the cutlass of a slave in place of the sword of a knight. And I came to know of many other things which tarnished in my eyes the noble breed of men I wanted to see devoted solely to the defence of the country. In the time of the Terror,[1] for instance, it happened that another ship's captain received – as did the whole navy – the Committee of Public Safety's monstrous order to shoot prisoners-of-war; he had the misfortune to capture an English vessel, and the even greater misfortune to obey the government's order. Coming back to shore, he reported his shameful executions, quit the service and shortly afterwards died of sorrow. This captain commanded *La Boudeuse*, a frigate that had first sailed around the world under the command of my relation, M. de Bougainville.[2] The great navigator shed tears for this, for the honour of his old ship.

Will we never evolve a law that in like circumstances would reconcile duty to conscience? Is the voice of the public mistaken when it resounds from age to age to pardon and honour the disobedience of the vicomte d'Orte, who, when ordered to extend the massacres of St Bartholomew in Paris[3] to Dax, replied to Charles IX:

'Sire, I have communicated Your Majesty's command to your faithful inhabitants and troops; I have found only good citizens, brave soldiers, and not one butcher.'

And if he was right to refuse to obey, how can we live under laws, and find them reasonable, when they deal out death to those who refuse this same blind obedience? We admire free will but we destroy it – an absurd state of affairs which cannot long be maintained. It must come about that we arrange things so that a man under arms is allowed discretion, and that we establish down to what rank free reasoning is allowed, and with it the exercise of conscience and of justice . . . It must come about that one day we progress from where we are now.

I am not in the least pretending that this is not an extremely difficult question, and one which bears on the very foundations of discipline. Far from wishing to weaken this discipline I think we need to reinforce it in many areas, and that in the face of an enemy regulations cannot be too draconian. When the army turns its front of steel towards the foreigner it ought to march and act as one man. Even so, when it turns home again and has nothing in front of it but the motherland, then at least it should meet with enlightened laws allowing it to show filial tenderness.

It is highly desirable also that immutable limits be set, once for all, on the absolute commands that can be given to armies by the sovereign power – a power that has fallen so often in our history into unworthy hands. It ought never to be possible that a few adventurers, suddenly assuming dictatorial powers, should be able to transform four hundred thousand honourable men into assassins, by laws which are as fleeting as their authority.

Often I did encounter, it is true, some compensations in the customs of the service, when – thanks perhaps to the carelessness and easy good nature of our national character – there flourished in the armies, side by side with the misery of military servitude, a kind of freedom of spirit that tempered the humiliation of passive obedience. And, seeing in every military man some quality of openness and noble detachment, I thought that this came from minds calmed and relieved from the tremendous weight of responsibility. I was extremely young then, and I found that, little by little, this sentiment allayed my conscience. I seemed to make out in every commander-in-chief a type of Moses who has to render up his terrible account to God alone, after having said to the sons of Levi: 'Go in and out from gate to gate throughout the camp, and slay every man his brother, and every man his companion, and every man his neighbour.' And there were twenty and three thousand men slain[4]

– that is according to Exodus (32:27). For I knew the Bible by heart, and the book and I were so inseparable that it followed me always, even on the longest marches. The first consolation it offered me is obvious. I reflected that it would be highly unfortunate should one of my Moses in gold braid order me to kill my whole family; but actually that never came about, as I had sagely enough foreseen. I thought also that even if the impracticable peace of the Abbé de Saint-Pierre[5] came to reign on earth, and if he himself was charged with ordering universal liberty and equality, he would still require for the work a few regiments of Levites whom he could tell to gird themselves with the sword, in the expectation that their obedience would attract the blessing of the Lord. Thus I sought to reconcile myself to the monstrous obligation of *passive obedience*, considering from what source it flowed, and how all social order seems to be founded on some obedience. But it was necessary for me to go through a great deal of reasoning and much paradox for this to take any hold on my mind. I was well content to impose obedience, but not at all to submit to it; I found it admirably wise under my feet, but ridiculous above my head. Since then I have seen plenty of men reason likewise who had not the excuse I had: I was a Levite of sixteen years old.

Then too I had not extended my views over the whole of our homeland of France, and over that other homeland that surrounds it, Europe – or from there over the homeland of humanity, the world, which, drawn together by the hand of civilization, happily grows smaller each day. I had not thought how the heart of a man of war would be lighter in his breast if he should feel the presence of two men within himself, one of whom obeyed the other; if he knew that after the harsh part he has to play in war, he had a right to a benevolent and equally glorious role in peace; if, according to his rank, he had a right of choice in politics; if, after having been so long mute in the camps, he had a voice in the cities; if in one capacity he were the enforcer of laws he had made in another, and if, to cover up the blood on his sword, he could wear the toga. – Well, it is not impossible that all this will one day come about.

We are truly pitiless if we require that a single man be strong enough to answer by himself, alone, for the nation in arms we put in his hands.

This is an arrangement that is itself dangerous to government: for the present practice, which makes the whole electric chain of passive obedience hang from a single finger, could, in a given case, render the ruin of the whole state all too simple. Any revolution, even half formed and recruited, need only win over the Minister of War to achieve complete success. All the rest would follow necessarily, according to our laws, for no link in the chain would be able to resist the shock imparted from above.

No – and here I call to witness the aroused conscience of every man who has shed the blood of his fellow citizens, or seen it shed – the weight of so many murders is too heavy for one head to bear. It would not be too much to ask that there be as many heads to bear as there are combatants. And it is only just that the agents of a law of blood should at least understand it if they are to be responsible for its execution. – Even so, the improved institutions suggested here would be themselves but temporary; for, I say once more, armies and war will only endure for a certain time. Despite the words of a sophist with whom I have fought elsewhere,[6] it is not at all true that war is *divine*, even against the foreigner; it is not at all true that *the earth thirsts for blood*. War is cursed of God, and of men themselves, who feel a secret horror even while waging it; and the earth cries to heaven only to demand fresh water for its rivers and for the pure dew of its clouds.

However, in my first youth – which was entirely given over to action – I was not as yet qualified to wonder whether there were modern countries where a man of war was the same individual as a man of peace, as opposed to a being separated from his family and situated almost as an enemy. Nor did I examine what we might well draw from the ancient world in this respect. Many projects for a more rational organization of armies have been produced, but fruitlessly. Very far from putting any of them into execution, or even giving such things the light of publicity, it is probable that an established power – whatever it is – will distance itself from them further and further, having an interest in surrounding itself with gladiators for the struggle which ceaselessly threatens. Nevertheless the idea will take shape one day, sooner or later, as do all necessary ideas.

Even as things are, what noble feelings there are to conserve –

feelings which could be elevated still further if blended with a sense of high personal dignity! I have gathered many examples of these in my memory; for I had all around me numerous close friends who were apt to furnish them, and who were so gaily resigned in their careless submission, so free in spirit while their bodies were in servitude, that their heedlessness won me over for a time – so that like them I acquired from it the perfect calm of the soldier and the officer, a calm which is precisely that of a horse nobly regulating his gait between bridle and spur, proud of being in no way responsible. May I therefore be allowed to give, in the simple story of a brave man and of a soldier's family – of whom I had but a glimpse – an example, less grim than the first, of one of those lifelong resignations, full of honesty, decency and good humour, which are very common in our army, and the sight of which refreshes the soul when one lives, as I have done, in the fashionable world – a world from which one descends with pleasure to study simpler customs, completely outmoded though they may be.

Such as it is, the army is a good book from which to learn about human nature; one gets to know there how to put one's hand to everything, to the basest things as well as the highest; the most refined men and the wealthiest are obliged to see poverty close to, and to live with it, to measure out its coarse bread and weigh out its meat. Without the army many a great noble's son could not even suspect how a soldier lives, grows, and flourishes all the year round on nine sous a day[7] and a pitcher of fresh water, carrying a pack on his back which, container and contents, costs his country forty francs.

This simplicity in living, this carefree and joyous poverty shared by so many young men, this vigorous and healthy existence, without false politeness or false sentiment, this manly bearing imparted to all, this uniformity of feeling imprinted by discipline, are ties of habit which are crude, but difficult to sunder, and not lacking in a special charm that is unknown to other professions. I have seen officers take to the life with such passion that they cannot quit it for any time without repining – even to resume the most elegant and the dearest habits of their lives.

Regiments are monasteries of men, although nomadic monasteries. Everywhere they take with them their customs marked by gravity, by silence, by restraint. And here the vows of poverty and obedience are amply fulfilled.

The characteristics of these recluses are as indelibly stamped on them as are those of monks, and I never see the uniform of one of my regiments without a throb of the heart.

2

A soldier's honourable scruples

One evening in the summer of 1819 I was strolling in the interior of
the fortress of Vincennes, where I was garrisoned, with Timoléon
d'Arc ***, who, like myself, was a lieutenant of the Guard. According
to our custom we had walked around the butts, attended the lecture on
ricochet fire, peaceably exchanged warlike stories, and discussed the
Polytechnic school, its formation, its uses, its faults, and the sallow-faced
individuals who had made that geometrical plot of ground flourish.[8]
Timoléon himself had the pale colour of the school on his brow. Those
who knew him will, like me, recall his regular but rather lean features,
his large black eyes topped by arched brows, and the serious expression,
so mild and so rarely troubled, in his Spartan face. That evening he
was much preoccupied with our long discussion of Laplace's theory of
probability.[9] I remember that he held this book – a work for which we
had a great esteem, and which often tormented him – under his arm.

Night was falling, or, rather, spreading – a lovely August night. I
contemplated with pleasure the chapel built by Saint Louis,[10] and the
crown of half-ruinous mossy towers which at that time ornamented
Vincennes. The keep rose above them like a king in the midst of his
guards. At the tops of their tall spires, the little crescents of the chapel
glittered among the first stars. The fresh and fragrant odour of the
woods came to us over the ramparts, and there was nothing, down to
the turf of the batteries, which did not give out the breath of a summer
evening. We seated ourselves on a great cannon of the period of Louis
XIV, and silently watched some young soldiers who were taking turns
to try their strength by lifting a cannon ball at arm's length, while others
drifted back in, crossing the drawbridge in pairs or groups of four with
all the indolence of the military off duty. The courtyards were full of

open artillery ammunition carts, charged with powder in preparation for the review next day. To the side of us, near to the gate to the wood, an old Artillery Quartermaster-Sergeant Major[11] kept on anxiously opening and closing the flimsy gate of a small tower, which was the field artillery's powder store and arsenal, and was full of barrels of powder, arms and ammunition. He saluted us as he passed. He was a tall man, but a little bowed. His hair was white and thin, his moustaches white and thick, his air open, strong and still fresh, happy, gentle and wise. He held three large ledgers in his hands, and was checking long columns of figures there. We asked him why he was working so unusually late. He replied with the tone of respectful calm one meets in old soldiers that there was a general inspection at five the following morning; that he was responsible for the powder, and was re-checking it over and over again to guard against the slightest reproach of negligence; that he wished to take advantage of the last rays of daylight because orders strictly forbade entry into the powder store at night with a torch, or even with a dark lantern; that there were still some shells to examine, and that he was disturbed at not having had time to inspect everything. He glanced with some impatience at the grenadier who was posted as sentry at the door, and who would hinder him from going in again.

Having given us these details he got down on his knees and looked under the door to check that there remained no trail of powder. He feared that some officer's spurs or boot irons might spark it off next day.

'But that's not what worries me most,' said he, getting up, 'it's my ledgers.' And he looked at them with regret.

'You are too scrupulous,' said Timoléon.

'Ah! Lieutenant, when you're in the Guards it's impossible to be too scrupulous about such matters. One of our camp marshals blew his brains out last Monday, because he'd been sent to the guardroom. And me, I have to set an example to the under officers. Since I've been in the Guards I've never had any reproach from my superiors, and to deserve punishment would devastate me.'

It is true that these fine soldiers, considered in the army as among the élite of the élite, hold themselves dishonoured by the slightest fault.

'Go on,' I said, clapping him on the shoulder, 'you're absolute puritans of honour, all of you!'

He saluted and went off towards the barracks where his quarters were. Then, with that simplicity of manners typical of the race of honest soldiers, he reappeared carrying some hemp seed in the hollow of his hands for the hen who was rearing her twelve chicks under the old bronze cannon on which we were sitting.

She was the most charming hen I have ever met; she was completely white, without a blemish; and, with his thick fingers mutilated at Marengo and Austerlitz,[12] this excellent fellow had tied a little red aigrette to her head, and on her breast fixed a little silver necklet with a plaque bearing his number. The good fowl was proud of this, and at the same time grateful. She knew that the sentinels always respected her, and she feared no one, not even the little sucking pig and the owl who had been lodged near to her under the neighbouring cannon. This beautiful hen was the mascot of the gunners; she would take crumbs of bread and sugar from all of us so long as we were in uniform; but she had a horror of civilian dress, and, no longer recognizing us under this disguise, would flee under Louis XIV's cannon with her family. Magnificent cannon on which was engraved the eternal sun with his *Nec pluribus impar*, and the *Ultima ratio Regum*.[13] Under it sheltered a hen!

The good Quartermaster-Sergeant Major talked of her in very warm terms. She supplied eggs to his daughter and himself with unparalleled generosity – and he loved her so much that he had not the heart to kill a single one of her chicks from fear of wounding her. While he was telling us stories of her excellent manners the drums beat and the trumpets sounded the evening retreat. The drawbridges began to be lifted, and their keepers made the chains clank. We were not on duty, so we departed by the gate to the wood. Timoléon, who had all the time been tracing angles in the sand with the point of his sword, rose from the cannon regretting his triangles, just as I regretted my white hen and my Quartermaster-Sergeant Major.

We turned to the left, following the ramparts; and, passing in front of the mound of turf raised over the duc d'Enghien[14] – his body shot through and his head crushed under a paving stone – we skirted the moat, looking down at the narrow white track that he had taken to come to that ditch.

There are two kinds of men easily able to walk together for five hours without exchanging a word: prisoners and officers. Condemned to see one another perpetually, they remain alone when they meet. We went along in silence, hands behind our backs. I noticed that Timoléon kept turning a letter over in the moonlight. It was a little letter and rectangular; I recognized its look and its feminine origin; and I was used to see him dream away a whole day over this small, fine and elegant handwriting. In this way we had come to the village opposite the fortress; had climbed the stair of our little white house, and were about to part on the landing of our neighbouring apartments, and I had uttered not a word. Only then he suddenly said to me:

'She absolutely insists that I resign my commission – what d'you think of that?'

'I think,' said I, 'that she's as beautiful as an angel, because I've seen her; I think that you love her like a madman because I've observed you for two years behaving as you have this evening; I think you have a pretty fine fortune, judging by your horses and your style of living; I think you've given proofs enough to the army to withdraw, and that in times of peace that's no great sacrifice; but I think also of one thing . . .'

'Which is?' said he smiling rather bitterly, because he guessed it.

'That she's already married,' said I more gravely; 'you know that better than I do, my poor friend.'

'It's true,' said he, 'there's no future in it.'

'And the service allows you to forget that sometimes,' I added.

'Possibly,' he replied, 'but it's not likely that my lot will improve in the army. You'll have seen that if ever I do anything good in this life it remains unnoticed or is misinterpreted.'

'If you read Laplace every night,' I said, 'you'd find a consolation for that.'

And I shut myself up in my quarters to write a poem on the man in the iron mask, which I entitled: THE PRISON.[15]

3

On the love of danger

No isolation is too complete for those who are pursued by the mysterious daemon of poetic fancy. The silence was profound, and the darkness thick on the towers of ancient Vincennes. The garrison had been asleep since nine in the evening. All lights had been extinguished at ten on the order of the drums. Nothing was to be heard but the voice of the sentinels stationed on the rampart calling out and echoing, one after the other, their long and melancholy cry: *'Sentry, take your guard!'* The crows in the towers answered with a still more mournful sound, and, still feeling insecure, flew up higher to the keep. There was nothing more to disturb me – yet something did disturb me, which had neither sound nor light. I wished to write, and could not. I was aware of something inside my thought, like a flaw in an emerald; it was the idea that there was someone close by me who also watched, and watched without consolation, suffering profoundly. This disquieted me. I was sure that he needed to confide, and I had brusquely fled his confidence out of a desire to give myself over to my favourite thoughts. I was now being punished by confusion in these very thoughts. They would not soar freely and widely, and it seemed to me that their wings were weighed down, wet perhaps with the secret tears of a neglected friend.

I rose from my chair. I opened the window and breathed in the night-scented air. The odour of the forest came to me over the walls, mixed a little with a slight whiff of gunpowder. That put me in mind of the volcano on which three thousand men lived and slept in perfect safety. On the great wall of the fortress, separated from the village by a track about forty paces wide, I perceived a gleam sent forth by the lamp of my young neighbour; his shadow passed back and forth on the wall, and I saw from the outline of his epaulettes that he had not even thought of going to bed. It was midnight. I briskly left my room and went into his. He was not at all astonished to see me, and immediately said that, if I found him still up, he was finishing a reading from Xenophon that interested him greatly. However, since there was not a single book open in the room and he had his little letter from the lady still in his hand, I was not deceived; though I pretended to be. We stationed ourselves at the window, and, in an effort to attune my thought to his, I said:

'For my part I've been working too, and I've been trying to account to myself for the essence of that attraction which resides for us in the blade of a sword. It's an irresistible pull which keeps us in army service in spite of ourselves, and makes us be for ever waiting for a crisis or a war. I don't know (and this is what I came to you to talk about) if it isn't true to say, or write, that there inheres in armies a passion which is peculiar to them and gives them their life; a passion that partakes neither of the love of glory nor of ambition, but is a sort of hand-to-hand combat against Destiny, a struggle which is the source of a thousand delights unknown to the rest of mankind, and whose secret victories are replete with magnificence: in brief – the *love of danger*!'

'It's true,' said Timoléon. I continued:

'What is it that sustains the sailor on the sea, pray? – that consoles him for the tedium of being a man who sees only other men? He sails, and says goodbye to the land; goodbye to women's smiles, goodbye to their love; goodbye to his chosen friends and to the gentle customs of his life; goodbye to his cherished old parents; goodbye to the natural beauties of the earth, to the trees, to the greensward, to the sweet-smelling flowers, to the shady cliffs and the melancholy woods thronged with wild and silent creatures; goodbye to the great cities, to the endless activity of the arts, to the sublime eruption of thought into the idleness of life, to the elegant, mysterious and passionate relationships of the great world: to all these he says goodbye – and sails. He sails to encounter three enemies: water, air, and man; and every moment of his life he will have to do battle with one of them. This magnificent tension frees him from tedium. He lives amidst continual victories; it's a victory in itself to sail across the ocean and not be swallowed up in shipwreck; a victory to go where one chooses, and to plunge through in the teeth of contrary winds; a victory to run before the tempest, and to make it follow like a servant; a victory to sleep in the midst of it and establish there a working place. The sailor reclines on the ocean's back with a regal feeling, like St Jerome on his lion, and rejoices in solitude, to which he is wedded.'

'That's magnificent,' said Timoléon; and I noticed that he put the letter on the table.

'And it's the *love of danger* which sustains him, which means that he's never idle for a moment, that he's conscious of a struggle and has a goal. We need constant struggle – if we were on campaign you wouldn't be suffering so much.'

'Who knows?' he said.

'You are now as much satisfied as you can be; you won't be able to increase your happiness. Your present happiness is a dead end, truly.'

'Too true! Too true,' I heard him murmur.

'You can't get round the fact that she has a young husband and a child, and that you can never win more freedom than you have; that's your torment for you!'

He grasped my hand: – 'And always to be lying!' said he. – 'D'you think there'll be a war?'

'I don't believe a word of it,' I replied.

'If only I knew whether she's at the ball tonight! I strictly forbade her to go.'

'I should have known well enough that it's midnight without your saying that,' I said to him; 'you have no need of an Austerlitz, my friend, you're busy enough; you'll be able to dissimulate and lie for many years to come. Goodnight.'

4

The family concert

As I was about to depart I paused with my hand on the latch of his door, astonished to catch the sound of some music quite near at hand, from the fortress itself. When we went to the window to listen, it seemed to us to be made up of the voices of two men, a woman and a piano. This had a pleasing oddity for me at that hour of night. I suggested to my friend that we go nearer to hear. The little drawbridge – parallel to the great one, and designed to let the governor and officers pass during part of the night – was still lowered. We re-entered the fortress, and wandering through the courtyards, were guided by the music to some open windows. I recognized them as belonging to the good Quartermaster-Sergeant Major of Artillery.

They were large windows on the ground floor, and as we stopped in front of them we could see the honest soldier's simple family within the apartment.

At the far end of the room there was a little mahogany piano decorated with old fashioned brass ornamentation. The Quartermaster-Sergeant Major – looking just as elderly and as modest as he had first seemed to us – was seated in front of the keyboard, playing a series of chords, decorations and modulations that were simple enough, but harmoniously united one with another. He had no music in front of him, and his eyes were raised to heaven; his mouth was half opened with delight under the thickness of his long white moustaches. His daughter, standing to his right, was about to sing, or had just left off – for she was glancing at him in question, her lips, like his, still parted. To his left a young non-commissioned officer dressed in the severe uniform of that splendid regiment, the Light Artillery of the Guard, gazed at this young woman as if he had never stopped hearing her voice.

Nothing could be so calm as their pose, nothing so becoming as their attitude, nothing so happy as their faces. The light which fell from high on their three faces revealed not a hint of care; and the finger of God had written on them nothing but good will, love and modesty.

The scraping of our swords on the wall alerted them to our presence. The worthy fellow saw us, and his face reddened with surprise – and I think with pleasure too. He got up briskly, and grasping one of the three candlesticks that lit them, came to open the door and invite us to sit down. We urged them to continue their family concert; and with a fine simplicity, without apologizing or begging indulgence, he said to the young people:

'Where were we?'

And the three voices rose in a chorus of inexpressible harmony.

Timoléon sat and listened, motionless; as for me, hiding my forehead and my eyes, I let myself drift into a melting mood which was – I know not why – full of sadness. What they sang transported my soul into a realm of tears and melancholy joys, and – pursued perhaps by the importunate themes of my evening labours – I transformed the floating modulations of their voices into floating images. It was one of those Scottish lays they sang, one of those ancient melodies that still echo in the sonorous chant of the Orkneys. For me the slow ascent and sudden vanishings of this melancholy harmony were like the mountain mists in Ossian[16] – those mists rising from the spray of the foaming torrents of Arven, gradually thickening as they rise, and seeming to swell and materialize into a gathering of innumerable phantoms tormented and writhing in the wind. – There are the warriors, who stand dreaming, helm in hand, their tears and their blood falling drop by drop into the black waters by the rocks. – There are the pale beauties, whose tresses stream out behind them like the glowing tail of a distant comet melting into the watery breast of the moon: they pass swiftly, and their feet vanish from sight enveloped in the folds of their vaporous white robes; they have no wings, yet they fly – fly bearing harps, with downcast eyes and innocently parted lips. As they pass they let out a cry, and then, rising, lose themselves in the soft light that calls to them. – There are the ships of ether which seem to dash against louring rocks, and sail on through deep seas – mountains lean to weep over them, and black hounds raise their misshapen heads and howl long at the trembling moon in the heavens, while the sea shakes the blanched columns of the Isles of Orkney, ranged like the pipes of an immense organ and pouring out heartrending harmonies over the ocean, a thousand times drawn out in the caverns that imprison the waves.

Thus the music translated itself into the sombre images of my soul, which was still very young, susceptible to every sympathy, and as if in love with imaginary woes.

Nevertheless to feel it in this manner was after all to recreate the thought of the original creator of those sad and powerful songs. The happy family themselves felt the strong emotion they generated, and a deep resonance sometimes made the three voices tremble.

The song stopped, and was followed by a long silence. The girl leant on her father's shoulder, as though tired. She was tall and a little stooping, as if from weakness; and she was slender and appeared to have grown too fast – her chest, which was rather slight, seemed to have been affected by this. She kissed her father on his bald, broad and wrinkled forehead, and gave her hand to the young non-commissioned officer, who pressed it to his lips.

As I was too reserved, wrapped up in my own dignity, for a frank avowal of my inner dreams, I contented myself with saying coolly:

'Heaven give long life and all sorts of blessings to those with the gift of interpreting music literally! I cannot be sufficiently amazed at the man who criticizes a symphony for being too Cartesian, or another for leaning towards the Spinozan system – who exclaims over the pantheism of a trio, or the utility of an overture for the improvement of the labouring class. If I had the pleasure of knowing how an extra flat on the clef is able to render a quartet for flutes and bassoons in favour of the Directory rather than of the Consulate or the Empire, I wouldn't speak at all, I'd always be singing; I'd trample words and phrases underfoot, for at best they'll be understood in a hundred or so provinces, while I'd have the pleasure of using my seven notes to explain my notions with the utmost clarity to the entire universe. But, since I'm devoid of this knowledge, my musical conversation is so limited that all I can do is to tell you, in plain language, of the pleasure you've given me – above all the sight of you, the spectacle of the harmony which reigns in your family, full of simplicity and good feeling. Indeed, what delighted me most in your little recital was the pleasure you took in it; your natures seem to me to be more beautiful than the most beautiful music that ever rose to heaven from our ever grieving, miserable earth.'

I held out my hand with great warmth to this excellent father, and he pressed it with an expression of grave acknowledgement. He was merely an old soldier; but he had in language and manner an indefinable touch of old-fashioned courtliness. This was to be explained by what followed.

'You've seen here, Lieutenant,' said he to me, 'the life we lead. My daughter, myself, and my future son-in-law take our relaxation in singing.'

As he spoke he looked tenderly at the fine young people, beaming with happiness.

'And here,' he added with a graver air, and pointing to a little portrait, 'here is the mother of my daughter.'

We turned to look at the white plastered wall of the modest room, and saw indeed a miniature which showed the most graceful, the freshest little peasant girl that ever Greuze[17] endowed with great blue eyes and lips the shape of cherries.

'It was a great lady who once had the kindness to do this portrait,' said the Quartermaster-Sergeant Major, ' – and it's a curious story how my poor little wife came to get her dowry.'

And, to our immediate requests that he tell the story of his marriage, he replied as follows, while we sat around three glasses of green absinthe which he ceremoniously offered us before beginning.

5

THE QUARTERMASTER-SERGEANT MAJOR'S STORY

The children of Montreuil and the stonecutter

'You should know, Lieutenant, that I was brought up in the village of Montreuil, by the Curé[18] of Montreuil himself. He taught me some rudiments of plainchant during the happiest times of my life – the times when I was a choirboy, when I had fresh, chubby cheeks that every passer-by wanted to pat. I had a clear voice, fair powdered hair, and was dressed in smock and clogs. I don't often look at myself, but I imagine that I don't look much like that any longer. However, that's how I was, and I could never bring myself to leave off playing a sort of jangling, discordant harpsichord the Curé had in his house. I used to tune it with a pretty accurate ear, and the good father, who at one time had a reputation at Notre Dame for singing and teaching plainchant harmony, made me learn an old sol-fa. When he was pleased, he would pinch my cheeks until they were blue and say: "Well, Mathurin, you're only a peasant boy, but if you really get to know your catechism and your sol-fa, and give up playing around the house with that rusty gun, we could make a master of music out of you. Go on as you've been doing." – This encouraged me, and I would bang away with all my fingers on the poor twin keyboards, on which nearly all the sharps were mute.

'There were times when I had permission to walk and run about; and my favourite recreation was to go and sit myself down at the end of the park of Montreuil, and eat my piece of bread with the masons and labourers who, a hundred yards down from the gate on the Avenue de Versailles, were building a little pavilion for music – by order of the Queen.

'This was a charming place. You can see it on the right as you go up the road to Versailles. When you make out a pavilion that looks

62

like a mosque or a box of sweets in the middle of a plot of lawn surrounded by great trees at the far end of the park of Montreuil — that's the one I watched them put up.

'I used to go along holding the hand of Pierrette, a little girl of my own age, who M. le Curé would make sing with me because of her pretty voice. She'd bring a big slice of bread and jam given to her by her mother, the Curé's housekeeper, and we'd go to see the building of this little house the Queen was having made as a gift for Madame.[19]

'Both Pierrette and I were about thirteen years old. She was already so pretty that people stopped on the street to compliment her, and I've seen beautiful ladies get down from their coaches to talk to her and kiss her! When she wore a red frock arranged in pleats and drawn in at the waist, one could see how beautiful she would be one day. She didn't think anything of this, and loved me like a brother.

'We'd always gone out hand in hand since our earliest infancy, and the habit was so well established that I never gave her my arm in my life. Our custom of visiting the workmen led to our making the acquaintance of a young stonecutter, who was about eight or ten years older than us. He'd make us sit on a block of ashlar or on the ground next to him, and, when he had a big stone to cut, Pierrette would pour water on the saw, and I'd take hold of the other end to help him — so he became my best friend in the world. In disposition he was quiet, very gentle, and sometimes light-hearted, though not often. He'd made up a little song about the stones he was cutting, how they were harder than the heart of Pierrette, and he played in a hundred ways on these words — *Pierre, Pierrette, Pierrerie, Pierrier, Pierrot*[20] — so that all three of us laughed a great deal. He was a tall young man, still growing, all pale and gawky, with long arms and big legs, and sometimes had the air of not paying attention to what he was doing. He said that he loved his work, because he could earn his living with a good conscience while dreaming of other things until the sun went down. His father had been an architect and had been ruined — I don't know how — which meant that the son had to start his work at the bottom. But he was quietly resigned to that. When he cut a great block, or sawed it lengthways, he always began a little song in which there would be a little fable which he would build up as he went along into twenty or thirty couplets or so.

'Sometimes he asked me to stroll up and down in front of him with Pierrette, and made us sing together, teaching us how to sing in part-song; then he'd amuse himself by having me go down on my knees in front of Pierrette, hand on heart, and do the words of a little scene that we had to repeat after him. But all this didn't prevent him knowing his profession, for he became a master mason before the year was out. He had to support his poor mother and two little brothers (who used to come with us to watch him working) by the labour of his square and hammer. When he saw all his little world around him it lent him courage and gaiety. We called him Michel: but, to tell you straight away, his name was Michel-Jean Sédaine.'[21]

6

A sigh

'Alas!' I said, 'there's a poet really in his place.'

The young woman and the non-commissioned officer looked at each other as if troubled to see their good papa interrupted; but the worthy Quartermaster-Sergeant Major, after tucking up each end of the black cravat he sported over a white stock, military style, continued his story.

7

The lady in rose

'It appears to me certain, my dear children,' said he, turning towards his daughter, 'that Providence has been pleased to take unto itself the shaping of my life. I can say before all the world that in the countless storms that have disturbed it, I've never ceased to trust in God and to wait upon His aid, after having done my utmost to make my way myself. So I may tell you that in walking upon the stormy waves I haven't deserved to be called *man of little faith*, as was the apostle; and when my feet began to sink I lifted up my eyes, and was raised up.'

(Here I looked at Timoléon, – 'He's worth more than we are,' I whispered.) – He continued:

'M. le Curé of Montreuil loved me very much, and I was treated by him with such fatherly affection that I used to forget entirely – though he was always reminding me – that I was born of humble peasant parents who were carried off by the smallpox, and whom I'd never even seen. At sixteen I was wild and foolish, but I knew a bit of Latin, a great deal of music, and was thought to be pretty well skilled in all kinds of garden work. My existence was extremely pleasant and joyful, because Pierrette was always there, and I could look at her while I worked, even though I didn't talk to her a lot.

'One day as I was cutting back the branches of one of the beeches in the park, and tying up a little bundle of sticks, Pierrette said to me:

'"Oh! Mathurin, I'm scared! Here are two fine ladies coming towards us by the end of the walk. What shall we do?"

'I looked up, and indeed there were two young women – not arm in arm but walking quickly over the dry leaves. One was rather taller than the other and was dressed in a short gown of rose-coloured silk. She almost ran as she came, and the other, even while accompanying her, was being left behind. Instinctively, like the poor little peasant that I was, I was seized with fright, and said to Pierrette:

'"We'll run away!"

'But heavens! – there was no time, and my fear redoubled when I saw the lady in rose beckon to Pierrette – who blushed high without daring to move, and hastily clutched at my hand for reassurance. As for myself, I whipped off my bonnet and pressed my back against the tree, completely petrified.

'When the lady in rose had come right up to us she went straight to Pierrette and unceremoniously took her chin to show her to the other lady, saying:

'"Aha! – just as I told you: it's my milkmaid costume for Thursday – and what a pretty little girl this is! My child, you'll give all your dresses, just as they are, to the people who'll come to ask you for them on my behalf, won't you? In exchange I'll send you mine."

'"Oh! Madame –" Pierrette said, stepping back.

'The other young lady started to smile with an air so delicate, so tender and melancholy, and with so affecting a mien that I can never forget her.[22] She advanced, her head on one side, and softly taking Pierrette's bare arm told her to come forward, for it was necessary for everyone to do the will of this lady.

'"Now don't think of changing anything in your costume, my pretty little girl," the lady in rose continued, threatening her with a slender gold-knobbed malacca cane she carried. "Here's a great big boy who is going to be a soldier, and I shall marry you to him."

'She was so lovely, that I remember an incredible temptation to throw myself on my knees; you'll laugh, and I've often done so myself since; but if you'd seen her you'd understand what I say. She had the air of a young and very benign fairy.

'She talked rapidly and vivaciously, and, giving Pierrette's cheek a little tap, left us totally speechless and completely stupefied, not knowing what to do. We watched the two ladies follow the avenue towards Montreuil, and then become lost to view in the park behind the little wood.

'So we looked at one another, and, still holding hands, went back to the Curé's house – not saying anything, but very happy.

'Pierrette was blushing furiously, and as for myself, I hung my head. The Curé asked us what was to do; and I said to him, very seriously:

' "Monsieur le Curé, I want to be a soldier."

'He almost fell over backwards – he who had taught me the sol-fa!

' "What, my dear child," he said, "you wish to leave me! Ah! Good heavens! Pierrette, what has happened to him, that he wants to be a soldier? D'you not love me any more, Mathurin? D'you not love Pierrette any more? What have we done to you – tell me? And what will you do with the fine education I've given you? It was all a waste of time, apparently. But answer me, you wicked fellow!" he went on, shaking me by the arm.

'I scratched my head, and answered with my eyes fixed to my clogs:

' "I want to be a soldier."

'Since M. le Curé had become extremely red, Pierrette's mother brought him a large glass of cold water, and she herself began to cry.

'Pierrette also cried, and didn't dare speak; but she wasn't angry with me, because she knew very well that it was in order to marry her that that I wanted to go.

'At that very moment two tall powdered lackeys came in, with a lady's maid who had the air of being a lady herself, and demanded if the little girl had prepared the clothes that the Queen and the princesse de Lamballe had asked for.

'The poor Curé had got up, but was so upset that he was unable to remain standing for long; and Pierrette and her mother trembled so much that they daren't open the chest which had been brought in exchange for the frock and bonnet, but went to change their clothes rather as if they were going to be shot.

'Alone with me, the Curé asked what had happened, and I told him what I've told you, only more briefly.

' "And it's for that you wish to go, my son?" said he taking both my hands. "But just think – the greatest lady in Europe would only speak to a little peasant like you by way of a distraction, and would hardly think twice about what she said. If someone told her that you'd taken it as an order or as a prediction, she would say that you're a simpleton, and that you can be a gardener all your life – it's all the same to her. What you earn by gardening, and what you earn by teaching singing, will belong to you, my friend; instead of which, what you earn in a regiment won't belong to you, and you'll have a thousand opportunities to spend it on pleasures forbidden by religion and morals; you'll lose all the good principles I've given you, and make me blush for you. You'll come back (if you come back) with a character changed from the one you were born with. You were gentle, modest, biddable – you'll become rough, impudent and blustering. Little Pierrette certainly won't submit to being the wife of a ruffian, and her mother would stop her if she did. And I, what can I do for you, if you forget all about God's Providence? You would forget about Providence, you know – I can assure you it would come to that."

'I remained with my eyes fixed on my clogs, my brows knit, lips pouting, and I said, scratching my head:

'"I don't care. I want to be a soldier."

'The good Curé could not brook this, and, opening the door wide, he sadly showed me the road. I understood the gesture, and went out. I'd certainly have done the same in his position. However, that's what I think now – then I didn't. I put my cotton bonnet over my right ear, turned up my smock collar, took up my stick, and marched straight to a little tavern on the Avenue de Versailles, without saying goodbye to anyone.'

8

Front-rank firing position

'In the little tavern I found three heroes with gold lace on their hats, white uniforms with rose-coloured lapels, waxed black moustaches, frosted powder in their hair – and talking as fast as quack doctors. These three fine fellows were your real recruiting sergeants. They told me that to obtain a fair idea of the perfect eternity of happiness one enjoyed in the Royal Auvergne Regiment, I had only to sit down at table with them. They gave me chicken to eat, then venison and partridge, Bordeaux and Champagne to drink, and excellent coffee. They swore on their honour that in the Royal Auvergne I'd never have anything else.

'I've seen since how truly they spoke.

'They also swore to me – they swore perpetually – that one enjoyed the most delicious freedom in the Royal Auvergne; that the soldiers there were incomparably happier than the commanding officers of other corps; that one enjoyed the society of agreeable gentlemen and lovely ladies, that much music was made, and above all that a piano-player would be mightily appreciated. This last circumstance decided me.

'The following day, therefore, I had the honour of becoming a soldier in the Auvergnes. It is a pretty good regiment, it's true; but I didn't see Pierrette any more, nor M. le Curé. I asked for chicken for dinner: and was given that pleasant mixture of potatoes, mutton and bread which then called itself, still calls itself, and undoubtedly will always call itself *ratatouille*. I was made to learn the correct stance for an unarmed soldier to such a pitch of perfection that I later served as a model for the artist who did the plates for the Ordinance of 1791 – an Ordinance which, as you know, Lieutenant, is a masterpiece of precision. I learnt individual drill and platoon drill, so as to be able to make charges in regular time, quick time or one's own time, by numbers or without, as perfectly as the smartest corporal of King Frederick the Great of Prussia – whom old soldiers still remember with that kind of affection felt by men who admire those who lick them hollow. I was done the honour of being promised that, if I bore myself well, I'd be admitted into a crack company of Grenadiers. – I soon had a powdered pigtail which fell pretty grandly on to my white shirt: but I didn't see Pierrette any more, nor her mother, nor M. le Curé of Montreuil, and I never made any music.

'One fine day, when I was confined to these very barracks – where we are now – for having committed three mistakes in weapons drill, I was made to assume the position of firing from the front rank: one knee on the paving, and a magnificent, dazzling sun full in my face at which I was forced to aim while keeping perfectly still – until fatigue made my arms crumple at the elbows. I was encouraged to keep my musket up by the presence of an excellent corporal, who from time to time used his butt to knock up my bayonet should it begin to wilt – this was a little punishment devised by M. de Saint-Germain.[23]

'I'd been endeavouring for twenty minutes to attain the highest degree of petrifaction possible in this pose, when at the end of my barrel I made out the gentle, mild face of my good friend Michel, the stonecutter.

'"You've come at exactly the right time, my friend," said I to him, "and you'll do me a great favour if you'll be so good as to slide your cane under my bayonet for a moment, without anyone seeing. My arms would be much better, and your cane none the worse."

'"Ah! Mathurin, my friend," he replied, "look at you – you're certainly being punished for having left Montreuil. You no longer have the good Curé's counsels and readings; and you'll end by entirely forgetting the music you love so much – bands on parade are no substitute."

'"I don't care," I said, lifting the end of the barrel of my gun from contact with his cane, out of pride; "I don't care – everyone has his own ideas."

'"You won't grow your espaliers any more, nor those beautiful

Montreuil peaches, with Pierrette at your side – who's as fresh as they are, and whose upper lip has a down as fine as theirs."

'"I don't care," I said again, "I've my own ideas."

'"You'll spend ages on your knees, shooting at nothing with a dud flint, before even making corporal."

'"I don't care," I repeated. "Even getting on slowly is still getting on – everything comes to him who waits, as they say, and when I'm a sergeant I'll be somebody, and I'll marry Pierrette. A sergeant; that's a great position, and honour be where honour's due."

'Michel sighed.

'"Ah! Mathurin! Mathurin!" he said to me, "you're not wise, my friend, and you've too much pride and ambition. Wouldn't you prefer to buy yourself out, if someone would pay for you, and come back to marry your little Pierrette?"

'"Michel! Michel!" I replied, "you've been too spoilt by the world. I don't know what it is that you do there, but you've no longer the look of a stonemason – for instead of your short jacket you're wearing a black taffeta suit. But you'd never have said that in the days when you were always telling me 'One has to make one's own way.' – Myself, I wouldn't want to marry on other people's money and, as you see, I am making my own way. – For the rest, it was the Queen who put this in my head, and the Queen couldn't be wrong in judging what's the correct thing to do. She herself said: 'He will be a soldier, and I will marry them'; she didn't say: 'He will go back home after having been a soldier.'"

'"But," said Michel to me, "if by chance the Queen wanted to give you enough to get married, would you take it?"

'"No, Michel, I wouldn't take her money, even if, which is hardly possible, she wanted me to."

'"But if Pierrette were to earn a dowry for herself?" he asked.

'"Yes, Michel, I'd marry her straight away," said I.

'The good fellow seemed quite touched.

'"Very well!" he said, "I'll tell the Queen that."

'"Are you mad," I said, "– or are you a servant in her household?"

'"Neither one nor the other, Mathurin, although I no longer cut stone."

' "What d'you cut then?" I asked.

' "Ha! I cut out plays, with pen and paper."

' "Heavens!" I said, "is that really possible?"

' "Yes, my boy, I make up simple little plays, very easy to understand. I'll show you them." '

'It's true,' said Timoléon, interrupting the Quartermaster-Sergeant Major, 'the works of the good Sédaine are not constructed around difficult questions; one doesn't find there any synthesis of the finite and the infinite, or arguments on ultimate causation, the association of ideas or the identity of the individual; there are no kings and queens murdered by poison or on the scaffold – and they don't have titles resonant with philosophical implication: instead they call themselves *Blaise*, *The Strayed Lamb*, *The Deserter*; or even *The Gardener and His Master*, and *The Unexpected Bet*; they are about straightforward folk, who speak truth, who are *philosophers without knowing it*, like Sédaine himself, whom I find more considerable than people think.'

I didn't answer.

The Quartermaster-Sergeant Major continued:

' "Oh, right, so much the better!" I said. "I'd like to see you working on that just as much as on your stone-cutting."

' "Well! What I built then was better value than what I do now. It doesn't go out of fashion, and it stays up much longer. Nevertheless if it fell it could crush someone, whereas now if my work falls flat, nobody's hurt."

' "Never mind, I'm still very pleased . . ." said I . . . or rather I would have said – for the corporal appeared, and gave my friend Michel's cane such a violent blow with his butt that he sent it over there – look! – over there by the powder store.

'At the same time he ordered six days in the guardroom for the sentry who'd let a civilian enter.

'Sédaine realized that he must leave; he calmly fetched his cane, and, going out by the door to the wood, said to me:

' "I promise, Mathurin, that I'll tell the Queen of all this." ' '

9

A sitting

'My little Pierrette was a beautiful girl, with a resolute character, calm and virtuous. She wasn't easily upset, and ever since she had talked to the Queen, she wasn't to be dictated to easily; she knew very well how to say firmly to the Curé and his housekeeper that she wished to marry Mathurin, and she stayed up at night to work on her trousseau, just as though I hadn't been put out of the house for a long time to come – if not for the rest of my life.

'One day – poor Pierrette always remembered that it was Easter Monday, and often told me about it – one day when she was seated outside the Curé's front door, working and singing as if she hadn't a care in the world, she saw a splendid carriage driving up fast – very fast – with six horses trotting down the avenue in great style, mounted by two little postilions with powdered hair and dressed in rose-coloured suits, very pretty, and so small that from a distance one could make out only their huge riding boots. They wore great bunches of flowers on their shirt fronts, and the horses sported flowers on their heads too.

'And then – then didn't the equerry who was running ahead of the horses stop precisely in front of M. le Curé's house! – and the vehicle was good enough to come to a halt there too, and deigned to open its door wide! It was empty. As Pierrette stared wide-eyed, the equerry swept off his hat very politely and asked her if she would be so good as to climb into the carriage.

'You think, perhaps, that Pierrette made a fuss? Not at all; she had too much good sense for that. She simply took off her clogs, which she laid on the doorstep, put on her silver-buckled shoes, folded up her work neatly, and climbed into the carriage, leaning on the footman's arm as if she'd never done anything else in her life – because since she'd exchanged dresses with the Queen she never lacked confidence in anything.

'She has often told me since that she had two great anxieties in the carriage: the first was that it went so fast that the trees of the Avenue de Montreuil seemed to chase after one another like madmen; the second that she thought that sitting on the white cushions of the carriage might stain them with the blue and yellow from her skirt. So she gathered it into folds and held herself very straight on the edge of the cushion – not at all worried by her adventure, and realizing that in circumstances like these it's best to do what everyone wants, freely and without hesitation.

'Secure in this sensible judgement of the situation – which was the gift of a happy and gentle nature, disposed to find goodness and truth in everything – she was perfectly prepared to take the arm of the footman, and be conducted to the Trianon – into the gilded apartments, where her only concern was to walk on tiptoe out of respect for the lemon wood and teak parquets, which she was afraid of scratching with the nails on her shoes.

'As she came into the last of the rooms she heard the joyous laughing murmur of two soft voices, which frightened her a bit and made her heart beat rather fast – but, on entering, she was immediately reassured, for it was only her friend the Queen.

'Madame de Lamballe was with her, but seated in a window embrasure and settled in front of a miniaturist's stand. Under the green cover of this stand lay an ivory fully prepared; next to the ivory, some paint-brushes; next to the paintbrushes, a glass of water.

' "Ah! here she is!" said the Queen gaily, and ran to take her by both hands.

' "How fresh she is, and how pretty! What a pretty little model she'll make for you! Come, don't fail to get her likeness, madame de Lamballe – Put yourself there, my child."

'And the lovely Marie-Antoinette forced her to sit down on a chair. Pierrette was quite speechless, and her chair was so high that her little feet hung down swinging.

' "Now just look how well she holds herself," continued the Queen, " – one doesn't have to tell her twice what to do. I'll wager she's intelligent as well. Hold yourself straight, my child, and listen to me. Two gentlemen are coming here. Whether you know them or not doesn't signify; it doesn't concern you. You'll do everything they tell you to. I know you can sing – and you will sing. When they ask you to go out and come in, to go there and come here, then you'll enter – you'll leave – you'll go there – you'll come here, precisely as they say, d'you understand? All this is for your benefit. Madame and I are going to help them teach you something I'm interested in, and for our pains we ask only that you pose for Madame one hour every day; that won't hurt very much, will it?"

'Pierrette only replied by blushing and turning pale at each word; but she was so happy that she could have wished to kiss the Queen, like a friend.

'As she posed, with her eyes turned towards the door, she saw two men come in, one fat and the other tall. When she saw the tall one, she couldn't prevent herself from crying out: – "Heavens! it's . . ."

'But she bit her finger to silence herself.

' "Well now! how do you find her, gentlemen?" said the Queen, "was I wrong?"

' "Isn't she just *Rose* herself? said Sédaine.

' "A single note, Madame," said the fatter of the two, "and I will know if this is Monsigny's Rose[24] as well as Sédaine's."

' "Let's see, my child, repeat this scale after me," said Grétry,[25] and he sang *do, re, mi, fa, so*.

'Pierrette sang it after him.

' "Her voice is lovely, Madame," said he.

'The Queen skipped and clapped her hands.

' "She shall earn her dowry," said she.'

10

A wonderful evening

At this point the worthy Quartermaster-Sergeant Major sipped some of his little glass of absinthe, and urged us to do the same. Then, having wiped his white moustache with a red handkerchief and rolled it a moment in his big fingers, he continued thus:

'If I knew how to produce surprises, Lieutenant, as they do in books, and make the audience wait for the end of the story by holding it up high like a sugar plum, giving their lips a little taste, then taking it away, then releasing it to be gobbled up, I'd find a new way to tell you what followed. But I go from one thing to another, simply, as my life has been from day to day. So now I'll tell you that since that day when my poor Michel had come to see me here at Vincennes and found me in the front-rank firing position, I'd grown ridiculously thin, because I'd heard no word of our little family at Montreuil, and so had come to think that Pierrette had forgotten me completely. The Auvergne Regiment had been at Orléans for three months, and homesickness took hold of me. I became jaundiced-looking, and was unable to bear the weight of my musket. My comrades began to feel contempt for me – like they always do with sickness in the army, as you know.

'There were some who scorned me because they thought I was seriously ill, others because they maintained I was pretending to be so – and in the latter case there was nothing for me but to die to show I spoke the truth, because I wasn't able to recover all at once, nor was I ill enough to retire to bed – a nasty predicament . . .

'One day an officer from my company came to find me and said:

' "Mathurin, you know how to read, look at this."

'And he led me to the Place de Jeanne d'Arc, a square which was dear to me, where I read a big theatre poster on which was printed:

77

BY ORDER

Monday next, a special performance of
IRÈNE, a new play by M. de VOLTAIRE,
and of *ROSE AND COLAS*, by
M. SÉDAINE,[26] music by M. MONSIGNY,
for the benefit of mademoiselle Colombe,
celebrated singer of the Italian Comedy,
who will appear in the latter piece. HER
MAJESTY THE QUEEN has condescended
to promise that she will honour the
performance with her presence.

' "Very well, Captain," said I, "what has it to do with me – this?"

' "You're a reliable chap," he said to me, "and handsome. I'm going to have you powdered and curled to make you smarter, and then station you as sentry outside the door of the Queen's box."

'And what he said was done. The hour of the performance came – and there I was in the corridor, in the Auvergne's full-dress uniform, standing on a blue carpet, and surrounded by garlands and festoons of flowers that had been arranged everywhere, with lilies in bloom on each step of the theatre staircases. The manager was running about all over the place with an expression of anxious happiness. He was a fat little man with a red face, dressed in a suit of sky-blue silk, with a frilled shirt front flowing out of it boldly. He busied himself everywhere, and never stopped standing in front of the window and crying out:

' "That's the livery of the duchesse de Montmorency; there's the courier of M. le duc de Lauzun; M. le prince de Guéménée is just arriving; after him comes M. de Lambesc. You've seen them? – you know them? How kind she is, the Queen! How kind the Queen is!"

'He went distractedly to and fro seeking Grétry, and then met him face to face in the corridor just where I was.

' "Tell me, monsieur Grétry, my dear monsieur Grétry, tell me I beg of you, is it not possible for me to speak with this celebrated singer you've brought along for me? Certainly it isn't for an illiterate ignoramus like me to raise the slightest doubt about her talent, but I'd still very much like you to assure me that there's no danger that the Queen will not be pleased. There's been no rehearsal."

' "Aha!" Grétry answered, with a teasing air, "it's impossible for me to answer for that, my dear sir; but what I can assure you is that you won't meet her. An actress like this one, sir, is a spoilt child. But you'll see her when she comes on stage. In any case, supposing it was somebody other than mademoiselle Colombe, what difference would that make to you?"

' "What, sir! I, Director of the Theatre of Orléans, haven't I the right . . . ?" he replied, puffing out his cheeks.

' "No right at all, my good Director," said Grétry. "Come," he pursued more seriously, "how can you bring yourself to doubt of a talent approved by both myself and Sédaine?"

'I was much pleased to hear that name cited as an authority, and I paid closer attention.

'The Director, a man who knew his profession, wished to take his opportunity.

' "But do I count for nothing then?" said he. "What kind of person d'you think me? I have lent my theatre with infinite pleasure, too delighted to receive that august princess who . . ."

' "Talking of that," said Grétry, "you should know that I've been commanded to tell you that this evening the Queen will remit to you a sum equal to half the gross takings."

'The Director, stepping back, bowed deeply with annoyance, which also betrayed the pleasure this news gave him.

' "For shame, sir, for shame! I was not speaking of that – in spite of the respect with which I shall receive this favour; but you've told me nothing of what we may hope for from your genius, and . . ."

' "You know too that there is some question of your directing the Italian Comedy in Paris?"

' "Ah! monsieur Grétry . . ."

' "At court we speak of nothing but your merits; everybody admires you very much, and that's why the Queen has wished to see your theatre. A Director is the soul of the enterprise: from him derives the genius of the authors, and that of the composers, the actors, the decorators, the designers, the lighting men and the cleaners; he is the beginning and the end of it all; the Queen knows this well. You've trebled the price of your seats, I hope?"

' "Better than that, monsieur Grétry, they're a louis each; I couldn't show lack of respect for the court by pricing them lower than that."

'Just at that moment everything resounded with a great commotion of horses and loud joyful cheers, and the Queen came in so fast that I, like the sentry positioned opposite me, hardly had time to present arms. She was followed by handsome, scented gentlemen, and by a young lady who I recognized as being the same as had accompanied her at Montreuil.

'The performance started immediately. Le Kain[27] and five other actors from the Comédie-Française had come to play the tragedy of *Irène*, and I was aware of this drama running its course, because the Queen talked and laughed as long as it lasted. Out of respect for her no one applauded – as I believe is still the custom at court. But when the comic opera came on she spoke no more, and no one breathed a word in her box.

'All of a sudden I heard a wonderful female voice rising from the stage, and it moved me to the core; I was trembling, and was forced to support myself on my musket. There was only one voice like that in the whole world, one voice coming from the heart, reverberating in the breast like the sound of a harp, a voice of passion.

'I listened, putting my ear to the door of the box, and through the gauze curtain of the window I glimpsed the players and the piece they were playing. A girlish figure was singing:

> "There was a little bird who dressed
> In grey as a mouse;
> And to give her chicks rest
> Built them a nest,
> As a house."[28]

'And saying to her lover:

"Love me, love me, my little King."[29]

'And, as she was sitting on the window sill, she feared lest her sleeping father should wake up and see Colas; so she changed the refrain of her song and sang:

"Oh! draw up your legs, for they can be seen."[30]

'An extraordinary thrill ran through my whole body when I saw how closely this Rose resembled Pierrette; it was her figure, she had the same dress, the same red and blue skirt, her white petticoat, her little unaffected, serious air, the same well-shaped leg and little silver-buckled shoes worn with red and blue stockings.

'"Good God!" I said to myself, "how clever these actresses must be to take on the appearance of other people just like that! Here's this famous mademoiselle Colombe, who lives in a beautiful house in town, who has come here by post-chaise, who has hundreds of servants, and goes round Paris dressed like a duchess – and she looks as much like Pierrette as that! Still, one can tell that it isn't her. My poor Pierrette couldn't sing so skilfully, even though her voice is at least as pretty."

'Even so, I wasn't able to stop looking at her through the glass, and I stayed there up to the moment when the door was pushed briskly open in my face. The Queen was too hot, and wanted her box open. I heard her voice speaking loud and quickly.

'"I'm very pleased – the King will be much amused at our adventure. The first Gentleman of the Bedchamber may tell mademoiselle Colombe that she won't repent having lent me the honour of her name. Oh! how droll this is!"

'"My dear princess," she was saying to madame de Lamballe, "we've enticed the whole world here . . . everyone is doing a good deed without suspecting it. See the people of the good town of Orléans enchanted by the great singer, and the whole court longing to applaud her. Yes, yes, we'll applaud."

'At the same time she gave the signal for clapping, and the whole house, their hands freed, didn't let a word of *Rose* go by without rapturous applause. The enchanting Queen was delighted.

'"There are three thousand lovers here," said she to M. de Biron, "but this time they belong to Rose, not to me."

'The performance ended and the ladies were throwing their bouquets to Rose.

'"And the real lover now, where is he?" said the Queen to M. le duc de Lauzun. He came out of the box and made a sign to my Captain, who was roaming the corridor.

'I began to tremble again; I felt that something was going to happen to me, without daring to guess what it could be, comprehend it, or even think of it.

'My Captain bowed low and spoke in a low voice to M. de Lauzun. The Queen looked at me; I leant against the wall to save myself from falling. People were coming up the staircase, and I saw Michel Sédaine, followed by Grétry and the important and foolish Director; they were leading Pierrette, real Pierrette, my own Pierrette, my sister, my wife, my Pierrette of Montreuil.

'The Director cried from a distance: "Here's a wonderful evening, worth eighteen thousand francs!"

'The Queen turned, and, speaking out of her box with a manner at once full of candid gaiety and delicate benevolence, she took Pierrette's hand.

'"Come, my child," she said, "there's no other walk in life in which one can earn a dowry in an hour without sinning. Tomorrow I shall lead my pupil back to M. le Curé of Montreuil, who will absolve us both, I trust. He'll certainly pardon you for having played a comedy once in your life – it's the least an honest woman can do."

'Then she greeted me. Greeted me! – me, who was more than half dead – what cruelty!

'"I hope," said she, "that M. Mathurin will now be willing to accept Pierrette's fortune; I add nothing to it, she has earned it herself."'

I I

The end of the Quartermaster-Sergeant Major's story

Here the good Quartermaster-Sergeant Major got up to take down the portrait, which he gave us to pass again from hand to hand.

'There she is,' said he, 'in the same costume, the same bonnet and neck scarf; there she is, as the princesse de Lamballe chose to paint her. It's your mother, my child,' he said to the pretty young woman he had next to him, and whom he sat on his knee; 'she played no more comedy, because she was never able to learn any but the part of *Rose and Colas*, taught her by the Queen.'

He was moved. His old white moustache trembled a little, and there was a tear on it.

'This is a child who killed her mother by being born,' he added; 'one must love her a great deal to forgive that; but, truly, one can't have everything at the same time. It would have been too much for me, apparently – as Providence didn't will it so. Since then I've followed the guns of the Republic and of the Empire – and I can say that, from Marengo to Moscow, I've seen some splendid actions; but I've never had a finer day in my life than the one I've just told you about. The day when I joined the Royal Guard was also one of the best. I took such great joy in wearing once again the white cockade that I used to have in the Royal Auvergne! But then, Lieutenant, I'm anxious to do my duty, as you've seen. I believe I'd die of shame if, at the inspection tomorrow, there was a single cartridge missing; and I suspect someone's taken a barrel of powder for infantry loading at the last firing practice. I'd almost be tempted to go and see, if it weren't forbidden to go in there with lights.'

We begged him to rest and remain with his children – which dissuaded him from his idea; and, while finishing his little glass, he told us some more assorted facts about his life. He hadn't been promoted to commissioned rank because he'd always loved the élite corps too much, and had been too attached to his regiment. Gunner in the Consul's Guard, sergeant in the Imperial Guard, these had always seemed to him greater positions than being an officer of the line. I have met many veterans of the Old Guard like that. For the rest of it, everything in the way of honours a soldier can have, he'd had: Musket of Honour with silver bands, Cross of Honour with a pension – and above all fine and noble deeds done in the service, which filled the column that records distinguished actions. Only he didn't tell us about these.

It was two o'clock in the morning. We made an end to the evening by getting up and cordially shaking hands with this brave man; and we left him happy amongst the lifetime of feelings that had been revived in his good honest heart.

'How many times more worthy,' I said, 'is this old soldier, with his resignation, than we others – we young officers with our silly ambitions!' It made us thoughtful.

'Yes, I really believe,' I went on as we crossed the little bridge, which was raised behind us, 'I believe that there's nothing so pure, in our times, as the soul of a soldier like that – scrupulous about his honour and believing himself soiled by the least hint of indiscipline or negligence; without ambition, without vanity, without luxury, always a slave and always proud of his servitude, holding nothing so dear in his life as a single memory of having been remembered.'

'And believing that Providence watches over him!' said Timoléon – as, with an air of being profoundly impressed, he left me to re-enter his own quarters.

12

The awakening

It was four o'clock in the morning; and I had slept for an hour. It was the 17th of August – I have never forgotten it. Suddenly both of my windows burst open instantaneously, and all their shattered panes fell into my room with a pleasant silvery tinkle. I opened my eyes and saw white smoke gently drifting towards me and forming countless ringlets around the bed. At first I looked at it with mild surprise, but quickly recognized the colour, and the smell. I ran to the window. Dawn was starting to break and its soft rays illuminated the whole of the old castle, which was silent still, and motionless – seemingly in a stupor upon receipt of this first blow. I could see no movement there, save that the old grenadier stationed on the rampart – and locked out there with a key as was the custom – was striding up and down quickly, his musket at the ready, and peering down into the courtyards. He paced there like a lion in a cage.

Since everything remained quiet, I was beginning to think the cause of this disturbance must be the testing of some armaments in the moat, when a more violent explosion made itself heard. At the same instant I saw a sun, which was not the natural sun, lift itself from the tower furthest away on the side of the forest. Its rays were red, and at the end of each was an exploding bomb; in front was a pall of powder smoke. This time the keep, the barracks, the towers, the ramparts, and the villages and woods trembled, and seemed to slide left to right and back again like a drawer opened and shut in one swift movement. In that moment I understood earthquakes. A clashing sound, like that which would be made if all the Sèvres porcelain in the world had been thrown out of the window,[31] made me realize that, of all the windows of the chapel, all the windows of the castle, all the panes of the barracks and of the town, there would not now remain one piece of glass held in its putty. The white cloud began to disperse in little wreaths.

'It's very good powder when it forms wreaths like that,' said Timoléon as he entered my room, fully dressed and armed.

'It seems to me we're being blown up,' I said.

'I don't deny it,' he replied coolly. 'At the moment there's nothing we can do about it.'

Within three minutes I was dressed and armed like him, and we stared in silence at the silent castle.

Suddenly a score of drums beat out the general alarm; the walls shook off their stupor and impassivity, and cried out for aid. The arms of the drawbridge slowly began to descend, letting down their heavy chains on the far side of the moat to let the officers in and the inmates out. We ran to the portcullis: it opened to admit the strong and eject the weak.

An extraordinary sight confronted us: all the women were flocking to the gate – but at the same time all the horses of the garrison were there too. By a sound instinct for danger they had broken the halters in their stalls, or thrown off their riders, and now waited, pawing the ground, to be set free into the open fields. They were galloping through the courtyards between herds of women, whinnying with terror, their manes bristling, their nostrils wide, their eyes bloodshot, rearing against the walls, breathing the gunpowder with horror, and burying their scorched nostrils in the sand.

A young and beautiful girl wrapped in her bedclothes and carried by a soldier, followed by her half-clothed mother, came out first – and the whole crowd followed. At the time this appeared to me a useless precaution, for the country could not be safe for six leagues around.

We entered at the run, as did all the officers lodged in the town. The first thing that struck me was the calm in the faces of our veteran grenadiers of the Guard, positioned at the entrance. Their arms grounded, and leaning on their weapons, they were looking towards the powder magazine with the air of connoisseurs, but without saying a word and without moving from the correct stance – hand on musket sling. My friend Ernest d'Hanache commanded them; he greeted us with the smile natural to him, which was like that of Henri IV; I gave him my hand. He lost his life as recently as the last Vendée, when he died nobly.[32] All of those I have named in these recollections – which are still fresh – are dead now.

In running I stumbled on something which almost made me fall: it was a human foot. I could not prevent myself from pausing to look at it.

'That's what your foot'll be like any moment,' shouted a passing officer, roaring with laughter.

There was nothing to indicate that this foot had ever worn a shoe. It was as though embalmed and preserved like a mummy's – broken off two inches above the ankle like the feet of those statues used as models in an artist's studio; polished and veined like black marble, and pink coloured only at the nails. I had no time to draw it; I continued on my way to the furthest tower, in front of the barracks.

There our soldiers awaited us. In their first surprise, believing the fortress under attack, they had thrown themselves from their beds to the arms rack, and then gathered themselves together in the courtyard – most of them in their shirts with their muskets on their arms. Nearly all had bleeding feet, cut by the broken glass. There they had stayed, silent and inactive in front of an enemy that was not human, and they were delighted to see their officers arrive.

As for us, we ran to the very crater of the volcano. It was still smoking, and a third eruption was imminent.

The little tower of the powder store had been ripped open, and through its gaping sides one could see a column of smoke rising slowly in a spiral.

Had all the powder in the tower been ignited? – did enough remain to blow us all up? That was the question. But there was another factor which was not a question – that all the artillery ammunition wagons, full and half open in the neighbouring courtyard, would blow up should a spark reach them, and that – since the keep held four hundred thousand charges of powder for the cannons – Vincennes, its woods, town, fields, and part of the suburb of Saint-Antoine would be made to erupt in a mixture of stones, branches, roofs and even the most firmly fixed on of human heads.

The best stimulus to discipline is danger. When everyone is at risk, each man keeps quiet and fastens upon the first person to give an order or set a salutary example.

The first to leap towards the ammunition wagons was Timoléon. His face retained its composed and serious expression, but, with an agility which surprised me, he threw himself on a wheel which was about to burst into flame. For want of water he extinguished it by smothering it with his coat, with his hands, and by pressing his chest down on to it. At first we thought he was doomed; but, on coming to help him, we found the wheel blackened and extinguished, his coat scorched, his left hand a little black-powdered, but otherwise he was completely calm and uninjured. In a moment all the wagons were hauled out of the endangered courtyard and taken outside the fortress, into the field where the butts were. Every gunner, every infantryman, every officer put himself in harness to drag, roll and push the terrible vehicles with hands, feet, shoulders, foreheads.

Through the black rents in its breast the pumps swamped the little powder store. It was riven on all sides, and, tottering back and forth twice, it opened its flanks like the outsides of a great tree, and, falling outwards, revealed a sort of black smoking furnace in which nothing had recognizable shape, where all the weapons and missiles were reduced to a reddish-grey dust diluted in boiling water; a sort of lava, in which blood, iron and fire were compounded into a living mortar which flowed out into the courtyards, scorching the grass in its wake. That was the end of the danger; it remained to consider our position, and to count the survivors.

'They could have heard that in Paris,' said Timoléon to me, pressing my hand: 'I shall write to reassure her. There's nothing more to do here.'

Without another word to anyone he went back to our little white house with green shutters, as if returned from hunting.

13

A pencil drawing

It is when dangers are past that we assess them and find them formidable. A man is amazed at his good fortune; he pales at the fear he might have felt; congratulates himself on not having betrayed some weakness, and feels a sort of reflective, conscious terror he did not dream of at the time.

Gunpowder, like lightning, wreaks unpredictable horrors.

This explosion had done its wonders, not by its power, but by its skill. It seemed to have thought about its blows, and chosen their targets. It had played with us, and said: 'I will blow away that one there, but not this one next to it.' It had plucked up a freestone arch and transported it complete, with its shape intact, into the fields where it lay on the turf like a ruin that had been blackened by time. It had thrust three cannon balls six feet underground, ground up the paving stones with bullets, broken a bronze cannon in two, dashed out all the windows and all the doors in all the rooms, and thrown the shutters of the great magazine on to its roof without touching a grain of its powder; it had scattered ten great stone boundary posts as if they were pawns on an overturned chessboard; had broken the iron chains which held them as one might break silk thread, twisting the links as one twists hemp; it had ploughed up the courtyard with smashed gun carriages, and inlaid the pyramids of cannon balls into its stones, and – under the cannon nearest the destroyed powder store – it had spared the life of the white hen we had seen the previous evening. When this poor fowl strolled peaceably out of its bed with its little ones our good soldiers welcomed her with joyful cries as an old friend, and petted her with the unselfconsciousness of children.

She turned around coquettishly, marshalling her young, and wearing as always her red aigrette and her silver necklet. She had the air of

89

expecting the master who would feed her, and ran in bewilderment between our legs, surrounded by her chicks. Following her we came upon a terrible thing. At the base of the chapel lay the head and chest of the poor Quartermaster-Sergeant Major, without limbs or the remainder of his body. The foot I had stumbled on with my foot when entering the fortress had been his too. Undoubtedly the unfortunate man had been unable to resist his desire to check his powder barrels once more and count his shells, and – whether it was the iron on his boots or whether a displaced flint – some movement had set everything off.

His head and chest had been launched like a stone from a sling at the wall of the church some sixty feet up; and the powder with which this horrifying torso was covered had graven its shape deeply on the wall, to the foot of which he had fallen. We gazed at him a long time, and nobody said a word of mourning. Perhaps because to lament him would have been to pity ourselves for having run the same risk. Only the Surgeon-Major said: 'He won't have suffered.'

For myself, I felt that he was still suffering. But despite that – half from an invincible curiosity, half from an officer's professional bravado – I made a sketch of him.

In an organization where feeling is repressed things like that happen. One of the dark sides of the profession of arms is the posture of excessive strength into which one is constantly straining one's character. A man strives to harden the heart, to hide pity lest it look like weakness; and he makes an effort to conceal the divine feeling of compassion, without realizing that by forcibly shutting up a virtuous feeling he may stifle the prisoner.

I felt myself to be hateful at that moment. My youthful heart was swollen with grief at this death – yet with obstinate calm I continued my drawing, and I have kept it. Sometimes I feel remorse at having done it; sometimes it reminds me of the story I have just written, and of the unassuming life of that good soldier.

That noble head was now nothing more than a thing of horror, a kind of head of Medusa. It was coloured like black marble; the hair stood on end, the eyebrows were opened towards the top of the forehead, the eyes closed, the mouth gaping as though crying out. Sculptured on to this black bust one could see amazement at the flames which had suddenly erupted from the earth. I felt that he had had time for a terror which had been as swift as the powder – time perhaps for incalculable anguish.

'Did he have time to think about Providence?' said the calm voice of Timoléon d'Arc***, who was looking at my drawing over my shoulder with an eye-glass.

At the same moment a cheerful soldier, fresh, pink-cheeked and fair, bent down to take the black silk cravat from the burnt torso:

'It's still perfectly good,' said he.

He was a decent young man in my company, called Muguet, who had two stripes on his arm, and neither scruples nor fine feelings, but was *notwithstanding, the best boy in the world*.[33] This incident broke our train of thought.

At length a great clatter of horses' hoofs arrested our attention. It was the King. Louis XVIII had come in his barouche to thank his Guard for having preserved his veterans and his ancient fortress. He looked for a long time at the strange lithography on the wall. All the troops were drawn up. He raised his voice loud and clear to ask the battalion commander which officers and what soldiers had distinguished themselves.

'Each man has done his duty, sire!' answered M. de Fontanges[34] simply. He was the most chivalrous and the most lovable officer I have known, the man in the world who has best enabled me to form an idea of what the duc de Lauzun and the chevalier de Grammont[35] must have been like in manner.

Thereupon, instead of Crosses of Honour, the King merely took rolls of coin from his barouche and gave them to be distributed amongst the soldiers; and, crossing Vincennes, he left by the gate to the woods.

The ranks fell out, the explosion forgotten; no one thought of being discontented, or thought he had deserved better than another. In fact, it was a case of the ship's crew saving the ship in order to save themselves, and that was all. However, I have since seen less valorous acts valued higher.

I thought of the poor Quartermaster-Sergeant Major's family. But I was the only one who did. Generally speaking, when princes pass through somewhere, they pass too quickly.

Memories of Military Grandeur

BOOK 3

I

How often were we to see terminated thus, by some obscure accident, those humble lives which had been caught up and fed by the collective glory of the Empire! Our army had received the veterans of the Grand Army, and they died in our arms, leaving us with the memory of their primitive and singular character. These men seemed to us what was left of a race of giants, vanishing now, man by man, and for ever. We loved them for what was good and honourable in their ways; but our more self-conscious generation could not help detecting in them sometimes little touches of childishness and backwardness which the idle times of peace brought to the eye. The army seemed to us a body without motion. We stifled, shut up in the stomach of this wooden horse which would never open on another Troy. You will remember – you, my comrades – how we never ceased to read over the *Commentaries* of Caesar, Turenne, and Frederick II, and how unremittingly we devoured the lives of those generals of the Republic so cleanly seized by Glory: those candid and humble heroes like Marceau, Desaix and Kléber,[1] youths of an antique virtue; and how, after having studied their combat manoeuvres and their campaigns, we fell into bitter distresses comparing our destiny to theirs, and reckoning that their elevation had been so high because they had found their feet immediately, at the age of twenty, on the highest step of that ladder of promotion, each rung of which cost us eight years' climbing. You, who I have so often seen suffering the boredom and disgust of military servitude – it is above all for you that I write this book. Therefore, side by side with those recollections in which I have showed some few traits of what is good and honest in armies – but where I have depicted also some of the appalling pettiness of that life – I wish to put memories which will enable us to lift up our heads in the knowledge and the contemplation of its grandeur.

The grandeur of the warrior, or the beauty of the life of arms, seems to me to be of two kinds: that of command and that of obedience. The first, wholly on the surface, active, glittering, proud, egotistical and capricious, will become from day to day rarer and less in demand, the more pacific society becomes. The second, wholly inward, passive, obscure, humble, devoted, persevering, will daily be more honoured – for now the spirit of conquest declines, and the greatness which a high character can bring to the profession of arms seems to me less in the glory of combat than in the honour of silent devotion and the faithful accomplishment of duties which are often odious.

If the month of July 1830[2] had its heroes, it had in you its martyrs, O my brave comrades! – you who are all now separated and dispersed. After the tempest, many among you retired silent to your ancestral roofs, however poor they were, much preferring them to the shadow of a flag not their own. Others have chosen to seek their lilies[3] in the brambles of the Vendée, and have bathed them anew with their blood; others have gone to die under foreign kings; while others still, still bleeding from the wounds of the Three Days, have been unable to resist the call of the sword, and have taken it up again for France, and for her have conquered new fortresses.[4] Everywhere the same necessity of giving oneself up body and soul, the same need to devote oneself, the same desire to uphold and practise, somewhere and somehow, the arts of suffering well and dying well.

But everywhere too are those to be pitied because they found them-selves thrown where they could not fight. Combat is the life of the army. Where it starts, the dream becomes truth, knowledge glory, and servitude service. The flare of war consoles the slaves of the army for the ineffable miseries of lethargic peace. Yet, I repeat, it is not in fighting that the very purest grandeur is to be found. I shall often speak of you to others; but I wish once, before finishing this book, to speak of you to yourselves, and of one life and death which to my mind achieved greatness in its force and its candour.

THE LIFE AND DEATH OF CAPTAIN RENAUD,
OR, THE MALACCA CANE

2

A memorable night

The night of the 27th of July 1830 was silent and foreboding. For me its memory is more vivid than that of many more terrible scenes that destiny has cast before my eyes.

The awful calm of the earth and the sea on the point of a tempest is not more majestic than was the calm of Paris on the eve of revolution. The boulevards were deserted. After midnight I walked their whole length alone, avidly looking and listening. The pure sky shed on earth the empty light of the stars; but the houses were shut up, extinct like the dead. All the street lamps were shattered. A few groups of labourers still lingered near the trees, listening to an unknown orator slipping them his secrets in whispered words. Then they separated and ran, scuttling up dark narrow streets, flattening themselves against tiny alley gates which opened like traps and immediately shut upon them. Nothing further stirred. The city seemed to be inhabited only by the dead, in houses struck by plague.

At regular intervals one encountered a dim, unmoving mass, which was scarcely recognizable save to the touch: it was a battalion of the Guard, at arms, rigid and silent. Further on was an artillery battery crowned with its lighted matches, like two stars.

One could walk with impunity in front of these imposing, solemn troops; walk around them; walk away; return – and receive no question, no insult, no word even. They were neutral, without anger, without hate; they were resigned and were waiting.

As I approached one of the largest of the formations, an officer advanced towards me and asked, with extreme politeness, if the flames one could see lighting up the Porte Saint-Denis in the distance were due to incendiaries – he was preparing to take his company forward to make sure. I told him that they came from some great trees that the shopkeepers had chopped down and set alight, taking advantage of the troubles to destroy the ancient elms which overshadowed their shops. So, seating himself on one of the stone benches of the boulevard, he commenced tracing lines and circles in the dust with a malacca cane. It was by this that I knew him, though he had recognized my face. As I stood in front of him, he shook me by the hand and asked me to sit beside him.

Captain Renaud was a man of upright and severe temperament, and a highly cultivated soul – like many in the Guards of that period. His character and habits were long familiar to us, and those who read these memoirs will well know which grave face they should put to the *nom de guerre* given by the soldiers, adopted by the officers, and received without comment by the man himself. Like old families, old regiments that are preserved intact in peacetime adopt domestic customs and invent nicknames for their children. An ancient wound in the right leg was the reason for the Captain's habit of always leaning on this *malacca cane*, the head of which was curious enough to attract the attention of those who saw it for the first time. He nearly always had it in his hand and took it everywhere – but there was not a scrap of affectation in the habit, his temperament being far too simple and serious for that. Even so one did feel that he set very great store by it. In the Guards he was greatly honoured. With no special ambition, and not wishing to be other than he was, a Captain of Grenadiers, he was perpetually reading, spoke as little as possible, and then in monosyllables. – Extremely tall, extremely pale, and with an air of melancholy, he had between his brows a rather deep small scar, which would often turn from its bluish colour to black, and so sometimes give a ferocious air to that usually calm and peaceable face.

The soldiers loved him. In the Spanish campaign[5] in particular the joy with which they served in detachments commanded by *Malacca Cane* had been much remarked. And it really was *Malacca Cane* who led them; for Captain Renaud never drew his sword, even when, at the head of his sharpshooters, he came near enough the enemy to run the risk of hand-to-hand fighting.[6]

He was not only an experienced man of war: he had also a penetrating grasp of the grand politics under the Empire that no one knew how to explain – and that was sometimes attributed to profound study, sometimes to important and long-standing connections in high places. His perpetual reserve made it impossible to discover which.

In fact this very reserve is the dominating feature of modern men, and he only carried a general trait to an extreme. Nowadays a front of cool civility covers both character and action. I do not think that many would recognize themselves in the startling portraits that are made of us. Affectation is ridiculed in France more than anywhere else, and it is doubtless for this reason that, far from displaying the excessive force of our feelings in our language or manners, everyone is at pains to conceal violent emotions, whether of profound chagrin or involuntary happiness. I am far from thinking that civilization has weakened these impulses; I observe only that it has carefully masked them. And I think that this is for the good – I love the self-contained nature of our time. In this apparent coldness there is modesty, and that is a prerequisite of true feeling. Disdain also enters into it – an appropriate currency in human affairs.

We have already lost many friends whose memory yet lives in us. – You will recall them, oh my dear comrades in arms! – Some killed in war, some in duels, some by suicide destroyed – all men of honour and resolution, of strong passions; but in appearance simple, cold and reserved. Ambition, love, play, hate, jealousy racked them internally: but they scarcely spoke of these, and turned swiftly aside from any too direct implication that might touch their intimate being. One never saw them seeking attention in drawing-rooms by striking tragic poses;[7] and if some young lady, putting down her novel, had witnessed them so submissive to the disciplines of conventional manners, and issuing platitudes in a low voice, she would have held them in contempt; yet, as we know, they lived and died as strong a band of men as ever nature produced. Not Cato nor Brutus – for all that they wore the toga – was ever their better. Our passions have as much of fire as those of any age, but even the scrutiny of a friend recognizes them only in the traces of fatigue they leave. On the outside, in address, in conduct, we have in common a certain cold dignity – which is only disregarded by a few children who want to seem important and cut a figure at all costs. The supreme law of our manners now is Decorum.

There is no profession where habitual coldness in language and habits contrasts more strikingly with the main activity of life than that of the soldier. Contempt for exaggeration is there pushed very far indeed; and we disdain the talk of a man who seeks to show off his feelings or elicit sympathy for his sufferings. I knew all this – and was prepared to leave Captain Renaud quickly, when he took me by the arm and held me back.

'Did you see the Swiss Guard drilling this morning?' he asked; 'it was rather interesting. They did the *street combat advance* drill with perfect precision. Ever since I've been in the service I've never seen it taken seriously: it's something for parades and the Opera. But it could be valuable in the streets of a big city, so long as the sections on the right and left form up quickly in front of the platoon that's just fired.'

As he spoke he continued to trace lines in the ground with the tip of his cane; then he rose slowly; and as he walked along the boulevard avoiding the groups of officers and men, I followed him, and he went on talking with a kind of nervous exaltation that charmed me, and which one would never have expected from him, so commonly thought of as cold.

Fingering the button of my coat, he started with a very simple request:

'Would you forgive me,' he said, 'if I asked you to send me your Guard's gorget, if you've kept it? I've left mine at home, and I can't send someone to find it, nor go myself, because they're killing us in the streets like rabid dogs: – but since it's two or three years since you left the army perhaps you've no longer got yours? About a fortnight ago I too threw in my commission, because I'm horribly bored with the army. But the day before yesterday, when I saw the Orders in Council,[8] I said to myself: "There'll be fighting." So I packed up my uniform, my epaulettes and my bearskin, and went along to the barracks to join these good fellows who they're going to kill at every corner – and who would certainly have felt, at the bottom of their hearts, that I'd shamefully abandoned them at a time of crisis. That would have been contrary to honour – isn't that so? – completely contrary to honour?'

'Did you foresee the Orders before you resigned?' I asked.

'Good Lord, no! I still haven't read them.'

'Well then, what could you blame yourself for?'

'Nothing but the look of the thing, but I didn't want even that against me.'

'Why, that's admirable!' said I.

'Admirable! Admirable!' exclaimed Captain Renaud walking faster, 'that's the new word, and how puerile! I detest admiration: it's at the bottom of too many rotten actions. It's bestowed far too cheaply these days – and on everybody. We should beware of admiring lightly. – Admiration is corrupt and corrupting. A man ought to do good as he sees it – not for praise. Anyway, I have my own ideas about that.' He stopped abruptly, and was going to leave me.

'There is something as fine as a great man,' I remarked, 'and that is a man of honour.'

He took my hand with feeling. 'That's an opinion we have in common,' he said warmly. 'I've put it into practice the whole of my life, and it's cost me dear. For it's not so simple a matter as people think.'

Here the second-lieutenant of his company came up to ask him for a cigar. He pulled several from his pocket, and gave them to him without speaking. The officers began to smoke as they walked up and down in silence, in a calm undisturbed by the thought of the present situation. None deigned to speak of the dangers of the hour, nor of their duty – for all knew the hearts of the others.

Captain Renaud returned to me. – 'Fine weather,' he said, pointing to the sky with his malacca cane: 'I don't know when I'll stop seeing the same stars every night; there was a time when I imagined I'd see the sky of the South Seas – but I wasn't destined to change hemispheres. It doesn't matter! – the weather's marvellous: the people of Paris are asleep, or seem to be. None of us have had anything to eat or drink for twenty-four hours, and that makes one's ideas very clear. I remember that once on the way to Spain you asked the reason for my lack of promotion, and I hadn't time to tell you: but this evening I feel the temptation to go back over my life, which I've been mulling over in my memory. You like stories, I recall, and in your life of retirement, you'll like some memories of us. – If you'd care to sit with me on this street parapet we can talk at peace, for it seems to me that they've stopped sniping at us from the windows and cellar vents for the time. – I shall tell you only a few episodes of my story, and shall do no more than follow my own fancy. I've seen a lot and read a lot, but I know very well that I wouldn't have the skill to write it down. That's not my function, thank God! – and I've never tried it. – But, really, I do know how to live, and have lived as I resolved to do from the time I had the courage to make a resolve – and, in truth, that's something. Let's sit down.'

I followed him slowly, and we walked through the battalion to get to the left of his magnificent grenadiers. They were standing upright, serious, their chins resting on the muzzles of their muskets. A few of the younger men were seated on their packs, more exhausted by the day's work than the others. All kept silent, coolly occupied with going over their equipment and putting it in good order. Nothing suggested disquiet or discontent. They kept their ranks just as if after a day of parades, awaiting orders.

When we were seated, our old comrade began to speak. In his own style he told me of three important episodes, which gave me a sense of his life and an understanding of the strangeness of his ways and the darker side of his character. Nothing he said to me has faded from my memory, and I repeat it almost word for word.

3

Malta

'I'm nothing,' he began, 'and, at the moment, it makes me happy to think so. But if I were someone important, I could say like Louis XIV that *I have been too fond of war*.[9] – What could one expect? – Bonaparte had made me drunk in infancy like all the others, and his glory went to my head so violently that I hadn't room in my brain for any other idea. My father, an elderly senior officer who was perpetually on campaign, was quite unknown to me when one day it took hold of his imagination that I should accompany him to Egypt. I was twelve, and still remember that time as if I was there now – the feelings of the whole army, the feelings which had already taken possession of my soul. Two spirits swelled the sails of our ships – the spirit of glory, and the spirit of plunder. My father no more heard the second than he heard the north-west wind which carried us along; but the first boomed so loud in my ears that it made me deaf for a long time to every sound in the world save Charles XII's music – the cannon.[10] The cannon seemed to me to be the voice of Bonaparte; and when it grumbled and roared, I, child as I still was, blushed with pleasure, jumped for joy, clapped my hands, and answered it with great whoops. These first passions were the basis for that excessive enthusiasm which became the goal, and the folly, of my life. A single memorable meeting determined for me that species of fatal infatuation, of insane adoration, to which I became all too willing to sacrifice.

'The fleet had got under way on the 30th Floréal, year VI.[11] I spent night and day on deck, bowled over with happiness at the sight of the vast blue sea and our ships. I counted up to a hundred sail, and I couldn't count them all.[12] Our fighting line stretched for a league, and the half-circle formed by the convoy was at least six leagues.[13] I was

speechless. I saw Corsica very close to us, towing Sardinia in her wake
– and soon Sicily rose on our left. – For the *Junon*, which carried my
father and myself, was ordered to clear the way and to form an advance
guard with three other frigates.[14] My father took my hand and pointed
out Etna smoking, and then two other heights I've never forgotten:
Favignana and Mount Eryx. Marsala, the ancient Lilybaeum, passed
between the mists – I took its white houses for doves flying out of a
cloud: and one morning – it was . . . yes, it was the 24th Prairial[15] – I
saw rising before me at daybreak a spectacle which dazzled me for
twenty years.

'Malta was spread before me with her forts, her cannon on a level
with the sea, her long battlements glowing in the sun like newly-polished
marble, and her swarms of slender galleys darting about on long red
oars. One hundred and ninety-four French ships enfolded her with their
great sails, and with the blue, red and white pennants that were being
hoisted on all the masts at that very moment – while the standard of
religion slowly lowered itself on Gozo and the fortress of St Elmo.[16] It
was the descent of the last Cross Militant. The armada fired five hundred
guns.

'The flagship *Orient* lay opposite alone and apart, vast and still.[17] One
after another all the men-of-war passed slowly in front of her, and from
afar I saw Desaix salute Bonaparte. We climbed aboard the *Orient* close
to him: – at last, for the first time, I saw him.

'He was standing near the rail, chatting with Casabianca, the captain
of the flagship – that poor *Orient* – and he was playing with the hair
of a boy of ten, the captain's son.[18] I was immediately jealous of this
boy, and my heart gave a bound when I saw him touching the general's
sabre. My father went up to Bonaparte and talked with him for a long
time. I couldn't yet see his face. Suddenly he turned round and looked
at me: my whole body trembled at the sight of that sallow forehead
surrounded with long lank locks, moist as though just issued from the
sea; those great grey eyes, those hollow cheeks and that lip recessed on
to a sharp chin.[19] He had been speaking of me, for he said: "Listen, my
friend, since you wish it, you shall come to Egypt, and General Vaubois
can stay here with his four thousand men without you. But I don't like
people bringing children; I've only allowed it to Casabianca so far, and

I was wrong. You'll have to send this one back to France; I want him to be strong in mathematics, and if anything should happen to you out there I'll look after him – myself; I'll take care of him, and I'll make him a good soldier." As he finished speaking he bent down and, taking me by the arms, lifted me up to his mouth and kissed me on the forehead. My head whirled, I felt that he was my master and that he was spiriting my soul away from my father – whom indeed I scarcely knew because of his always being with the army. I believed I knew the terror of the shepherd Moses when he saw God in the burning bush. Bonaparte had lifted up a free being: when his hands set me gently down again on deck they released another slave.

'The day before that I would have thrown myself in the sea if any-one had taken me away from the army; but now I let them lead me wherever they wished. I left my father with indifference – and it was for ever! But we are sinful in that way from infancy, and, men or children, such unworthy things can grasp us and sweep us away from true natural feeling! My father was no longer my master, because I had seen his master, and from him alone seemed to emanate all the authority on earth. – Oh, delusions of command and servitude! Oh, corrupting notions of Power, fit for seducing children! False enthusiasms! subtle poisons! – what antidote can ever be found against you! – I was carried away, made drunk. I wished to work, and I worked to the point of madness! Night and day I applied myself to mathematics. I put on the uniform, the knowledge, and, on my face, the sallow colour of the school. From time to time the cannon would interrupt me, and in its demigod's voice told me of the conquest of Egypt, of Marengo, the 18th Brumaire,[20] and the Empire . . . and the Emperor kept his word to me. – As to my father, I no longer knew what had become of him – when one day this letter, here, came for me.

'I carry it always in this old wallet – which used to be red – and I re-read it often to convince myself once more of the futility of the advice given by one generation to the next, and to reflect on the absurd obstinacy of my illusions.'

Here the Captain opened his tunic and extracted from his breast, first a handkerchief, then a little wallet which he opened carefully. We went into a café which was still lit, where he read me the following fragments of the letter – a letter which was to remain in my hands, as will soon appear.

4

A plain letter

'On board the English ship *Culloden*,
off Rochefort, 1804

'Sent to France with Admiral Collingwood's permission[21]

'It is not necessary, my child, that you[22] should know how this letter
comes to you, nor by what means I have been able to learn of your
conduct and present circumstances. It will suffice you to know that I
am satisfied with you, and that I am virtually certain that I shall never
see you again. It is probable that this will disturb you but little. You
have known your father only at that time of life when memory is still
unborn and the heart as yet closed to others. It develops in us later than
is generally thought, which has often surprised me. But there it is. –
You are no worse than others, as it seems to me. I must be content
with that. All that I have to tell you is that I have been a prisoner of
the English since 14th Thermidor, year VI (or the 2 August 1798, old
style – which they tell me is coming back into fashion nowadays). I
went aboard the *Orient* to try to persuade the valiant Brueys[23] to set sail
for Corfu. Bonaparte had already sent his poor aide-de-camp Julien,
who had had the stupidity to let himself be taken by the Arabs. I arrived
myself, but uselessly. Brueys was as stubborn as a mule. He said that
he was going to find the channel to Alexandria to allow his ships in –
but he added some words proud enough to let me see that at bottom
he was rather jealous of the land forces. – "Do they take us for *ferry-
men*?" he asked me. "Do they think we're frightened of the English?"
– He would have served France better if he had been afraid. But if he
made mistakes, he expiated them gloriously; and I may say that I am
expiating in tedium the mistake I made in staying by his side when we

were attacked. Brueys was wounded first in the head and the hand. He continued the fight until a cannon ball ripped out his entrails. He had himself put in a sack of bran and died on his quarterdeck. Towards ten in the evening we knew clearly that we were going to blow up. What remained of the crew shipped into the longboats and saved themselves – except for Casabianca. He stayed to the end, of course; but his son, a fine boy whom you have seen, I think, came to find me and said: "Citizen, what would honour have me do?" – Poor little fellow! He was ten, I think, and to prate of honour at such a time! I took him on my knees in the boat and prevented him from seeing his father on the *Orient*, which showered into the air like a spout of fire. We were not blown up, ourselves, but were taken prisoner – which is an even sadder fate; and I went to Dover under the guard of a fine English captain, called Collingwood, at present in command of the *Culloden*. He is a gallant gentleman if ever anyone was, who, since he joined the navy in 1761 has had only two years ashore, in which to marry and father two daughters. These children, of whom he talks incessantly, do not know him; and his wife knows only a little of his splendid character through his letters. But I feel strongly that the wretchedness of our defeat at Aboukir has shortened my own days – which have already lasted too long since I was witness to such a disaster and the deaths of my glorious friends. My advanced age has touched the hearts of everyone here; and, since the English climate makes me cough a great deal and has exacerbated all my wounds to the point of depriving me entirely of the use of one arm, the excellent Captain Collingwood has asked and obtained for me (that which he could never obtain for himself, to whom the land is forbidden) the boon of being transferred to Sicily, under a warmer sun and a purer sky. I believe that I shall come to my end there: for seventy-eight years, seven wounds, deep disappointments and captivity are incurable illnesses. My poor child, I have nothing to leave you but my sword! – and at present not even that, for a prisoner has no sword. But I have at least one piece of advice to give you, and that is that you should be wary of your enthusiasm for men who rise quickly, above all for Bonaparte. If I know you, you will become a Seid,[24] and it is necessary to guard against *Séidisme* when one is French – that is to say terribly susceptible to that contagious disease. The amount of tyrants it has produced, great and small, is amazing. We love braggarts far too well, and give ourselves over to them so heartily, that it is never long before we find ourselves gnawing our own fingers. The source of this flaw in us is a great need of action, and a great intellectual laziness. It follows from it that we are delighted to give ourselves body and soul to someone who will think for us and take the responsibility – never mind how laughable we find ourselves, and him, afterwards.

'Bonaparte is a good fellow, but he really is too much of a charlatan. I fear that he will become the instigator amongst us of a new species of foolery; and we have had enough of that in France. – Charlatanism is impudent and corrupting – there have been so many instances of it in our era, and they have led to such a clamour of drumsticks banging on drums in the marketplace, that it has insinuated itself into every profession – and there is no one so insignificant as not to be puffed up. One could not count the number of frogs who have burst. I fervently desire that my son shall not be one of them.

'I am much relieved that he has kept his word to me in *taking care of you*, as he calls it; but do not rely too much on this. Consider a scene someone told me of, which occurred at a certain dinner shortly after my melancholy departure from Egypt. I wish to tell you about it in order that you may think it over, often.

'Being in Cairo on the 1st Vendemaire, year VII,[25] Bonaparte, as a member of the Institute,[26] ordered a civic fête to mark the anniversary of the establishment of the Republic. The garrison of Alexandria celebrated this at the column of Pompey, around which a tricolour was draped; Cleopatra's needle was illuminated, rather badly; and the army of Upper Egypt rejoiced as well as they could between the pylons, the columns, and the caryatids of Thebes, on the knees of the colossus of Memnon, and at the feet of the figures of Tama and Chama. In Cairo the First Army Corps held manoeuvres, marched around, and let off fireworks. The commanding general had invited the whole staff, the civilian commissioners, the scholars, the Pasha's Kehayah, the Emir, the members of the Divan and the Agas,[27] to dinner round a table of five hundred covers laid on the ground floor of the house he had in the Place d'El Béquier. The Bonnet of Liberty and the Crescent were amorously intertwined: the Turkish and the French colours made a

convenient bower and a carpet on which to celebrate the wedding of
the Koran with the Rights of Man. After the revellers had feasted –
with their fingers – on chicken and saffron rice, water-melon and fruits,
Bonaparte, who had said nothing, darted a sharp glance at the assembled
company. The good Kléber – who was stretched out next to him because
he could not fold his long legs Turkish fashion – gave a great shove
with his elbow to his neighbour Abdallah-Menou,[28] and said to him in
his half-German accent:

'"See there! – there's Ali-Bonaparte going to give us one of his turns."

'He called him that because, at the feast of Mahomet, the General
had amused himself by wearing oriental costume, and at the moment
when he declared himself the Protector of all the religions, someone
had grandly bestowed on him the title of son-in-law of the Prophet,
and named him Ali-Bonaparte.

'Kléber had not finished speaking, and was still running his hand
through his long blond hair, when the little Bonaparte was already on
his feet, and, raising his glass to his narrow chin and his enormous
cravat, said in a curt, clear, abrupt voice:

'"A toast to the year three hundred of the French Republic!"

'Kléber burst out laughing on Menou's shoulder, almost spilling his
glass on to a venerable Aga, while Bonaparte looked askance at both
of them, knitting his eyebrows.

'Certainly he was right, my boy; for a divisional general ought not to
behave indecorously in the presence of the Commander-in-Chief – not
even a gay blade like Kléber. But they were not entirely wrong either, for
at this very hour Bonaparte calls himself Emperor, and you are his page.'

*

'– True enough,' said Captain Renaud, taking the letter from my hands,
'I'd been appointed page to the Emperor in 1804. – Ah, what a terrible
year that was! – Had I been able to think over anything then, how
attentively I'd have considered the events it brought in its train! But I
had neither eyes to see nor ears to hear anything but the Emperor's
deeds, the Emperor's voice, the Emperor's gestures, the footsteps of the
Emperor. His approach stupefied, his presence magnetized. The glory
of being attached to such a man seemed to me the greatest thing in the

world, and never has a lover felt the ascendancy of his mistress with fiercer and more devastating emotions than those which the sight of him bestowed on me every day. Admiration for a military commander becomes a passion, a fanaticism, a frenzy, which makes of us slaves and madmen, blind agents. – This poor letter I've given you to read had not much more immediate effect on my spirit than what schoolboys call a *talking to*, and I felt only the impious relief of children when they find themselves freed from natural authority, and imagine themselves at liberty because they've embraced the chains which the general folly has riveted around their neck. – However, a residue of healthy native feeling did make me keep this writing sacred, and its authority over me grew in proportion to the decline in my dreams of heroic subjection. It has stayed always next my heart and in the end it put down invisible roots there, as good sense began to clear the fumes which obscured my vision. On this particular night I couldn't resist re-reading it with you, and I pity myself when I consider how slow and twisting a road I've followed in returning to a more solid and straightforward basis for considering the conduct of man. You'll know to how small a compass it can be reduced: – but truly, sir, I think that that suffices for the life of a decent man, and it has taken me long enough to come to find the origin of that real grandeur which can still be achieved in the nearly barbarous profession of arms.'

Here Captain Renaud was interrupted by an old Sergeant of Grenadiers who came to stand at the door of the café, carrying his weapon NCO fashion and pulling a letter written on grey paper from the sling of his musket. The Captain got up calmly and opened the order he had received.

'Tell Béjaud to copy this into the Order Book,' he said to the Sergeant.

'The Sergeant Major didn't come back from the arsenal,' said the NCO, in a voice as soft as a girl's, lowering his eyes without even troubling to explain how his comrade had been killed.

'The Quartermaster will replace him,' said the Captain, not asking anything further; and he signed an order on the Sergeant's back, which served as a desk.

He gave a little cough, and went on calmly:

5

An unreported conversation[29]

'Completely intoxicated though I was, and quite infatuated by the jangle of my spurs, my poor father's letter – and his death, of which I learnt shortly afterwards – made a strong enough impression on me to give a definite check to my blind ardour; and I started to analyse more closely and calmly the scarcely canny nature of the glamour that enthralled me. I asked myself for the first time: in what precisely consists that ascendancy we allow men of action to exercise over us when they are dressed up in absolute power? – and I dared try to establish some limits within my own mind as to the voluntary submission made by so many men to one man. This first check half opened my eyes, and I had the courage to look in the face of that splendid eagle who had swept me up as a child, and whose talons were still fixed in my entrails.

'I didn't delay seeking opportunities to examine him more closely, to attempt to seek out the spirit of this great man in the hidden movements of his intimate life.

'As I've told you, they'd had the ostentation to appoint pages – though we wore officer's uniform while waiting for the green livery and red trousers we were to sport at the coronation. Up until then we served as equerries, secretaries and aides-de-camp, according to the will of a master who took up what came to hand. It already pleased him to fill up his antechambers; and since the need to dominate accompanied him everywhere he couldn't help indulging it in the most trifling things, and constantly tormented his entourage with the ceaseless drivings of his restless will. He was amused by my timidity; he made fun of my fears and my awe. Sometimes he would call me sharply to him and, seeing me enter pale and stammering, would divert himself by making me talk at length in order to witness my astonishment and confuse my ideas. Sometimes when I was writing to his dictation he would suddenly pull my ear in his special fashion, and ask me an unforeseen question on some ordinary subject like geography or algebra, posing a childishly easy problem. Then it seemed as though a thunderbolt had struck. I knew a thousand times what he asked; I knew more than he thought I knew; often, even, I knew more than he did – but his eye paralysed me. When he was out of the room I was able to breathe again, blood flowed again in my veins, memory returned and with it an inexpressible shame. Seized with rage, I would write out what I ought to have answered: then I would roll on the carpet, weep, and want to kill myself.

'"What!" I would say to myself, "are there really minds strong enough to be certain of everything, and never to falter in front of anybody? Men who can on all occasions subdue thought to action, and whose confidence crushes others and makes them believe that the key to all knowledge and all power, the key for which everyone incessantly searches, is in their pocket, and that they only have to use it to open the door into light and infallible authority!" – And yet I felt that this force was unsound, and had been usurped. I rebelled. I cried: "He deceives! His pose, his voice, his gestures are nothing but a pantomime act, a miserable parade of sovereignty, of which he himself must realize the vanity. It isn't possible that he sincerely believes in himself like that! He forbids us to lift the veil, but he sees himself naked beneath it. And what does he see? – a poor ignorant man like the rest of us, and underneath that, the mere frailty of the creature!" – Nevertheless I didn't know how to penetrate into the core of this masked soul. Power and glory encircled him on every side. I went around and about without succeeding in taking anything by surprise – and this ever-armed porcupine turned in front of me, presenting sharp spines at each point. – One day, however, chance – which rules in all things – parted them a little, and flashed a momentary light between the darts and the spikes. – One day, for perhaps the only time in his life, he encountered one stronger than he and recoiled an instant before a star greater than his own. – I witnessed it, and I felt avenged. This is how it happened:

'We were at Fontainebleau. The Pope had just arrived. The Emperor had impatiently awaited him for his coronation, and had received him in a carriage they entered simultaneously from either side, using an etiquette apparently careless, but actually profoundly calculated neither to give nor to take precedence – an Italian trick. He was now returning to the palace, where there was a great bustle; I had left several officers in the chamber just before the Emperor's, and was alone in his. – I was looking at a long table, dressed with Roman mosaics in place of marble, and heaped over with an enormous pile of petitions. I'd often seen Bonaparte come in and submit these to a peculiar test. He took them up neither by order nor at random; but when the number of them irritated him he would sweep his hand over the table from left to right and from right to left, like a haymaker, and scatter them until they were reduced to five or six, which he would open. I'd been singularly affected by this haughty kind of game. All those records of grief and suffering shoved and thrown on the polished floor, blown away as if by an angry wind, those vain pleas of widows and orphans who found their only hope of relief dependent on the arbitrary wave of the consular hat; all those papers of lamentation, moist with the tears of families, lying about haphazardly under his boots and trampled upon as though they were the dead on one of his battlefields: – they all represented to me the present destiny of France as a kind of sinister lottery. And I thought that, however magnificent the harsh indifferent hand which drew these lots, it was unjust to abandon so many obscure destinies to the blows of caprice in this way, when they might one day be as great as his, had a single trifle of support been given them. I felt my heart rise against Bonaparte, and rebel: but in secret shame – for it was the heart of a slave. I thought on those forsaken letters, on the cries of woe unheard that rose from their desecrated folds; and taking them up to read, then casting them down again, I made myself the judge between them and the master they had brought upon themselves – and who today was about to seat himself even more firmly above their heads. I was holding one of these scorned petitions in my hand when the rattle of drums beating the general salute warned me of the imminent arrival of the Emperor. For you know that, just as one sees the flash of the cannon before hearing its report, so one always saw him at the same moment as being struck by the noise of his approach – so rapid was his gait, and so much he seemed driven to live apace, piling action upon action. When he rode into a palace courtyard his escort could hardly keep up with him, and the guard hadn't time to snatch up their arms before he'd already dismounted and was going up the steps. On this occasion he'd left the papal coach to return himself alone – ahead, and at a gallop. I heard his spurs jingling at the same time as the drums beat. I hardly had time to dash into the alcove of a great ceremonial bed that no one ever used, encircled by a princely balustrade which was, happily, more than half covered over by curtains sewn with bees.[30]

'The Emperor was much agitated: he strode alone in the chamber as though waiting with impatience, covering its length three times in a trice; then he went to the window and set himself to drumming a march on it with his fingernails. A carriage rolled into the courtyard. He stopped drumming and stamped his foot two or three times as if exasperated at the sight of something done slowly, then marched brusquely to the door and opened it to the Pope.

'Pius VII came in alone. Bonaparte hastened to close the door behind him – with the swiftness of a gaoler. I confess I felt extremely frightened at finding myself a third party with such personages. However, I stayed silent and still, looking and listening as hard as I could.

'The Pope was a man of considerable height. He had a long face, sallow and sickly, but full of a noble holiness and boundless good will. His black eyes were large and fine, his lips parted in a benevolent smile to which his prominent chin imparted an expression of lively spiritual delicacy – a smile which had no politic dryness but was full of Christian charity. A white skull-cap covered his long black hair, which was streaked with silver. He wore a large capuchin of red velvet carelessly draped over his rounded shoulders, and his robe trailed over his feet. He advanced slowly, with the sedate and wary step of an old woman. With lowered eyes he sat down on one of the great gilded Roman chairs, covered with eagles, and waited for what his fellow Italian had to say.

'Ah! What a scene that was, sir! What a scene! I see it still. – It was not the man's genius that was shown me, but his character; and if his vast intellect wasn't revealed, at least his heart blazed forth. – Bonaparte wasn't then as you've seen him since. He hadn't that financier's belly, that puffy ill-looking face, those gouty limbs, and all that unhealthy flesh that art has unfortunately seized upon to make a *type*, as the current jargon goes, and which has left the people God knows what common and grotesque image – an image fit for children's toys, which will perhaps end one day in making him as fabulous and unnatural a shape as the preposterous Punch. He wasn't like that then, sir, but vigorous and supple, lithe and swift and slender, sudden in his movements, at times graceful, and elegant in manner; his slim chest was drawn back level with his shoulders – and his face was still the one I'd seen in Malta, sharp and melancholy.

'The Pope's entrance didn't stop him moving about the room. He started to prowl round the armchair like a careful hunter, and, stopping suddenly in front of it rigid and motionless as a corporal on parade, he took up the conversation begun in the carriage and interrupted by their arrival, which he was impatient to pursue.

'"I repeat to you, Holy Father, that I'm not in the least a free-thinker, and personally I don't like intellectuals and ideologues. I can assure you that, in spite of my old Republicans, I shall go to mass."

'He threw these last words brusquely at the Pope as though swinging a censer in his face, and stopped to watch for their effect, thinking that the rather unreverential events that had preceded this interview ought to give a special force to his sudden and unqualified avowal. – The Pope lowered his eyes and placed his hands on the eagle heads that formed the arms of his chair. By assuming the attitude of a Roman statue he seemed clearly to say: "I'm resigned in advance to listen to all the profane things it pleases him to force me to hear."

'Bonaparte circled round the chamber and round the chair placed in the middle of it, and I perceived by the sideways glance he threw at the aged pontiff that he was pleased neither with himself nor with his adversary, and that he regretted having begun the renewal of their conversation so lightly. He therefore started to talk more connectedly, pacing meanwhile round and round and throwing stealthily piercing glances at the wall mirrors reflecting the grave face of the Holy Father – looking at his profile when he passed near to him, but never in his face, for fear of seeming uneasy about the impression his words made.

'"There's something else that weighs upon my heart, Holy Father," said he, "which is that you consented to the coronation in the same manner as you did previously to the Concordat – as though you'd been forced. You have the air of a martyr in front of me, you sit there as though resigned, as though offering your sorrows to Heaven. But really this isn't your situation, you're not a prisoner, by God! – you're as free as air."

'Pius VII smiled sadly and looked him in the face. He understood the exorbitance which accompanied the demands of this despotic character, with whom – as with all such natures – being obeyed wasn't enough unless the very act of obedience appeared also to have been what you ardently desired.

'"Yes," resumed Bonaparte even more forcefully, "you're perfectly at liberty; you can take yourself off back to Rome – the road is open, nobody is detaining you."

'The Pope sighed, and lifted up his eyes and his right hand to Heaven without speaking. Then very slowly he lowered his wrinkled forehead and began to contemplate the golden cross hung around his neck.

'Bonaparte circled more slowly as he continued to talk. His voice softened and his smile was full of charm.

'"Holy Father, really, if the severity of your character didn't prevent me, I might say that you're a little ungrateful. You don't seem to remember at all well the good turns France has done you. Your election as Pope at the Conclave of Venice had to me a little the air of being inspired by my Italian campaign – and by a word I dropped about you. Austria didn't treat you very kindly then, and I was much pained by it. Your Holiness had to return to Rome by sea, I believe, being unable to pass through their territory."

'He paused, awaiting a response from this silent guest he had brought upon himself; but Pius VII only made a scarcely perceptible inclination of the head, and remained as if plunged in a despondency which prevented him from listening.

'Bonaparte then used his foot to push a chair next to the Pope's great armchair. I trembled, because in going to find this seat his epaulette had brushed the curtain of the alcove where I was hidden.

'"It was in truth as a Catholic that I was pained," he continued. "I haven't had time to study much theology myself; but I still entertain great faith in the power of the Church – Holy Father, she has prodigious vitality. Voltaire certainly cut you up a bit – but I don't like him, and

I'm going to set a veteran defrocked Oratorian[31] on him. You'll be pleased – you'll see. Look here, if you wanted, we could do a lot of things together in future."

'He assumed an air of innocence and beguiling youthfulness.

' "Myself – I don't know, I've tried hard enough – but I don't really see why, really, you've such a revulsion from settling the papacy in Paris for good! Good Lord, I'd let you have the Tuileries if you want it. I hardly ever use it myself. You'd find there your own room in Monte Cavallo, ready and waiting. Now look here, *Padre*, don't you see that it's the true capital of the world, there? As for me, I'd do anything you wanted; and to begin with I'm a nicer fellow than people think. – So long as war and those tedious politics were left to me, you could arrange the Church just as you please. I'd be your soldier in everything. Look, it'd be really fine: we'd have our Councils like Constantine and Charlemagne, I'd open them and close them; then I'd put the true keys of the world into your hands. And, as Our Lord said: 'I come with a sword' – I'd look after the sword myself – and I'd bring it back to you only for a blessing after each of our victories."

'He bowed slightly on saying these last words.

'The Pope, who up to then had remained motionless as an Egyptian statue, gently lifted his half-inclined head, gave a melancholy smile, raised his eyes on high and said, with a peaceful sigh, as if confiding the thought to an invisible guardian angel:

' "*Commediante!*"

'Bonaparte shot out of his chair, springing like a wounded leopard. A real rage seized him – one of his black fits. At first he marched about without speaking, gnawing his lips until they bled. No longer did he circle round his prey with delicate looks and cunning step; now he paced firm and upright, to and fro, quickly, stamping his feet and making his spurred heels ring. The room shook; the curtains trembled like trees at the approach of thunder; it seemed to me that something terrible and tremendous was about to happen; my hair began to creep, and in spite of myself I put up my hand to feel it. I looked at the Pope, but he didn't move except that both hands gripped the eagles' heads on the arms of his chair.

'The bomb exploded all at once.

'"Comedian! Me! Hah! – I'll show you comedies that will make you weep like a woman or a child! – Comedian! – Ah! you're nowhere if you think you can offer me such cold-blooded insolence! My theatre is the world, and the part I play is master and author. For actors I have you all – Pope, Kings, Peoples! – and the string by which I move you around is fear! – Comedian! Ah! – it needs a much bigger man than you to dare to clap or boo me, *Signor Chiaramonti*! Don't you realize that you'd be nothing more than a poor parish priest if I willed it? You and your tiara! – France would laugh in your face, if I didn't take care to look serious when I meet you.

'"– Only four years ago people didn't dare speak about Christ out loud. Who would have mentioned the Pope then, I ask you? – Comedian! Hah! – and now you gentlemen have moved back in amongst us fast enough! You're in a foul mood because I'm not fool enough to sign away the liberties of the French Church like Louis XIV![32] But you won't catch me like that. – It's I who hold you in my hands; it's I who carry you from south to north like puppets; it's I who make you seem to count for something, because you represent an ancient idea I want to revive; and you haven't the wit to perceive that, and to act as though you didn't notice. – Oh no! It's necessary to spell everything out! – it's necessary to rub your nose in things for you to understand them. And you really do think there's a need for you, so you stick your head in the air, and dress yourselves up in women's clothes! – But get it into your head that those don't impose on me in the slightest – and as for you! if you go on like this – I'll serve yours like Charles XII served the Grand Vizier's: I'll cut them up with my spurs."

'He was silent. I didn't dare breathe. Not hearing that voice thundering out any more I edged my head forward to see if the poor old man had died of fright. The same calm posture, the same calm face. He raised his eyes to Heaven a second time and, after having sighed deeply once more, he smiled bitterly and said:

'"*Tragediante!*"

'At that moment Bonaparte was at the end of the chamber leaning on a marble chimney as tall as himself. He left it like a thunderbolt, dashing at the old man; I thought, to have killed him. But he stopped short, grabbed from the table a Sèvres porcelain vase on which the

Capitol and the Castel Sant'Angelo were painted, and flinging it against the marble surround and the firedogs, ground it beneath his feet. Then he sat down suddenly and remained formidably still, in profound silence.

'I was relieved. I knew that the power of reflection had returned to him and his brain resumed its empire over the seething of the blood. He became sad, his voice subdued and melancholic, and from his first word I knew that he had returned to reality, and that this Proteus, subdued by two words, now showed his true self.

'"What a miserable existence!" he began. Then he sat musing, picking at the brim of his hat, not speaking for another minute, after which, alert again, he resumed, speaking to himself:

'"It's true! Tragedian or Comedian. – It's all acting, everything has been a costume drama for me for years past, and will be for ever. What weariness! What pettiness! To be posing – always posing! – full face for that man, profile for this, according to what they expect. To appear to them to be whatever they want me to be – correctly divining their imbecile dreams. To dangle them between hope and fear. To dazzle them by bulletins and days of remembrance, by the glamour of distance and the ring of names. To be their absolute master and not know what to do about it. My God, that's all there is! And at the end of it all to be as bored as I am – it's too much. – For, in truth," he continued, crossing his legs and settling into his chair, "I am colossally bored. – The moment I sit down I die of tedium. – I can't hunt for three days at Fontainebleau without curling up with ennui. For me it's essential to be on the go and to keep others going – but I'll be hanged if I know in what direction, by God! I'm speaking to you quite frankly. I have enough plans for the lives of forty emperors, I make one every morning and one in the evening; my imagination is insatiable; but I won't have enough time to carry out even two of them before I'm worn out body and soul – our little lamp burns for so short a time. And, frankly, if all my schemes were to be put into practice I couldn't swear to you that the world would be much happier: only, it would be more beautiful, and ruled by a majestic unity. – I'm no philosopher, myself, and our Secretary of Florence[33] is the only one I know who had much common sense. I don't understand certain theories. Life is too short to stop for them. So soon as I think, I act. After my death people will find quite enough explanations of my actions to exalt me if I succeed, or diminish me if I fall. The paradoxes are all there, ready, they abound in France; I shut them up in my lifetime, but afterwards they'll be evident. – It doesn't matter – my business is to succeed, and I'm good at it. I create my Iliad by my actions, create it day by day."[34]

'Here he got up cheerful and easy, with a lively, alert air. At that moment he was natural and genuine, and not at all calculating his effect, as he did later in the conversations on St Helena; he was not straining to idealize himself, and not in the least fashioning a personality fit to realize the best philosophical models. He was himself, seeing himself objectively. – He returned to be near the Holy Father, who had not moved, and paced in front of him. There, working himself up a little, and laughing half ironically, he delivered the following speech, or something like it, mixing up the trivial and the grandiose as was his wont, and speaking with phenomenal volubility – the rapid expression of an easy, swift genius who understood everything spontaneously, without study.

' "Birth is everything," said he, "and those who come into the world in naked poverty are born to desperation. This results in vigour or suicide according to temperament. When men have the courage to put their hand to anything, like me, by God they're the devil! What d'you expect? You have to live. You've got to find your place and make your mark. Myself, I've done it like a cannon ball. So much the worse for those who've been in my way. – Some are content with a little, others can never have enough. – What of it? Everyone eats with their own appetite – and myself I've been ravenous! – Listen, Holy Father, at Toulon I didn't have enough to buy a pair of epaulettes – instead my shoulders had to support a mother and I don't know how many brothers. They're all situated comfortably enough now, I should hope. Josephine married me almost out of pity, and now we're going to crown her, and pull the beard of her lawyer Raguideau who said that I had nothing except my cloak and sword.[35] But he wasn't far wrong, my God! – The imperial mantle, the crown – what is all this? What are they to me? – Costume! an actor's costume! I shall put them on my back for an hour, and that'll be enough for me. Then I'll get my ordinary officer's uniform back on, and mount a horse. – Always on horseback, all my life on horseback! I won't be able to sit on my throne for a single day without running the risk of being turfed off it. What is there to envy in all this, eh?

'"I'll tell you this, Holy Father: in this world there are only two kinds of men – those who have and those who take.

'"– The first sit around, the others are on the move. Because I understood this pretty well and early on, I shall go far – and that's all there is to it. There are only two men who have started at the age of forty and succeeded – Cromwell and Jean-Jacques Rousseau. If you'd given one a farm and the other two hundred francs and a servant, they'd neither of them have preached, nor commanded, nor written. There are workers in buildings, in colours, in forms and in words – myself, I'm a worker in battles. It's my calling. – At thirty-five I've already made eighteen of them, called Victories. – I have to be paid for my work. And it's not expensive to pay with a throne. – Besides, I shall always go on working. You'll see plenty more. Parvenu as I am, you'll see all of the dynasties dating from mine – an elected one at that. Elected, like yourself, Holy Father, and drawn from the crowd. On that point we can shake hands."

'And, coming up to him, he held out his swift white hand to the lean and timid one of the good Pope, who, perhaps softened by the friendly nature of the Emperor's last movement, perhaps by private recollections of his own destiny and a sad thought for the future of Christian societies, gently gave up the tips of his still trembling fingers with the air of a grandmother being reconciled to a child whom she has had the pain of scolding too harshly. However, he shook his head with sadness, and I saw a tear come from his fine eyes and roll quickly down his pale and wasted cheek. It seemed to me the last farewell of dying Christianity, abandoning the earth to egoism and contingency.

'Bonaparte shot a furtive glance at this tear wrung from an unhappy heart, and I even caught a rapid movement of one side of his mouth which resembled a smile of triumph. – In that moment this all-powerful nature seemed to me less refined and less elevated than that of his holy adversary. It made me blush – behind my curtain – for all my past ardours; I felt a sadness completely new to me in discovering how trivial the highest political grandeur could become by the frigid vanity of its

manoeuvres, its miserable traps and base sharp practice. I perceived that
he had not really wanted anything from his prisoner, and that it gave
him a secret joy not to have weakened in this interview, and, having
been surprised into losing his temper, to have then made his captive
bend under fatigue and fear and all those weaknesses which could bring
an inexplicable tear to an old man's eye. He'd wished to have that, and
left without adding a word, as abruptly as he had come in. I didn't see
whether he saluted the Pope. I believe not.'

6

A man of the sea

'As soon as the Emperor had left the chamber, two ecclesiastics came up to the Holy Father and, supporting him under each arm, led him out, cast down, emotional, and trembling.

'I stayed in the alcove where I'd heard this encounter until night fell. My thoughts were in turmoil, but it was not the frightening aspect of the scene that dominated them. What I'd witnessed had upset all my ideas: and, understanding now to what base stratagems personal ambition could lower genius, I hated the obsession that had tarnished, under my very eyes, the most brilliant of leaders – he who will perhaps give his name to this century, having held its destiny in check for ten years. I saw that it was futile to dedicate oneself to one man, because despotic power can't fail to corrupt our frail nature; but what I didn't know was to what ideal I should thenceforward devote myself. I've told you, I was only eighteen then, and had nothing but the vaguest inklings of the True, the Good, and the Beautiful – though these were persistent enough to commit me to a ceaseless search for them. That is the only thing I respect about myself.

'I judged it my duty to keep quiet about what I'd seen. But I've reason to believe that my momentary absence from the Emperor's suite had been noticed – for this is what followed. I perceived no difference in my master's attitude towards me. But I spent only a few more days near to him, so that the close study I wished to make of his character was abruptly broken off. One morning I received an order to depart immediately for the camp at Boulogne,[36] and on my arrival, another to embark on the flat-bottomed boats which were being tested at sea.

'I went away with less reluctance than if I'd been told of this voyage before the scene at Fontainebleau. Indeed I breathed more freely in getting away from the old palace and its forest – and at this involuntary lightening I knew that my *Séidisme* was being eaten away at the core. At first I was saddened by the realization of this new mood, and trembled for the glittering illusion that had raised up a duty for me out of my blind devotion. The great egotist had shown his true nature in front of me: but the further I travelled from him the more I began to judge him through his achievements – and so he regained over me, in that perspective, some of the magical ascendancy by which he'd fascinated the world. – However, it was more the gigantic conception of war itself which impressed me thenceforth, rather than the man who so formidably represented it: and at that terrific prospect I felt a redoubling of mindless intoxication about the glory of battles; I was stunned by the master who ordained these things, and looked with pride at the perpetual labour of those who seemed to me only his humble serfs.

'Indeed the scene really was Homeric, and well suited to carry school-boys away by the astounding multiplicity of its action. – Even so there was something spurious mixed in with it, which I vaguely sensed, but always imprecisely – and I felt the need of a better-informed vision than mine to pierce to the bottom of it all. I had learnt to evaluate the Captain: now I must sound out war itself.

'And here is the new event that gave me my second lesson: – I've received three rude awakenings in my life, and, having thought of them daily for years, I'm now telling you about them. All three gave me a violent shock – and the last quite overthrew the idol of my soul.

'The ostentatious plans for the landing in England and its conquest, the invocation of the memory of William the Conqueror, the discovery of Caesar's camp at Boulogne, the rapid assembly of nine hundred vessels in that harbour under the protection – which was daily heralded – of a fleet of five hundred sail; the establishment under four marshals of camps at Dunkirk, Ostend, Calais, Montreuil and Saint-Omer; the military throne from which rained the first stars of the Legion of Honour; the revues, fêtes, and mock attacks – all this brilliant display when reduced (in the language of geometry) to its simplest expression, had three aims: to disturb England, to lull Europe, and to concentrate and galvanize the army.[37]

'These three points gained, Bonaparte let the specious machine he'd put into motion at Boulogne fall apart piece by piece. When I arrived there it was playing in a void, like the machine at Marly.[38] The generals were still busy arranging mock manoeuvres, and feigning an ardour they did not feel. And they still shoved a few unfortunate vessels out to sea, which the English scorned, and from time to time sank. I received a summons to one of these sailings the day after my arrival.

'That day there was in the offing a single English frigate. It tacked to and fro with a majestic lack of urgency, it came, it went, it turned about, heeled over, righted itself, preened on the water, glided along, slowed down, and played in the sun like a swan bathing. Our wretched-flat ship, of novel and stupid design, had put itself at risk far out to sea with four others of similar type; and we were feeling proud of our daring, having been afloat since morning, when we suddenly discovered the frigate playing its peaceful games. Undoubtedly these would have appeared exceedingly graceful and poetic when viewed from dry land, or even if she had only been amusing herself by gambolling between England and us: but, on the contrary, she lay between us and France. The coast at Boulogne was more than a league distant – which made us thoughtful. We pressed on hard with our poor sails and worse oars, and while we floundered about, the peaceful frigate continued to take her swim in the sea and described a thousand elegant figures around us, going through her paces, changing from one tack to the other like a well-trained horse, and tracing the letters S and Z in the water in the most agreeable manner. We noticed that she had the goodness to let us pass several times in front of her without firing a shot, and even suddenly withdrew all her guns inboard, and closed the ports. At first I thought this a completely pacific move, and didn't understand the politeness at all. – But a burly old sailor gave me a dig with his elbow and said: "That looks bad." Indeed, after having let us run in front of her like a mouse before a cat, the beautiful and agreeable frigate bore down on us under full sail without deigning to open fire, broke us up with her prow like a horse with its chest, smashed us, crushed us, sunk us, and blithely sailed over us leaving a few boats to fish for prisoners – of which I was the tenth and last to be rescued, out of two hundred men who had set sail. This beautiful frigate was called the *Naiad*, and, not to forgo the French habit of punning, you may well believe that we never failed subsequently to call her the *Noyade*.[39]

'I had taken so violent a ducking that they were on the point of throwing me back into the sea, when an officer flicking through my wallet found there the letter from my father which you have read, and on it Lord Collingwood's signature. He ordered that I be given more attentive treatment; signs of life were found – and when I recovered consciousness it was not aboard the gracious *Naiad*, but on the *Victory*. I asked who commanded this new ship. Someone replied laconically, "Lord Collingwood."[40] I thought this might be the son of the man who had known my father; but when I was taken to him I learned differently. It was the same man.

'I couldn't conceal my surprise when he said to me, with a truly paternal kindness, that he'd never expected to have care of the son after having been in charge of the father, but that he hoped to find it not less pleasant; that he'd been present at the old gentleman's deathbed, and that on hearing my name he'd wished to have me on board. He spoke in beautiful French, with a soft melancholy intonation I've never forgotten. And he offered to keep me on his ship, on my word of honour that I'd make no attempt at escape. I gave him my parole without hesitation – just like a boy of eighteen – and found myself much better off on the *Victory* than on some hulk. Astonished to find nothing that justified the warnings we'd been given against the English, I easily made friends with the ship's officers, who were mightily amused by my ignorance of the sea and of their language, and entertained themselves with teaching me both – all the more politely since their admiral treated me like a son. Nonetheless I was gripped by a great sadness when I saw the white coastline of Normandy in the distance, and I would go below to prevent myself from weeping. I put up a resistance to this yearning because I was young and full of courage; but later, when my will no longer governed my heart, when I was in bed and asleep, tears flowed from my eyes in spite of myself and soaked my cheeks and bedlinen until I awoke.

'One evening, especially, a fresh conquest had been made of a French brig. I had seen it perish from a distance, without there being a chance of saving a single man of the crew, and, despite the gravity and reticence of the officers, I had been forced to hear the yells and huzzays of the sailors who joyfully saw our forces fading away and the sea swallow up drop by drop the avalanche that threatened to overrun their native land. I had withdrawn, and hidden all day in the closet Lord Collingwood had given me next to his own quarters, the better to demonstrate his protection of me; and when night came I climbed alone on to the deck. I was more than ever conscious of the enemy on all sides of me, and started to reflect with even greater bitterness on my so abruptly curtailed career. I had been a prisoner-of-war for a month, and Admiral Collingwood, who treated me in public with such benevolence, had spoken to me in private only for a moment on that first day on board. He was kind, but in his manners, as in those of all the English officers, there was a point where all openness came to a halt and the forms of etiquette rose like a barrier to anything further. It is then that one realizes one's in a foreign country. I felt a kind of terror in thinking of the abjectness of my position, which could well be the same until the end of the war, and I saw the sacrifice of my youth as inevitable – swallowed up in the shameful, useless life of a prisoner. The frigate[41] sailed swiftly on, under full sail, but I felt no motion. I put both hands on a cable, and rested my forehead on them, and, leaning thus, looked down into the sea. Its green and sombre depths caused a sort of giddiness in me, and the silence of the night was broken only by English voices. For a moment I hoped that the ship would transport me far from France, and that the next morning I would no longer see the level white coasts cutting across the good, beloved soil of my poor country. I thought I'd be delivered then from the perpetual longing the sight aroused in me, and that I'd be spared, at least, the torture of not being able even to dream of escape without dishonouring myself – a torture of Tantalus, by means of which an agonizing thirst for my homeland would devour me for the foreseeable future. I was overwhelmed by my loneliness and longed for an early occasion to get myself killed. I dreamed of an artistically composed death in the grand and dignified manner of the ancients. And I conjured up in my imagination a heroic end – of the kind that had been the subject of so much talk amongst us pages and budding warriors, and which would be the envy of my companions. I was caught up with that species of dream which at eighteen is more like a continuation of action and combat than a serious meditation – when I felt myself gently taken by the arm and, turning, saw the good Admiral Collingwood standing behind me.

'He had his night-glass in his hand and was in full dress uniform according to the rigid conventions of England. He put a paternal hand on my shoulder, and I noticed a look of deep melancholy in his large dark eyes and on his brow. His lightly powdered white hair fell somewhat negligently about his ears, and, under the unchanging calm of his voice and air there was a private fount of sadness which struck me especially that evening, and immediately inspired in me an enhanced respect and attention.

'"You are already disheartened, my boy," said he. "I've one or two little things to say to you. Will you talk with me a while?"

'I stammered some vague words of recognition and respect, which probably had little meaning, for he didn't listen to them, but sitting on a bench, took my hand. I stood up in front of him.

'"You've been a prisoner only a month," he continued, "and I for thirty-three years. Yes, my friend, I'm a prisoner of the sea; it guards me on every side – always waves – and then more waves; I see nothing but them, and hear nothing but them. My hair has turned white beneath their spray, my back is stooped with their damp. I've spent so little time in England that I know it only from the map. My country is an ideal being that I've only glimpsed, but which I serve as a slave, and which increases its rigour the more necessary I become to it. It is a common fate – and it is even our duty to desire to wear such chains. – But they are sometimes very heavy to be borne."

'He paused a moment and we were both silent, for, seeing that he was about to continue, I daren't interpose a word.

'"I've thought a great deal," he went on, "and I asked myself what my duty was when you came on board. I could have let you be taken to England, but there you might have fallen into a wretched state against which I ought always to protect you, and a despair from which I hope always to save you. I felt a genuine friendship for your father, and I give him proof of it now – if he can see us he will be content with me, don't you think?"

'The Admiral fell silent again, and pressed my hand. He even leaned forward in the dark and looked at me attentively to see what my feelings were as he spoke. But I was too tongue-tied to respond. He went on more quickly:

' "I've already written to the Admiralty, so that you'll be sent back to France at the first exchange. But," he added, "I'll not conceal from you that this could be a long time, for, apart from Bonaparte's not favouring exchanges, few of us are made prisoner. – I want to say that it would give me pleasure to see you studying your enemy's language while waiting – you can see that we know yours. We can work together if you care to, and I can lend you Shakespeare and Captain Cook. – Don't be distressed, you'll be free before I am, for, if the Emperor doesn't make peace, I shall be here for the whole of my life."

'The kindness of his tone – by which he associated himself with me and made us comrades in his floating prison – made me feel for him. I sensed that in his self-sacrificing and isolated life he had a need to do good, as secret consolation for the harshness of his mission in making perpetual war.

' "My Lord," I said, "before teaching me the words of a new language, let me know something of the thinking through which you have arrived at this perfect calm, this perfect balance of spirit which resembles happiness, and masks perpetual care . . . Forgive me what I am about to say, but I fear this virtue is only a continual façade."

' "You're very much deceived," he replied. "The feeling of duty comes to master a man's spirit so much that it pervades his character and becomes one of its principal features, just as a healthy diet, continuously absorbed, can change the quality of the blood and become one of the elements of the constitution. I have experienced, perhaps more than anyone, how easy it is to abnegate oneself completely. – Nevertheless one can't strip out everything human, and there are things that keep their grasp on the heart more than could be wished."

'Here he interrupted himself and took up his long glass. He put it on my shoulder to inspect a light which gleamed far away on the horizon, and knew instantly what it was by its movement. "Fishing boats," he said; and sat down next to me on the side of the ship. I reckoned that he had had something to say to me for a long time, which he hadn't yet mentioned.

' "You never speak of your father," he said suddenly. "I'm amazed that you never ask me about him, about his sufferings, about what he said, what he wished."

'And since it was a very clear night, I saw once more that he was intently observing me with his big black eyes.

' "I was afraid of being tactless . . ." I said, embarrassed.

'He gripped my arm, as if to prevent me saying more.

' "It's not that, *mon enfant*,"[42] said he, "it isn't that."

'And he shook his head with kindly scepticism.

' "I've had only a few chances to speak to you, my Lord."

' "It's still less that," he interrupted – "you could have spoken of this every day, if you'd wished."

'I noticed some agitation and a little reproach in his tone. It was this that he had at heart. I thought of yet another stupid answer in justification; for nothing makes one seem more foolish than bad excuses.

' "My Lord," I said, "the humiliation of being a captive absorbs one more than you might imagine." – And I remember that in saying this that I thought to adopt the countenance of a Regulus,[43] in order to inspire him with respect for me.

' "Ah! poor boy! poor child! – *pauvre garçon*!"[44] he said, "You're not looking at reality. You're not looking at yourself. Look clearly and you'll find a lack of feeling in yourself – for which the military career of your poor father is responsible, and not you."

'He had opened the way to the truth, and I took it.

' "It's quite true," I said, "that I didn't know my father – I saw him once, for a short while, at Malta."

' "There's the truth!" he cried. "There's the cruel truth, my friend! My two daughters will one day speak just like that. They'll say: *We didn't know our father!* Sarah and Mary will say that! – and yet I love them with a tender and fervent love, and I bring them up from a distance; I supervise them from my ship, I write to them every day, I direct their reading, their work, I send them ideas and suggestions, and in return receive their childish confidences; I scold them, I relent, I make it up with them; I know everything they do! I know on what day they went to church too finely dressed – I give their mother instructions for them, I predict who will fall in love with them, who will ask for their hand, who they will marry – and their husbands will be my sons. I'm making devout and uncomplicated girls of them – one couldn't be more the father than I am . . . Well! – all this is nothing, because they never see me."

'He said these last words in a voice full of feeling, behind which I sensed tears. After a moment of silence, he continued:

'"Yes, Sarah hasn't sat on my knee since she was two, and I last took Mary in my arms when her eyes were still unopened. – Yes, it is fair that you should have been indifferent to your father, and that's what they will become, one day, to me. You can't love an invisible parent. – What do they have of their father? – a daily letter. Counsel, more or less cold. – One doesn't love counsel, one loves a person – and a person who can't be seen isn't there, one doesn't love him – and when he's dead, he is no more absent than he was already – and one doesn't weep."

'He was overcome with emotion, and ceased. – Not wanting to go further into these painful feelings before a stranger, he moved away and paced up and down the deck for some time. I was at once much moved at the sight – and then began to experience the regrets it bred in me for never having had sufficient sense of a father's value. I owe to that evening the first decent, natural and blessed emotions my heart ever felt. I came to understand, from the sight of his profound repining – his unappeasable sadness in the midst of a most brilliant military reputation – all that I had lost in never having known that feeling of devotion to home which could cause such bitter longings in so great a heart. I understood the falsity of our barbarous, brutal education, of our insatiable need to be drugged by action. I saw, by a sudden revelation of the heart, that there existed an adorable, desirable life from which I'd been violently torn, a real life of paternal love – instead of which we had constructed a factitious existence, composed entirely of resentments and all kinds of childish vanities. I understood that there is only one thing more lovely than the family, and to which one might righteously sacrifice it – and that is that other family, one's country. And while the gallant old gentleman stood aside from me weeping because he was good, I put my head in both hands and wept because up to that moment I had been so lacking.

'After a few minutes the Admiral returned to me:

' "I should tell you," he resumed in a firmer voice, "that soon we'll be approaching the shores of France. I'm a perpetual watcher stationed over your ports. I've only one word to add, and I want it to be between ourselves: remember that you're here on your word of honour, and that I don't watch you at all. But, my child, the longer this goes on, the more difficult it will become for you. You're still very young: if a temptation threatens to overcome your resolution, come and seek me out when you fear you might succumb – don't hide from me; I'll save you from a dishonourable action which has been committed by some officers to the ruin of their good names. Remember that it's permissible to break a galley chain, if you can, but not your word of honour." – And with these last words he shook my hand and left me.

'I don't know whether you have noticed, sir, that in our lives the revolutions that take place in the soul often derive from a specific day, or hour, or from an unforeseen but memorable conversation which disturbs us and plants new seeds that slowly grow, and of which the rest of our actions are simply the consequences and natural development. Of such a kind, for me, were that morning at Fontainebleau and that night on the English ship. Admiral Collingwood left me the prey to a new dilemma. What had up to then been in me only a profound boredom with captivity and a broad youthful desire for action, now became a wild need for my native land; at the sight of such suffering, wearing down over the years a man who had been perpetually separated from his motherland, I conceived an urgent need to know and worship mine; I invented passionate ties which had no counterpart in fact; I imagined a family and dreamed of relatives whom I had scarcely known, and reproached myself with not having held them sufficiently dear, whereas they, used to thinking me of no account, lived on in their cold selfishness, perfectly indifferent to my forsaken and deprived existence. Thus even the good in me turned to evil; for the wise counsel that the gallant Admiral thought he'd given me had been enveloped in a personal emotion which spoke more distinctly than his words; his troubled tone had affected me more than the wisdom of his opinions; so that, while he believed himself to be securing my chains, he had excited in me a wild desire to break them. – It's almost always like that with written or spoken advice. We can only be taught by experience, and by the reasoning which comes from our own observations. Consider, since you are involved in it, the uselessness of literature. What does it accomplish? – who is changed by it? – and who, may I ask, ever understands it properly? You almost always achieve a success for the cause opposite to the one you plead. For example, the most beautiful epic poem possible about female virtue has been written about Clarissa – and what's the result? Readers take the opposite view and rave about Lovelace, whom she has crushed by her virginal splendour, splendour unsullied even by rape – about Lovelace, who drags himself on his knees to implore in vain the pardon of his saintly victim, and is unable to sway this soul the fall of whose body has left it unstained.[45] Everything goes wrong when literature tries to teach. You do nothing so much as stir up the vices, who, proud of what you've depicted, come to admire themselves in your picture and find themselves very fine. – It's true that this doesn't matter much to you: but my good, straightforward Collingwood had conceived a real affection for me, and my conduct did matter to him. So at first he was very pleased to see me take up serious and sustained study. He also found something congenial to his English gravity in my habitual reserve and discretion, and became accustomed to talk openly to me on many occasions, confiding not unimportant matters to me. After some time I came to be considered as his secretary and relative, and spoke English well enough to be no longer thought much of a stranger.

'However, it was a sad life for me to lead, and I found the melancholy days at sea very long. For year after year we ceaselessly patrolled the coasts of France, and I would constantly see etched on the horizon the cliffs of the land that Grotius[46] called the most beautiful kingdom after the kingdom of Heaven. Then we would head back to sea, and I would be surrounded for month after month with nothing but mists and mountains of water. When a ship passed, nearby or far off, it would always be an English one – no others being allowed to let the wind fill their sails, and the ocean not hearing a word that wasn't English. Even the English themselves were saddened by this, and complained that the sea had now become a desert in which they continually met each other, and Europe a fortress which shut them out. Sometimes my wooden prison came so close to land that I could make out men and children walking on the shore. Then my heart would beat wildly, and I would be seized by an inner frenzy so violent that I would go and hide deep in the hold of the ship, so as not to succumb to my desire to plunge into the waves. But when I returned to the indefatigable Collingwood I would feel ashamed of my childish weakness – and I never tired of marvelling at how he united so very active a courage with so deep a sadness. This man, who for forty years had known nothing but war and the sea, never ceased to apply himself to their study, as though they were inexhaustible subjects. When a ship became tired out he would, like an implacable rider, get on another – he wore them out and killed them under him. He wore out seven while I was with him. He spent the nights fully dressed, sitting on a cannon, endlessly calculating the art of holding his vessel immobile without casting anchor, at the same point on the sea, on sentry, between the gusts and storms. He constantly exercised his crews,[47] and watched over them and for them.[48] This man had never enjoyed any riches; and, even though they made him an English peer, he enjoyed his soup from a tin plate like a sailor; then, on going below to his quarters, he became the father of a family again, and wrote to his daughters not to become fine ladies; to read not novels, but stories of voyages, and essays – and Shakespeare just "as often as they pleased".[49] After the battle of Trafalgar – which I had the unhappiness to see him win, and of which he had made out the plan with his friend Nelson, whom he succeeded – he wrote: "We fought on my little Sarah's birthday." Sometimes he felt his health failing and asked for mercy from England: but she inexorably replied: *Remain at sea* – and sent a new honour or a gold medal for each distinguished action, so that his chest was crowded with them. Again he wrote: "Since I left my country I have not spent *ten days* in port. My eyes are weakening, and when I am allowed to see my children the sea will have made me blind. I lament that out of so many officers it is so difficult to find one of superior skill to take my place." England replied: *You will remain at sea, always at sea.* He remained there until he died.

'Even after a single day spent contemplating its grave and thoughtful resignation, this imposing, Roman, life overwhelmed me by its loftiness and moved me in its simplicity. I – who was nothing, nothing as a citizen, nothing as a father, nor as a son, a brother, family man, or public figure – I held myself in great contempt for complaining about my plight while he made no complaint. He had revealed himself once only, and in spite of himself; whilst I – a useless boy, an ant among the heap of ants that the Sultan of France trod underfoot – reproached myself for my secret longing to return and deliver myself over to the chanciness of that man's caprice, to be once more one of those grains of dust which he stamped into blood. – The vision of this true citizen, devoted, not, as I had been, to one man, but to Country and Duty, was a fortunate experience for me – for in his strict school I learnt the nature of the real nobility that can be sought in modern times through arms, and how much – when it is constituted like that – it may elevate our profession above all others, and make some of us worthy of admiration whatever be the future of war and of armies. Never has a man possessed in such a high degree that inner peace which is born of a sense of sacred duty, and the modest military unselfconsciousness which cares little about personal fame so long as the public weal prospers. I saw him write one day: "My greatest desire in life is to maintain the independence of my country, and I would rather that my body were added to the rampart of my native land than trailed in useless pomp through an idle throng. My life and my strength belong to England. Pray do not talk about my last wound, or people may think I am vapouring about my dangers."[50] His sadness was deep, but full of grandeur. It didn't at all impede his unwearying activity, and he gave me the pattern of what an intelligent man of war should be, practising the *art of war* not out of ambition, but as an artist, judging it at the highest level and often scornfully, like Montecucculi;[51] – who, Turenne being dead, retired from the field and didn't deign to continue the game against an inferior player. But I was still too young to understand all the virtue of his character, and what compelled me most was an ambition to hold in my own country a rank comparable to his. When I saw the Kings of the South asking his protection,[52] and even Napoleon moved with the hope that Collingwood might be in the Indian seas, I started wishing with all my heart for a chance to escape – and I pushed the urgency of my perpetually hungry ambition almost to the point of breaking my word. Yes, I came even to that.

'One day the ship carrying us, the *Ocean*, put in to Gibraltar. I went ashore with the Admiral, and walking in the town met an officer of the seventh Hussars, who'd been taken prisoner in the Spanish campaign and sent to Gibraltar with four of his comrades. They had the whole town for their prison, but were closely watched. I'd known this officer in France, and we met again with pleasure, finding ourselves in comparable positions. It'd been so long since I'd spoken French with a Frenchman that I found him eloquent, even though he was actually completely stupid – and by the end of a quarter of an hour we'd confided our situation to each other. He told me straight off, and frankly, that he was going to escape with his comrades; that they'd found an excellent opportunity, and that he didn't need asking twice to follow them. He strongly urged me to do the same. I replied that he was very lucky to be under guard: but as to me who was not, I couldn't escape without dishonour, and that he and his companions were not at all in the same case. This was too subtle for him.

'"Good Lord! I'm no casuist," he said, "and if you like I'll get a bishop to give you his opinion. But in your place, I'd go. I see only two alternatives, to be free or not to be free. D'you realize that you'll have lost five years of your promotion trailing about in that English tub? – lieutenants made at the same time as you are colonels by now."

'Thereupon his companions arrived and took me off to a seedy-looking house, where they drank sherry; and they described so many captains who'd become generals, and second-lieutenants who'd become viceroys, that my head was turned, and I promised that they'd find me at the same place at midnight the day after tomorrow. A little boat would take us – hired from some honest smugglers who'd guide us to a French ship commissioned to take the wounded from our army to Toulon. The idea seemed to me excellent, and my good friends, having made me drink numerous toasts to quiet the murmurings of my conscience, finished their speeches with a triumphant argument, swearing on their heads that whilst strictly speaking one should have some regard for an honest man who'd treated one well, everything confirmed them in the belief that an Englishman was not a man.

'I returned on board the *Ocean* full of thought; and, when I'd slept, awoke seeing my position more clearly, and asking if my fellow countrymen hadn't been making fun of me. However, my longing for freedom, and that ever pricking ambition which had been excited in me since childhood, urged me towards flight, despite the shame I felt at breaking my word. I spent the whole day near to the Admiral without daring to look him in the face, and tried hard to find him inferior and narrow-minded. – I talked loudly at table, arrogantly, of the greatness of Napoleon; I exalted him, and vaunted the universality of his genius, which divined the very nature of law in the creation of his codes, and the nature of the future by his moulding of events. I insolently upheld the superiority of this genius – compared with the mediocre talent of mere tacticians and manoeuvrers. I hoped to be contradicted; but, contrary to my expectation, I found still more admiration for the Emperor amongst the English officers than even I was able to show for their implacable enemy. Lord Collingwood in particular, emerging from the grave silence of his perpetual meditations, praised him in terms so just, so forceful, so precise, setting so clearly in front of his officers at once the grandeur of the Emperor's projects, the magical celerity of their execution, the firmness of his orders, the sureness of his judgement, his subtlety in negotiation, his soundness in councils, his greatness in battle, his calm amidst danger, his thoroughness in the preparation of his enterprises, his pride in the stature he'd given to France, and, in short, all the qualities that compose a great man, that I asked myself what history could add to this eulogy; and I was confounded, because I'd sought to inflame myself against the Admiral, hoping to hear him make unjust accusations.

'I'd wished, spitefully, to put him in the wrong – and that an inconsiderate or insulting word from him would give me justification for the disloyalty I contemplated. But it seemed, on the contrary, as if he took care to redouble his kindnesses, and – his alacrity making the others suppose that I had some new trouble for which it would be right to console me – they were even more attentive and indulgent to me than ever. I became moody and left the table.

'To my misfortune the Admiral took me to Gibraltar again the following day. We were to spend eight days there. – The evening of the escape came. – My head was on fire, and I constantly debated within myself. I gave myself specious reasons for action and benumbed myself by their falsity; they set off a violent conflict within me; but, while my soul writhed and twisted around itself, my body – as if it had been made the arbiter between ambition and honour – followed the road to flight of its own accord. Hardly aware of what I was doing I'd made a bundle of my goods and was going to take myself from the house we stayed in in Gibraltar to the rendezvous – when, suddenly, I stopped, and I felt that it wasn't possible. – In shameful actions there is something poisonous that a man of spirit tastes on his lips the moment they touch the cup of perdition. He can't even sip this without sensing the approach of death. – When I realized what I was about to do, and that I was going to break my word of honour, I was so struck with horror that I thought I'd go mad. I ran down to the shore, fleeing from the fatal house as though it were infected with the plague, not daring to look back. – I threw myself into the waves and swam through the dark to the *Ocean*, our ship and my floating prison. I boarded her in haste, clambering up by the cables; and when I came on deck I grabbed at the mainmast, embracing it with passion as a sanctuary that would protect me from dishonour. At the same time, the magnitude of my sacrifice rent my heart, and falling on my knees and resting my head on the iron bands which circled the mast, I melted in tears like a child. Seeing me in this state the Captain of the *Ocean* thought, or pretended to think, that I was ill, and had me carried to my cabin. I cried aloud and implored him to post a sentry at the door to prevent me going out. They locked me in and I breathed easier, absolved at last from the torture of being my own gaoler. The next day, at dawn, I saw myself to be in open sea, and enjoyed a little more calm, having lost sight of the land – the object of all dreadful temptation for me. I was thinking of things with more resignation, when the little door opened and the good Admiral stepped in, alone.

'"I've come to say goodbye," he began, with a rather less grave air than usual. "You leave for France tomorrow morning."

'"Oh God! D'you say that to test me, my Lord?"

'"That would be a cruel game indeed, my child," he replied, "I've already done you enough harm. I ought to have left you a prisoner in the *Northumberland* – which is surrounded by land – and given you back your parole. Then you'd have been able to plot against your gaolers without feeling guilty, and been ruthlessly cunning in making your escape. You've suffered much more in having greater liberty; but yesterday – thanks be to God! – you resisted an opportunity which would have dishonoured you. – And that would have been scuttling yourself as you reached port, because for the last fortnight I've been negotiating your exchange, which Admiral Rosily is now going to confirm. – I trembled for you yesterday, because I knew of your companions' project. I let them get away on your account, for fear that in arresting them you too would have been arrested. And what could we have done to conceal that? You'd have been lost, my child, and, believe me, you'd have been ill received by Napoleon's veterans. They have the right to be precise on points of honour."

'I was so moved that I didn't know how to thank him. He saw my embarrassment, and hastened to cut off the sorry phrases in which I was trying to stammer out how I would miss him:

' "Come, come," he said, "none of these French compliments,[53] as we call them. We like each other – that's all; and you have, I believe, a proverb which says *There's no such thing as a good prison*. – Leave me to die in mine, my friend; I've got used to it, for myself, because I've had to. But it won't last very long now. I feel my legs tremble under me and I get thinner. For the fourth time I've asked Lord Mulgrave[54] to grant me rest, and he has again refused; he writes that he doesn't know how to replace me. However, when I'm dead he'll surely have to find someone, and he'd do well to make some preparations. – I shall stay on guard in the Mediterranean – but you, *mon enfant*,[55] don't lose any more time. There's a sloop can take you off. I've only one piece of advice to give you – devote yourself to a principle rather than to a man. The love of your country is a great enough principle to fill the heart and occupy the mind wholly."

' "Alas! my Lord," said I, "there are times when one can't easily know what one's country needs. I shall go to ask it of mine."

'We bade each other farewell once more, and, my heart full, I left this noble man, of whose death I learnt shortly afterwards. – He died at sea, as he had lived for forty-nine years, without complaint or self-glorification, and without having seen his two daughters again. Lonely and sombre he was, like one of those ancient hounds in Ossian who guard the coasts of England behind the waves and the mists.

'I'd learned by his schooling everything that those exiled by war could suffer – and also how completely the sentiment of Duty can master a great soul. Thoroughly permeated by this example, graver through my own sufferings and the sight of his, I came to present myself in Paris, with my experience of prison, to the all-powerful master I'd left behind.'

7

A reception

Here Captain Renaud paused, and I looked at the time by my watch. It was two in the morning. He got up, and we walked in amongst his grenadiers. Everywhere there reigned a profound silence. Many were sitting on their packs and had gone to sleep. We seated ourselves a few paces away on the parapet, and after having relit his cigar from a soldier's pipe he continued his story. None of the houses gave any sign of life.

'From the moment I came to Paris I wanted to see the Emperor. I had my opportunity at a court performance to which one of my old comrades, now a colonel, took me. It was over there – at the Tuileries. We placed ourselves in a little box opposite the Imperial box, and waited. Up to that point only the kings were in the house. Each one had established his court around him in a box in the dress circle, and had his aides-de-camp and favourite generals in the galleries in front of him. The Kings of Westphalia, Saxony and Württemberg, and all the princes of the Confederation of the Rhine were seated at the same level. Upright, close to them, speaking out loud and quickly was Murat, King of Naples,[56] shaking his mane of black curls and looking round him like a lion. Higher up was the King of Spain,[57] and alone, at a distance, the Russian Ambassador, Prince Kourakim, wearing diamond epaulettes. In the pit was a mob of generals, dukes, princes, colonels and senators. Up above, everywhere, were the naked arms and bare shoulders of the ladies of the court.

The box with the eagle over it was still empty. We watched it constantly. After a short while the kings got up, and remained standing. Walking quickly the Emperor entered his box alone, threw himself without ado into his armchair and stared in front of him with his

lorgnette; then, remembering that the whole theatre was standing awaiting his notice, he nodded his head twice, brusquely and with an ill
grace, and quickly turned around and allowed the kings and queens to
seat themselves. His red-uniformed chamberlains stood erect behind
him. He talked to them without looking at them, and from time to time
extended a hand to receive a golden box that one or the other offered
him and then took again. Crescentini sang *Les Horaces*,[58] – the voice of
a seraphim issuing from an emaciated, wrinkled face. The orchestra was
soft and low, by order of the Emperor – who perhaps wished, like the
Lacedaemonians, to be soothed rather than excited by music. He looked
in front of him through his lorgnette, and frequently in my direction.
I knew his great grey-green eyes again, but I hated the yellowish fat
which had engulfed his severe features. As was his custom he put his
left hand over his left eye in order to see better, and I felt that he had
recognized me. He faced about abruptly, looking only at the stage; and
soon he went out. I was already standing in his line of passage. He
strode quickly down the corridor, and the fat legs swathed tightly in
white silk stockings, the swollen figure under the green coat, made him
almost unrecognizable to me. He stopped short in front of me, and
spoke to the colonel presenting me, instead of directly to me:

' "Why have I seen him nowhere around? – Still a lieutenant?"

' "He has been a prisoner since 1804."

' "Why didn't he escape?"

' "I was on parole," said I quietly.

' "I don't like prisoners," he said, "one should fight to the end."

'He turned his back on me. We all stood motionless in a row; and,
when his whole suite had filed out: "My dear fellow," said the colonel,
"see what an imbecile you've been; you've lost your promotion, and
you'll get no gratitude for that." '

8

The Russian guard-post

'Is it possible?' I exclaimed, stamping my foot. 'When I hear stories like that I congratulate myself that the officer in me died years ago. – Which leaves me no more than a solitary but independent writer, contemplating what may become of his liberty – and hoping not to have to defend it against his old friends.'

And I thought to find in Captain Renaud some remnants of indignation at the memory of what he had just told me. But he smiled gently and contentedly.

'It was very simple,' he continued. 'That colonel was the best fellow in the world; but there are types who pretend to be, in the famous phrase, *braggarts about their crimes*,[59] and about their callousness. He wanted to treat me badly because the Emperor·had given the lead. It was the crude flattery of a guardsman. – But what a fortunate turn it was for me! – From that moment I began to respect myself from within myself, to have confidence in myself, to feel my character purifying, taking form, rounding out, completing itself. From that moment I saw clearly that what happens to one is nothing, that what counts is the inner self – and I rated myself well above my judges. In short I realized my independent consciousness – and determined to rely on it alone, and to consider public opinion, rapid advances in fortune, glittering rewards, swift promotions, and newspaper reputations as vapid frippery, and a game of chance not worth playing.

'I went off quickly to the war, and plunged myself right into the unsung battalions, the infantry of the line, the fighting infantry, where the peasants of the army get mown down thousands at a time, and are as undifferentiated and as indifferent as the heads of corn in the rich fields of the Beauce. – There I hid myself like a Carthusian in his cloister; and in the depths of this armed multitude, marching on foot like the common soldiers, carrying a pack like them and eating their bread, I fought the great wars of the Empire as long as the Empire stood. – Ah! if you knew how at ease with myself I felt during those terrible hardships! How I loved the obscurity, and what savage pleasure the great battles gave me! The beauty of war lies in the midst of the troops, in the life of the camps, in the mud of the marches and the bivouacs. I took my revenge on Bonaparte by serving my country – and I took nothing from Napoleon; when he reviewed my regiment I hid myself because I dreaded a favour. Experience had shown me how to value power and honours at their true worth; I wanted nothing more from the conquests of our armies than to take my proper part of natural pride in them. I wanted to be a citizen, where one was still allowed to be one, and in my own style. Sometimes my services weren't noticed; sometimes they were elevated above their merits; but I never ceased keeping them dark to the best of my ability – particularly anxious that my name shouldn't become too prominent. There was such a mob of people set on following the very opposite course that obscurity remained easy, and I was still only a lieutenant in the Imperial Guard in 1814, when I received this wound in the forehead that you can see, and which tonight gives me more pain than usual.'

Here he ran his hand several times across his forehead, and, since he seemed to wish to stop talking, I pressed him to go on, with enough urgency for him to give in.

He rested his head on the knob of his malacca cane.

'How strange it is,' he said, 'that I've never told anyone of all this, yet this evening I have the desire to do so. Bah! it doesn't matter! I'm pleased to confide in an old comrade. It'll be something for you to think about seriously when you've nothing better to do. It seems to me not unworthy of that. Maybe you'll think me feeble or completely mad; but it doesn't matter. Until the event I'm going to tell you of – which might be ordinary enough to others, but which in spite of myself I've recoiled from telling up till now because of the pain it gives me – my passion for the glory of arms had become sober, serious, devoted and perfectly concentrated, like the simple and peerless feeling of duty; but from that day onwards different ideas came to cast a shadow over my life once more.

'It was in 1814, at the beginning of the year and the end of that grim war when our poor army defended the Empire and the Emperor, while France looked on in dejection. Soissons had just surrendered to the Prussian Bülow.[60] The armies of Silesia and of the North had made a junction there. Macdonald[61] had quitted Troyes and abandoned the Yonne basin in order to establish a defensive line from Nogent to Montereau with his thirty thousand men.

'We were going to attack Rheims, which the Emperor wished re-taken. The weather was overcast and the rain perpetual. The previous day we'd lost a senior officer while he was dealing with prisoners. The Russians had surprised and killed him during the night, and rescued their comrades. Our Colonel, who was known as a *tough nut*, wanted his revenge. We were near Épernay and had been turning the heights which surround it. Evening came, and, having spent the whole day in regrouping, we were marching past a pretty white château with turrets, called Boursault, when the Colonel called me over. He led me aside while the arms were being stacked and said in his hoarse old voice:

'"See that barn up there on the steep side of the hill; there, where that great clod of a Russian sentry is walking around in his bishop's bonnet?"

'"Yes, yes," I replied, 'I can see the grenadier and the barn perfectly."

'"Good, well you're a veteran officer, so you must know that's the position the Russians took the day before yesterday – and it preoccupies the Emperor just at this moment. He's told me it's the key to Rheims, and that could well be so. In any case we're going to play a trick on Woronzoff.[62] At eleven in the evening you'll take two hundred of your lads and surprise the guard-post they've set up in that barn. But, for fear it might raise the alarm, you'll take it with the bayonet."

'He took a pinch of snuff and offered some to me; then, letting the rest blow away bit by bit, as I'm doing now, he continued, enunciating one word to each grain carried away in the wind:

'"You may be sure I'll be there behind you with my column. – You shouldn't lose more than sixty men, and you'll take the six guns which are set up there . . . and turn them towards Rheims . . . Eleven o'clock

. . . by half-past eleven the position will be ours. And then we'll sleep till about three to recuperate from that little scrap at Craonne – which was a tidy piece of work, as they say."

'"Very well," said I; and I went with the lieutenant who was my second-in-command to make some preparations for the evening's work. The essential thing, as you can appreciate, was to make no noise. I held an arms inspection, and ordered the charges from any muskets that were loaded to be extracted with a wad-hook. Then I walked around for a while with my sergeants, waiting for the hour. At half-past ten I ordered cloaks to be put on, and muskets under the cloak, for as you can see tonight a bayonet is always visible whatever one does – and even though it was darker than it is now, I wasn't going to trust to that. I'd noticed little hedge-lined paths leading up to the Russian post, and up these I sent the most determined fellows I've ever led. – There are two of them still around, over there in the ranks, and they remember it well. – They were used to the Russians, and knew how to deal with them. The sentries we came across during the ascent vanished without a sound, like reeds flattened to the earth by the sweep of a hand. The one who stood in front of their piled arms demanded more care. He was motionless, his musket butt on the ground and leaning his chin on the barrel – the poor devil was swaying like a man drugged with tiredness and about to fall over. One of my grenadiers grabbed him in his arms, squeezing the breath out of him, and another two, having gagged him, threw him in the undergrowth. I came up more slowly, and I couldn't help being aware, I must tell you, of a certain sensation I'd not had in previous combats. It was the shame of attacking sleeping men. I saw them lying there, rolled up in their cloaks and illuminated by a dark lantern, and my heart beat violently. But suddenly, at the point of action, I suspected that this was a weakness such as a coward feels, and fearing that I'd experienced fear for the first time, I drew my sabre from its concealment under my arm and went in first, swiftly, giving the lead to my grenadiers. I made a gesture they understood, and they threw themselves on to the arms, and then on the men like wolves on to a flock. Oh! what a confused and horrible butchery it was! – the bayonet stabbed, the butt smashed, the knee throttled, the hand strangled. All their scarcely uttered cries of pain were stamped out under the boots of our soldiers, and no head was raised without receiving its death stroke. Upon entering I'd struck a terrible blow at random in front of me, at something which I pierced through and through; an elderly officer, a big powerful man with a mane of white hair, rose like a phantom, let out a terrible cry when he saw my deed, struck me a powerful blow in the face with his sword, and then instantly fell dead under the bayonets. I too fell into a sitting position at his side, stunned by the stroke between my eyes, and then I heard beneath me the soft dying voice of a child saying: "Papa . . ."

'I realized then what I'd done, and stared at my work in desperation. I beheld one of those officers of fourteen years of age who were so common in the invading Russian armies of those days, and whom someone had sent to this terrible school. His long curled locks fell on his breast, as fair and as silky as a woman's, and his head leant forward as though he'd dropped back to sleep again. His rosy lips, full like those of a new-born child, seemed still plump from his nurse's milk, and his large half-open blue eyes were beautifully shaped, trusting, feminine, and affectionate. I raised him with one arm, and his cheek leaned against my bloody cheek as though to hide his head for warmth between a mother's chin and shoulder. He seemed to crouch against my chest for shelter from his murderers. On his dead face lay filial tenderness and surety, and the repose of sweet slumbers – and he seemed to me to be saying: Sleep in peace . . .

' "Was this an enemy!" I cried. – And that fatherly feeling that God has planted deep in every man stirred and trembled in me. I drew him to my breast – and at that felt the hilt of my sabre pressing against me – the sabre with which I'd killed this sleeping angel, running it through his heart. I wanted to rest my head against his head – but my blood covered it with great stains. Then I felt the wound on my brow and remembered that it had been inflicted on me by his father. I looked aside in shame, and saw only the mass of corpses that my grenadiers were dragging by the feet and throwing outside, taking nothing from them but their cartridges. At that moment my Colonel arrived followed by his column, who I recognized by their step and the clatter of their arms.

' "Bravo! my dear fellow," he said, "you've taken this place smartly. But you're wounded?"

' "Look there," I cried, " – what difference is there between a murderer and me?"

' "God dammit, old fellow, what d'you expect? It's our profession."

' "That is so," I replied; and I got up to resume my duties. The child sank back into the folds of his cloak, with which I'd covered him, and his delicate hand, which was ornamented with great rings, let slip a malacca cane which fell into my hand as though he'd given it me. I grasped it; I resolved that in whatever danger I should find myself in future I should never carry any other armament – and I hadn't the heart to pull my murderous sword from his breast.

'I hastily left that den, which reeked of blood, and when I found myself in the open air I mustered the strength to stanch my red and dripping brow. My grenadiers had formed ranks; and each of them was calmly wiping off his bayonet with grass and securing the flint in the firelock. My sergeant-major, followed by the quartermaster, paced in front of the ranks, and, holding his roster in his hand and reading by the light of a candle-end stuck like a torch in the muzzle of his musket, calmly took the roll call. I leant against a tree and the surgical officer came to dress my forehead. A copious March rain fell on my head, and did me some good. I couldn't help letting forth a great sigh:

' "I'm sick of war," I said to the surgeon.

' "And so am I," said a grave voice, which I recognized.

'I lifted the bandage over my eyebrows and saw – not the Emperor Napoleon, but Bonaparte, the soldier. He was standing on foot in front of me, alone, melancholy, his boots covered in mud, his coat torn, water streaming from the brim of his hat. He felt that his last days had come, and was looking round him at the last of his soldiers.

'He gazed at me attentively – "Haven't I seen you somewhere, old soldier?" said he.

'At that last phrase I sensed that this was only a set formula, and I knew I'd aged in appearance more than in years, so that my labours, my moustaches and my wounds disguised me well enough.

' "I've seen you everywhere, without being seen myself," I replied.

' "D'you want promotion?"

'I said: – "It's too late."

'He folded his arms without answering for a moment, then:

"You're right – in truth, in three days we'll both have quit the service, you and I."

'He turned away from me and remounted his horse, which was being held a few paces away. At that moment, the front of our column had attacked and someone started sending shells over at us. One of them fell right in front of my company, and a few men ran back by an instinctive movement – of which they were ashamed. Bonaparte rode his horse up alone to the shell, which flared and smoked in front of them, and made him sniff the fumes. Everyone stood silent and without moving; then the shell burst, hurting no one. The grenadiers appreciated the grim lesson he'd given them; for myself, I sensed in it something akin to despair. France was failing him, and for a moment he'd doubted his veteran troops. I thought that such a desertion was too much of a revenge for me and too great a punishment for him. I struggled to my feet, and going up to him, took and pressed the hand he extended to some of us. He didn't know me at all – none the less it was for me a tacit reconciliation between the most obscure man of our time and the most illustrious. The drums beat out the charge, and by dawn the following day we had retaken Rheims. But a few days after, Paris fell to the others.'

Captain Renaud was silent for a long time after this recital, and sat with head bowed, so that I was loath to interrupt his reverie. I regarded this brave man with the deepest respect, and while he spoke I had attentively followed the gradual transformations in this good and simple soul – whose generous dedication of himself had always been repulsed, always crushed by an invincible power, but who had come to find peace in the humblest and most austere devotion to duty. – His obscure career seemed to me as fine a spectacle, in its inner life, as the most glittering deeds of any man of action could be. – Each wave of the sea adds a milky veil to the beauty of a pearl, each billow slowly works to render it more perfect, each flake of foam streaming over helps to impart that mysterious tinge, half-golden, half-transparent, through which one can only guess at the light which makes up its heart; it was just so that this character had been formed amidst vast upheavals and in the course of dark and unrelenting trials. I knew that up to the death of the Emperor he had considered it his duty not to serve – respecting, despite the entreaties of his friends, what he called the decent thing to do; and since then, when freed of the obligation of an ancient promise to a master who no longer knew him, he had returned to command the remnant of the Old Guard, within the Royal Guard; and since he never spoke of himself no one had thought of him, and he remained unpromoted. – He minded this very little, and used to say that unless one was a general by the age of twenty-five, an age when one can translate one's imagination into action, it is best to remain a humble captain so that one can live with the men like a father of a family, or the prior of a convent.

'See there,' he said to me after this interval of repose, '– look at our old Grenadier Poirier, with his dark squinting eyes, his shaven head and sabre cuts across his cheek – that's the man who Marshals of France stop to admire when he presents arms at the King's gate; see Beccaria with his profile like a Roman veteran, Frechou with his white moustaches; look at the whole front rank with their medals and three chevrons on their sleeves! – what would they have said, these old monks of the old army, who never wanted to be anything but grenadiers, if I'd failed them this morning – I who was still in command of them fifteen days ago? – If I'd got used to home life and rest for a few years, or started another profession, that would've been different; but, in truth, as it is I've no other virtue than they have. Anyway, look how calm it is in Paris tonight – as still as the air itself,' he added, as we both got to our feet. 'Dawn is coming; it's not very likely they'll start smashing the street-lamps again, and tomorrow we'll go back to our quarters. As for me, in a few days I'll probably retire to a small piece of land I have in another part of France, where there's a little tower in which I'll amuse myself by rounding off my studies of Polybius, Turenne, Folard and Vauban.[63] Nearly all my comrades were killed with the Grand Army, or have died since; it's a long time since I've had anyone much to talk to – and now you know the road by which I've come to hate war, while prosecuting it so vigorously.'

Upon this he shook me warmly by the hand, reminded me again about the gorget he needed, if mine wasn't rusty and if I could lay my hands on it at home. Then he called me back and said:

'Look, as it's not entirely out of the question that we might be shot at out of some window, I'd be obliged if you'd take this packet full of old letters, which are interesting to me, but only to me, and if we don't meet again you might burn them.

'Many of our old comrades have come to us, but we asked them to go home. We're not fighting any kind of civil war. We're as calm as firemen whose job is to extinguish the blaze. Someone will explain it all later, but that's not our business.'

And smiling, he left me.

9
A marble

Even the revolution could not make me forget this conversation; and a fortnight afterwards I was still engaged in solitary meditation about self-forgetful heroism, and about disinterestedness – both of them so rare! I was trying to forget the innocent blood which had recently flowed, and was re-reading the history of America in 1783: how the victorious Anglo-American army, having freed the country and laid down its arms, was on the point of revolt against the Congress, which – being too poor to pay the soldiers – was preparing to disband it. Washington, generalissimo and conqueror, had only to say one word or nod his head to be Dictator; he did what he alone could do: he disbanded the army and then resigned. – I had laid down my book and was comparing this serene grandeur with our anxious ambition. I was melancholy, and put myself in mind of those pure and soldierly souls who without spurious display or charlatanism had embraced command and power only for the public benefit; had worn them without pride; and had entertained no thought of turning them against their country, or of converting them into gold; I was thinking of all the men who had waged war with a full consciousness of its nature; I was thinking of the good Collingwood, so resigned to the life, and finally of the obscure Captain Renaud – when I saw a tall man entering, clad in a blue and rather tattered cloak. From his white moustaches and the scars on his copper-coloured face I recognized one of the grenadiers of Renaud's company; I asked him if the Captain was still alive – for from the emotion the brave fellow showed I could see that something bad had happened. He sat down, wiped his forehead, and when he was composed – after some little while and some effort – he told me.

Throughout the two days of the 28th and 29th of July Captain

Renaud had done nothing but march in column through the streets at the head of his grenadiers; he had put himself in front of the first section of his troops, and calmly passed through a hail of stones and gunshot from the cafés, balconies and windows. When he halted it was only to close up the ranks opened up by those who fell, and to see if the markers on his left were maintaining their proper distance and their dressing on the file-leaders. He had not drawn his sword, and walked cane in hand. At first precise orders had been conveyed to him; but – whether it was that the aides-de-camp had been killed on the way, or that headquarters had not sent any orders – he was left in the Place de la Bastille on the night of the 28th to 29th[64] with no further instructions than to retire on Saint-Cloud, destroying the barricades on his way. This he did without firing a shot. Arriving at the Pont d'Iéna, he halted his company to make a roll call. He had fewer losses than any of the other Guards detachments engaged – and in addition his men were less fatigued. He had the art of making them rest at proper times in the shade and out of the sweltering heat, and of searching out food for them in abandoned barracks when it was refused in hostile parts of the city. The appearance of his column was such that he had found every barricade deserted, and had only the trouble of ordering their demolition.

Thus he was standing upright at the head of the Pont d'Iéna, covered in dust, and shaking it from his feet. He was looking across the barrier to see if there was anything to hamper the exit of his detachment, and choosing scouts to send on ahead. There was no one in the Champ de Mars save two masons lying on their bellies, seemingly asleep, and a small boy of about fourteen who marched about barefoot playing at castanets with two shards of broken faience. He scraped these along the parapet of the bridge from time to time, and so came up, playing, to the stone post where Renaud stood. At that moment the Captain was indicating the heights of Passy with his cane. The boy approached him, gazed at him with big, startled eyes, and, drawing a horse pistol from his jacket, grasped it in both hands and pointed it at the Captain's chest. The latter deflected the barrel with his cane, and, when the child fired, the ball caught him high on the thigh. The Captain fell into a sitting position, not saying a word, and looked at his strange enemy with pity. He stared at this youngster, who still held the weapon in both hands, and stood terrified at what he had done. While this was happening the grenadiers had been standing sadly leaning on their guns; and even now they did not deign to strike the little urchin. Some of them raised their Captain up, others contented themselves with taking the child by the arms and leading him in front of the man he had wounded. He burst into tears; and when he saw the blood flowing copiously from the officer's wound and on to his white trousers he was appalled at the grisliness of the sight and fainted. They took man and child into a little house near Passy, where they still were. The column, led by the lieutenant, pursued the road to Saint-Cloud, and four grenadiers, after shedding their uniforms, had stayed in this house of refuge in order to look after their old commander. One (the one who was speaking to me) had taken work as a labourer with a Paris armourer, the others as fencing-masters; and, by taking their pay to the Captain they had made sure that he had lacked no care up until now. His leg had been amputated; but he had a fierce and malign fever, and, since he feared a dangerous paroxysm, he had sent to find me. There was no time to lose. I left immediately with the worthy soldier – who had told me all these details with moist eyes and a trembling voice, but without complaint, abuse, or accusation, repeating only: 'It's a great misfortune for us.'

The wounded man had been carried to the home of a small shop-keeper, a widow who lived alone with her young children in a little shop on a street on the outskirts of the village. She had not worried for a single moment about being compromised, and no one had thought of taxing her on the subject. On the contrary, her neighbours had been anxious to help her in her care of the invalid. Since the medical officers they called in had not thought him fit to be moved after the operation, she had kept him, and often spent the night next to his bed. When I arrived she came to meet me with such a grateful, timid look that I felt a pang of compunction. I sensed how many difficulties she must have concealed out of natural kindness and charity. She was excessively pale, and her eyes were red with tiredness. She went in and out of a very narrow back room that I could see from the door, and I understood from her bustle that she was arranging the sick man's little chamber with the sort of stylishness that she thought a stranger might think fitting. – So I took care not to enter too quickly, and to allow her all the time she needed.

'Look, sir, he's suffered very much! Come and see!' she said, opening the door.

Captain Renaud was seated on a little bed curtained with serge and set in a corner of the room, and his body was propped up on numerous bolsters. He was reduced to skeletal thinness, and the skin on his cheekbones was a hectic red; the wound in his forehead had gone black. I could see that he had not far to go, and his smile told me this too. He gave me his hand, and indicated that I should sit. On his right was a young boy who held a glass of gum-water which he was stirring with a tablespoon. He rose and carried his chair over to me. From his bed Renaud took him by the ear lobe and said gently to me, in an enfeebled voice:

'Here, my dear fellow, allow me to introduce my conqueror.'

I shrugged my shoulders, and the poor child lowered his eyes and blushed. – I saw a large tear roll down his cheek.

'Come, come!' said the Captain, running his hand through his hair. 'It's not his fault. Poor boy! – he met two men who made him drink some brandy, then paid him, and sent him over to fire his pistol at me. He did it as though he'd been throwing a marble at the post on the bridge. – Isn't that so, Jean?'

And Jean began to tremble with so devastatingly grief-stricken a look on his face that I was touched. I inspected him more closely; he was a very handsome child.

'It really was a marble too,' said the young shopkeeper to me. 'See, sir.' – And she showed me a little agate ball, as big as the heaviest lead bullets, which someone had loaded into the heavy-calibre pistol that lay there.

'It doesn't take more than that to cut off a captain's leg,' said Renaud.

'You mustn't make him talk too much,' the shopkeeper said timidly to me.

Renaud did not hear this.

'Yes, my dear fellow, there's not enough of my leg left to fix a wooden one on to.'

I pressed his hand without replying: humbled to observe that to kill a man who had seen so much and suffered so much – whose breast was armoured over by twenty campaigns, and had sustained ten wounds, who had been tried by fire and ice, by lance and by bayonet – it took no more than the petty assault of one of those Parisian street boys that we call *gamins*.

Renaud answered my thought. He leant his cheek on the pillow, and, pressing my hand, said:

'We were at war. He's no more of a murderer than I was myself at Rheims. When I killed that Russian child, wasn't I perhaps also an assassin? – In the great war in Spain the men who put our sentries to the dagger didn't think of themselves as murderers, and since it was war, perhaps they weren't. Did the Catholics and the Huguenots murder one another or not? – How many murders are there in a big battle? – This is one of those questions in which reason loses herself and has nothing to say. – It's war that's to blame, not us. I assure you that this little chap is most gentle and most kind, and already he reads and writes pretty well. He's a foundling. He was apprenticed to a joiner. – He hasn't quit this room for a fortnight; and he loves me very much – the poor boy. He shows an aptitude for figures; one could make something of him.'

Since he spoke with ever greater difficulty and moved closer to my ear, I leant forward; and he gave me a small piece of folded paper which he asked me to look over. I saw that it was a short will by which he bequeathed an impoverished sort of smallholding he possessed to the poor shopkeeper who had taken him in, and, after her, to Jean, whom she should bring up under the condition that he never become a soldier. He assigned a sum for his replacement,[65] and gave his little plot of land as a refuge for his four old grenadiers. He entrusted all this to a lawyer in his part of the country. When I had this paper in my hands he seemed calmer and ready to doze off. – Then he gave a start and, re-opening his eyes, begged me to accept and to look after his malacca cane. – After that he dozed some more. His old soldier gave a shake of the head, and took one of his hands. I took the other and found it like ice. He said that his feet were cold, and Jean lay down and pressed his little child's body on to the bed to warm him. Then Captain Renaud started to pick at the sheets with his hands, saying that he could no longer feel them; which is a fatal sign. His voice was sepulchral. He carried a hand painfully to his brow, looked at Jean intently, and spoke again:

'It's curious! – That child there looks like the Russian boy!' – Then he closed his eyes, and clasping my hand, said with re-awakened presence of mind:

'You see! That was my mind wandering – it's the end.'

His look was altered and calmer. We understood the struggle that was taking place between his powerful, self-critical mind and the pains bewildering it. For me the sight on the wretched little bed was filled with a solemn majesty. He flushed up again, and said very loud:

'They were fourteen years of age . . . – both of them . . . – Who knows if this isn't that young soul come back in another young body to avenge itself? . . .'

Then he started again, grew paler, and gave me a tranquil and affectionate look:

'I say! . . . Can't you make me shut my mouth? I'm afraid to talk on . . . one gets weak . . . I don't want to speak any longer . . . I'm thirsty.'

We gave him a few spoonfuls, and he said:

'I've done my duty. That idea comforts me.'

Then he added:

'If the country feels better for all that's been done, we've nothing to say. But you'll see . . .'

Then he dozed off and slept for about half an hour. After that a woman came timidly to the door and indicated that the surgeon had arrived. I tiptoed out to speak to him, and, as I went with him into the little garden, and was about to stop at the well to question him, we heard a loud cry. We ran back and saw a sheet covering the head of that brave man, who was now no more . . .

IO

Conclusion

The era that yielded me up these scattered memories is passed now. The cycle opened with the battle of Paris in 1814 and closed with the Three Days of Paris in 1830. It was a time when, as I have said, the army of the Empire was dissolving away into the body of an army then coming into being, and which is now full-grown.

Having previously discussed the function of the poet in various lights, and deplored his situation in our society,[66] I have sought to show here the plight of that other modern pariah, the soldier. I should wish that this book might become for him what the altar of the Lesser Fortune was for a Roman soldier.[67]

I am satisfied with these stories because I value above all others those acts of self-dedication that seek no special recognition. There is something about the more celebrated sacrifices that smacks of self-glorification, and one cannot help being reluctantly aware of this. It would be vain to want to strip it away, because it inheres in them and constitutes their power and their substance – it is the bone beneath their flesh and the marrow in that bone. There was perhaps something inherent in combats and spectacles that inspired the early martyrs; the role they had to play in the scene was so grand that it could well have redoubled the fortitude of its pious victims. For two ideals sustained their arms on either side – canonization on earth and beatitude in heaven. May those ancient sacrifices to a sacred belief be for ever reverenced. But should we not value also, when we can detect them, those unsung acts of devotion which do not seek even to be noticed by their beneficiaries; those humble sacrifices, mute, obscure, neglected, and without a hope of any kind of crown, either human or divine? – Those silent deeds of resignation the examples of which – far more numerous than one might think – possess so compelling a merit that I can think of no virtue to compare with them?

It is not without a purpose that I have tried to direct the attention of the army to that PASSIVE GRANDEUR which consists wholly in *abnegation* and *resignation*. It will never equal in brilliance the grandeur of military action, in which men's energies and capacities are so comprehensively developed; but for a long time to come it will be the only grandeur that any man carrying arms can pretend to, since at present his arms are virtually useless. The dazzling glory of the conqueror is extinguished, and perhaps for ever. His former glamour fades in proportion – I repeat – as there grows in people's minds a contempt for war, and as their hearts fill with disgust at its cold-blooded cruelties. Standing armies embarrass their masters. Every sovereign looks glumly on his army: seated at his feet, the unmoving and silent colossus constrains and alarms him; he knows not what to do with it, and fears lest it turn against him. He sees it devoured by ardour, but unable to stir. A need for action that must not be satisfied constantly torments the blood of its great body – blood which cannot flow, and which therefore simmers incessantly. From time to time the rumours of great wars arise and growl like distant thunder; but their impotent clouds vanish, their whirlwinds sputter out in grains of sand, in treaties, protocols, or I know not what . . . Happily, philosophy has diminished war; diplomacy is replacing it; and at the last technology will succeed in annulling it through the progress of invention.[68]

But, while waiting for the world – which is still a child – to cast aside its ferocious toy, while waiting for this progress, which seems to me inevitable but extremely slow, the soldier, the substance of the armies, needs consolation for the harshness of his lot. He feels that his country, which used to love him for the glories with which he crowned her, begins to despise him for his idleness, or even hate him for the civil wars in which he is ordered to strike at his mother. – This gladiator who is no longer applauded in the arena needs to restore confidence in himself – and we ought to plead for justice for him, because, as I have said, he is blind and dumb; thrown wherever others desire him to go, and in arms today against the cockade of one faction, he must ask himself whether tomorrow he will not be wearing it in his own hat . . .

What idea can sustain him if not that of duty and his oath? And in the uncertainties of his path, in his doubts and hampering regrets, what feeling, in our cold despondent days, could excite, and might even exalt him?

What is there left that is sacred?

In the universal shipwreck of beliefs, what floating debris can still be clutched by a courageous hand? Beside the love of *comfort* and transient luxury nothing appears on the surface of the abyss. It seems as though egotism has drowned everything; even those who dive bravely in, seeking to save souls, feel themselves about to be engulfed. The party political chiefs take Catholicism as a watchword and a banner; but what faith have they in its mysteries, and how far do they follow its doctrine in their lives? – Artists illuminate it like a precious medallion and plunge themselves into its dogmas as into a magnificent source of imagery; but how many of them kneel in the church they embellish? – Numerous philosophers embrace its cause, and plead for it as though they were generous lawyers acting for an impoverished and forlorn client; they love to imbue their words and their writings with its forms and colours, to ornament their books with gothic gilding, to weave the clever web of their arguments around the cross in all their work; but in private this cross is rarely by their side.[69] – Modern warriors fight and die with scarcely a thought of God. Our age knows that this is so, wishes it were otherwise, and can do nothing about it. It looks at itself with a weary eye, and no other era has so powerfully felt how unhappy introspection can be.

From these dismal symptoms some foreigners have concluded that we have fallen into a state comparable to that of the later Roman Empire – and grave men have asked themselves if the national character is not sunk for ever. But those who have known how to look a little deeper have seen that in spite of the corrosions of sophistry that have worn us down so deplorably, the quality of virile resolution survives in us. In France manly action has not lost its ancient strength. Sacrifices as great and as complete as ever there were are accomplished with vigour and alacrity. Coldly calculated battles are executed with conscious ferocity. – Today the least inclination of the mind leads to actions as mighty as were once produced by the most fervent faith. Beliefs are weak amongst us, but men are strong. Every calamity finds a hundred Belzunces.[70]

The youth of today continually defy death – for duty or for a whim – with the smile of a Spartan; a smile the more severe in that not all of them believe in a banquet of the gods.

Yes, I believe I am able to make out one point that seems to me secure upon the darkling flood. At first I saw it fleetingly, and for the moment did not believe in it. I was afraid to look more closely, and for a long time turned my eyes aside. Then, because I was haunted by the memory of that first glimpse, I returned in spite of myself to this perceptible but still uncertain point. I approached it, went round about it, looked over it and under, put my hand on it; and I found it strong enough to serve as a refuge in the storm, and was reassured.

It is not a new faith, a newly-evolved cult, a vague concept. It is a sentiment born in us irrespective of time, of place, even of religions; a proud unshakeable sentiment, an instinct of incomparable beauty which has found a name worthy of itself only in modern times, yet was already producing sublime achievements in antiquity – and fertilizing them like those great rivers which at their source and first meanderings have as yet no name. This faith, which it seems to me still resides in everyone, and reigns sovereign within armies, is that of HONOUR.

I see no evidence that it has been weakened, or that it has been exhausted. It is not an idol. For most men it is a god – and a god around whom many greater gods have fallen. The collapse of their temples has not disturbed its statue.

This strange, proud virtue is animated by a mysterious vitality, and it stands erect in the midst of all our vices, blending so well with them that it is fed by their energy. – While all other virtues seem to descend from heaven to clasp our hands and lift us up, this one appears to spring from within ourselves and itself strives upwards. – It is a wholly human virtue which I believe to be born of the earth, without celestial reward after death: it is the virtue appertaining to life.

Its cult, as it is manifested and interpreted in diverse ways, is never a matter of arguments. It is a dynamic faith, without symbols or images, without dogma or rites, and whose laws are always unwritten. – How comes it that all men feel its formidable power? Modern men – men of the hour in which I write – are sceptical and ironical about everything else besides. But each becomes serious the moment its name is mentioned. – And this is not a theory, but an observation. – The name of Honour moves something in a man which is integral to himself, and the shock of it awakens all his pride and his primitive vigour. The thought of being the guardian of that pure tabernacle – which resides in his breast like a second heart, inhabited by a god – stirs an invincible resolution to defend it against others, and even against himself. From it there comes an inward solace which is all the more beautiful for his ignorance of its source and true causation; from there, also, come sudden revelations of the true, the beautiful, the just; from there a light that travels before him.

Honour is conscience, but conscience exalted. – It is respect for oneself and for what is most beautiful in one's life carried on to the highest plane, and with the most ardent feeling. – It is true that I cannot perceive any single unifying principle in it, and every time one tries to define it with precision the argument dwindles into mere terminology; but I cannot see that definitions of God have achieved any greater precision. And what does that fact prove against an existence which is universally felt?

Perhaps it is Honour's greatest advantage to be so powerful and constantly beautiful whatever its source! . . . Sometimes it persuades a man that he cannot survive an insult, sometimes that he must bear it with such self-possession and magnanimity that it is compensated for and its stain rubbed out. On other occasions it finds the way to hide both the injury and its expiation. On yet others it initiates great enterprises, and magnificent hard-fought struggles; it presides over unsung sacrifices, slowly accomplished, and more beautiful through their patience and obscurity than are the transports of sudden enthusiasm or violent indignation; it can produce acts of good will quite unsurpassed by gospel charity; it is capable of wonderful tolerances, divine indulgence and sublime forgiveness. Always and everywhere it sustains individual human dignity in all its beauty.

Honour is active decency.[71]

The shame of failing in honour is felt as a total shame.

Is it then the mysterious, the sacred, touchstone?

Consider the weight, amongst us, of the common expression – universally employed, decisive, yet simple: – To give one's word of honour.

Here the human word ceases to be simply the expression of ideas, it becomes the word in the highest sense, the word sacred among words, as if it issued with the primal utterance of human language.[72] And, as if thenceforward there was no further word worthy of being said, it became the promise of men to men, blessed by all the peoples; it became the substance of the oath itself, because to it was added the idea of Honour.

From that moment each of us possessed his word, and clung to it like life itself. The gambler has his, considers it sacred, and adheres to it. Even in the throes of passion it is given, taken, and – entirely profane as it is – religiously kept. This word is thought lovely everywhere, everywhere revered. And is not this principle – which one might well think to be innate, and that compels only by the inner assent of all – is it not of the most sovereign beauty when vindicated by a soldier?

The sworn word, which too often is a mere vocal act on the part of a statesman, becomes a terrible fact to the warrior; that word which one of them engages lightly or treacherously, the other writes with his blood in the dust – and that is why he should be honoured by all, above others, and why many of us should lower our eyes in his presence.

I trust that in the coming times the loftiest of religions will not attempt to belittle or to extinguish this sentiment of Honour, which burns in us like the last lamp in a ruined temple! – rather it should appropriate it, and unite it with its own splendours, placing it as another candle on the altar it strives to revive. That would be holy work. – For myself, struck by this happy insight, I have neither wished nor been able to write more than a humble and entirely human book – stating simply what I believe myself to have perceived as enduringly vital within us.

We should beware of calling this ancient god of Honour a false god, for the stone of his altar is perhaps that of the unknown God.[73] The magnetic power of the stone draws and fixes to itself the hearts of steel, the strong hearts.

Say if this is not so, you my brave comrades, you for whom I have written these tales – you, O reborn Theban Band,[74] whose heads have been bruised on the stone of the Oath – all of you, who are the saints and martyrs of the religion of HONOUR, say if this is not so!

Written at Paris, 20 August 1835

NOTES

Introduction

1. *Introduction*. In this Introduction I try to prepare for the reader's pleasure rather than anticipate it by giving away the details and the outcomes of Vigny's stories. Some features of them have to be touched on because arguments need to be illustrated, but I hope to have been discreet enough to allow the text to be read with appropriate freshness.

2. *Servitude and Grandeur of Arms*. After balancing the advantages and disadvantages of the many possible translations of *Servitude et grandeur militaires* – from the purely literal *Military Servitude and Grandeur* onwards – it seems that the present title, though slightly cumbersome, best reconciles the dignified resonance of the original with possible English.

The two nouns are usable in themselves: Royal Navy officers in Vigny's period referred to their hard apprenticeship as midshipmen as their 'servitude'; and 'grandeur' is still acceptable in English in spite of having a somewhat stiffer, more pompous feeling than in French. In the text – where the words are controlled and modified by the nuances around them – they present no difficulty at all.

The more daring renderings by previous modern translators, *The Military Necessity* by Humphrey Hare (1953), and *The Military Condition* by Margaret Barnett (1964), though intelligent and very sayable in English, lack specificity. So I have preferred to aspire to the precision, and a little to the glamour, of the French phrase.

3. *England . . . in theory*. English professional soldiers tended to be relatively few, tucked away overseas, and explained away in terms befitting a militia: for the English assumption since Charles I and the Commonwealth was that regular soldiers meant tyranny. Defence could best be left to the sea. This – the 'blue water' policy – often led to a dangerous unpreparedness for land wars. But one of its incidental benefits is illustrated by the not always beneficial political predominance of standing armies and their officer corps in most other European countries – those of Prussia being especially prominent until 1945.

4. *Dieu! . . . au fond des bois.* 'O God! How sad is the call of the horn in the depths of the woods!'. *'Le Cor'*, written in 1825.

5. *within strong literary conventions.* So much so that it may well be felt that in the inner, Marie-Antoinette, part of 'An Evening at Vincennes' – as opposed to its fine and elaborate frame – the Cinderella plot runs on a little too long, and too cosily, to remain pertinent to the rest of the work.

6. *offering no extenuation. Lord Jim*, Chapter 13. See on this subject: Ian Watt, *Conrad in the Nineteenth Century* (1980); Norman Page, *A Conrad Companion* (1986); and Yves Hervouet, *The French Face of Joseph Conrad* (1990).

7. *the abstract, dry idea . . . human entrails.* Letter to Louis Colet, December 1846.

8. *not simply an auxiliary.* Paul Bénichou, *Les Mages Romantiques* (1988).

Memories of Military Servitude

1. *Ave, Caesar, morituri te salutant.* 'Hail Caesar, we who are about to die salute you'. (See n.13 to Book 1, below.)

BOOK I

1. *. . . there is no greater grief . . . in times of misery.* Dante, *Inferno*, V, 121–3:

> . . . Nessun maggior dolore,
> che ricordasi del tempo felice
> nella miseria . . .

2. *as I write.* 1835 (Vigny's note).

3. *the great Frederick.* Frederick II of Prussia (1712–86), the celebrated intellectual, disciplinarian, musician and warrior king. Through his brilliant and hectic fighting of cleverly aggressive wars; his genius for heroic and desperate defence; his amazing talents and resource as a strategist and tactician; and through a hard policy of internal economic and intellectual modernization, he raised up Prussia to the status of a European power, successfully rivalling Austria in middle Europe. It is said that he increased his kingdom's territory twofold and its prestige tenfold.

4. *the Seven Years War.* Or the third Silesian war, 1756–63, fought by Prussia, as pre-emptive aggressor, against an alliance of Austria, Russia and France. This was the war of Frederick the Great's most astonishing victories – Rossbach and Leuthen – and his worst defeat – Kunersdorf. It exhausted all the main participants, but Prussia survived. It also cemented the Prussian alliance with

England, La Belle Alliance, which bore its greatest fruit at Waterloo. 'Were he still alive,' said Napoleon at Frederick's tomb at Potsdam, 'we should not now be here in Prussia.' (The tomb has recently been restored to its place, with symbolism, after a removal in 1945.)

5. *Soubise and M. de Clermont.* As Vigny remarks, the personal rivalries and quarrels over precedence among French generals during the Seven Years War were notorious.

Charles de Rohan, prince de Soubise (1715–87), was the French marshal who managed to lose the pivotal battle of Rossbach to Frederick the Great in 1757. He commanded three times as many French and Austrians as Frederick had Prussians. Nevertheless he was shortly afterwards made Marshal of France, and gained two victories in the following year.

The prince de Clermont commanded the army of the Lower Rhine in 1758. On the grounds – it is said – that he was a prince of the blood, he refused to be aided by Soubise against the Prussian threat, and was routed at Krefeld in June. Vigny's uncle was killed in this battle.

6. *intrigues in the* Œil *de Bœuf.* The *Œil de Bœuf* was an antechamber at Versailles lit by a circular window, and a byword for backstairs gossip and plots.

7. *for M. de Chevert and for M. d'Assas.* These were two French heroes of the Seven Years War. Chevert was one of Louis XV's best generals, and was celebrated for his defence of Prague in the War of the Austrian Succession (1740–2). The heroic death of Chevalier d'Assas at Klosterkamp was made famous by Voltaire – he was a captain in the Royal Auvergne Regiment (for which see Book 2, Chapter 8).

8. *star of the Legion of Honour.* The Legion of Honour was created to reward civil and military distinction – with a typical classicizing flourish – by Napoleon in May 1802, specifically to replace the old chivalric orders of Saint-Louis and of the Holy Ghost, which had been abolished at the Revolution.

9. *the Champ-de-Mars.* An area in Paris named after the Campus Martius in ancient Rome, and, like that, a ground set aside for military exercises. It stretches from the front of the École Militaire to the Seine, and is now a rectangular park with the Eiffel Tower at the river end.

10. *M. de Louvois.* François Michel le Tellier, marquis de Louvois (1641–91). Louis XIV's energetic, centralizing and reforming Minister of War, who also took a leading part in the persecution of Protestants.

11. *Turenne.* Henri de la Tour d'Auvergne, vicomte de Turenne, Marshal (1611–75), was perhaps the most highly regarded French soldier before Napoleon. He fought in the Thirty Years War, conquered Roussillon from Spain in 1642, fought for and against the Fronde rebellion (when he beat Condé), in the

Netherlands, and finally against the Imperialists under Montecucculi in Southern Germany, where he was accidentally killed by a cannon ball. (See n.51 to Book 3.)

12. *Mirabeau.* Honoré Gabriel Riqueti, comte de Mirabeau (1749–91), was an audacious French revolutionary, writer, and politician, at one time imprisoned for three years by the King at Vincennes (for which castle, see Part 2). He was a great force in revolutionary politics and was elected President of the National Assembly just before he died. An expert on England and Prussia, he advocated a constitutional monarchy.

13. *Those who are about to die salute you.* This, also used as the epigraph to the whole work, is from the section of Suetonius which deals with Claudius (paragraph 21). In it Claudius makes a sarcastic riposte to the gladiator's salute – 'Or not, as the case may be,' he says – and is faced by a strike on the part of the offended fighters.

14. *I sang* Joconde. *Joconde* was a comic opera by Nicolo Isouard and d'Étienne, which was the hit in Paris during the Hundred Days in 1814. Possibly the young warrior was singing 'I've roamed the whole world over' or 'You always come back to your first love'.

15. *his white cockade . . . the sleeve of my red tunic.* The white cockade is the Bourbon emblem. The four Red Companies of light horse, to which the narrator belongs, were created out of the scions of the older nobility in 1814 to mark Louis XVIII's first restoration. They were part of the Royal Household. Their aristocratic and privileged nature provoked the resentment of the regular army – see below – and the formation was dropped after the second restoration in 1815.

16. *the Legion of Honour.* One of the concessions that the Bourbons deemed it wise to make at their restoration was the retention of the Legion of Honour.

17. *pigtail's ribbon.* In French, *ruban de queue* – a piece of eighteenth-century army slang for which there is no convincing equivalent. It refers to a military fashion of the time of Louis XV, according to which troops bound their hair with a ribbon behind their neck like a horse's tail. Sometimes the fashion was for very long pigtails.

18. *the* Marat. The ship is named after an appropriate hero. Jean Paul Marat (1743–93), a moderately distinguished doctor and scientist, was, of course, also a violent journalist and one of the most daring and ferocious French revolutionaries. He is held to be largely responsible for inciting the disgusting September massacres in 1792 (see also n.22 to Book 2). He was already dying when assassinated in his bath, on a principled impulse, by Charlotte Corday.

19. *the 28th Fructidor 1797.* The revolutionary project to erase history (as well as Royal Naval officers) involved the re-naming of the months – Fructidor

was the invention for the twelfth month of the new calendar, from 18 August to 16 September.

At this time the executive power of France consisted in a Directory of five members (one of them annually elected), whose rivalry and internecine intrigues supplied much of the interest of political life. This date (14 September) was ten days after one of the numerous *coups d'état*, 18th Fructidor, when Barras and his fellow republican Directors struck down their royalist colleagues with the support of the army, including General Bonaparte. The large number of deportations to Cayenne in French Guiana – known as the 'dry guillotine' – here recorded or imagined by Vigny must be a reflection of this event.

Two years afterwards Bonaparte, on becoming one of three Consuls, and effectively military dictator, was able to proclaim that 'The Revolution is established upon the principles which began it: it is ended.'

20. *the custom in those days*. Powdered hair was associated with the *ancien régime*.

21. *forbidden all noises and lights*. Probably not just an aesthetic preference, but a reminder that France was at war.

22. *Paul and Virginia*. In *Paul et Virginie* (1786), by Bernardin de Saint-Pierre. This was one of the most celebrated novels of the culture of Sensibility. Saint-Pierre was a follower of Rousseau, and his hero and heroine are brought up in Mauritius and nurtured and moulded far from the snares of European civilization. Though the story ends in tragic shipwreck, part of its striking proposition is that human nature, like the revolutionary state, can be subject to rational and enlightened formation. It is a seminal Romantic text, much emulated and mocked (for example by Maria Edgeworth in *Belinda*).

Laure's touchingly naive view of the reality of fiction confirms our sense of her young lady's notion of the world; but it might also convey a hint of Vigny's intended genre in this tale.

23. *one solitary louis*. A louis = 24 francs, an *écu* = 6 francs.

24. *La Force*. This was originally the *hôtel* of the duc de La Force and was converted into a prison in 1788. It was destroyed in the nineteenth century, but has such a dreadful name because it was the scene of some of the most bloody episodes in the September massacres of 1792 (see n.18 above; and n.22 to Book 2). For the dates, see above.

25. *the Paris Panorama*. The Panorama, invented by the Scots painter Barker in 1792, was a large circular device sited in a rotunda for the presentation of spectacular scenes. These could extend over sixty feet from the viewing platform, and be forty feet high. Napoleon planned to use the Panorama to show propaganda pictures of his great victories.

26. *Charenton*. The famous lunatic asylum of Saint-Maurice in the Val de Marne.

27. *the Napoleon's month allowance*. Napoleon's birthday on the 15 August was celebrated by double pay for that month for some officers of the Guard.

28. *went bareheaded at the Beresina*. The Beresina was a particularly awful defeat for the French during their retreat from Moscow, on 28–9 November 1812. A demoralized and ill-supplied army sustained 25,000 casualties in trying to cross the river in the freezing snow. 'There ended the career of the Grand Army, which had made Europe tremble; it ceased to exist in the military sense, its only safety now lay in headlong flight' (marquis de Chambray).

29. *a campaign of Marshal Masséna*. André Masséna (1758–1817), duc de Rivoli, Prince of Essling, has the reputation of being the ablest of Napoleon's marshals. After a career in the Corsican and revolutionary armies he crushed a Russian force under Suvorov at Zürich in 1799, beat the Austrians in Italy, and covered himself in glory against them in 1809. In 1810 he compelled Wellington to retreat to the lines of Torre Vedras in Portugal, but was blocked by these and conducted an admired retreat when forced to retire because of lack of supplies. But he was recalled by Napoleon in disgrace and adhered to the Bourbons at the restoration.

BOOK 2

1. *the time of the Terror*. The Reign of Terror is the name given to the phase of absolute revolutionary administration by the Jacobin Committee of Public Safety from around October 1793. It was conceived, at least by its most radical exponents – Robespierre and Saint-Just – as a means of totally reforming human society, economy, property, custom and belief, most obviously by the guillotine and propaganda, but in many other modes too. It relied heavily for its immediate powers on the *sans-culotte* mobs of Paris, and is famous for intensifying and feeding on its own fury to the point of destroying its exponents – first Danton and Desmoulins (April 1794), eventually Robespierre and his allies (July 1794–10 Thermidor). After that the apparatus was fairly quickly dismantled.

2. *my relation, M. de Bougainville*. Louis Antoine, comte de Bougainville (1729–1811), Field Marshal and Admiral, was a navigator, mathematician and soldier who accomplished the first French circumnavigation of the world. He served with distinction in Canada and Germany, and colonized the Falkland Islands for France (later transferred to Spain, then Britain). He was also the author of an important treatise on integral calculus. The largest of the Solomon Islands is named after him, as well as the plant bougainvillaea.

3. *the massacres of St Bartholomew in Paris*. The fearful massacres of the Parisian Huguenot Protestants by Catholics on St Bartholomew's Day, 1572. Generally

held to be the responsibility of the King's mother Catherine de Medici and his younger brother the duc d'Anjou, later Henri III.

4. *twenty and three thousand men slain.* 'about three thousand' in the Authorized Version.

5. *peace of the Abbé de Saint-Pierre.* Charles Irénée Castel, Abbé de Saint-Pierre (1658–1743), was the author of a *Plan for a Perpetual Peace* (1713) which proposed an organization of sovereigns to enforce peace on its members – a little like the United Nations. His theories were influential in the formation, after 1815, of the reactionary Holy Alliance.

6. *a sophist with whom I have fought elsewhere.* This is a reference to Joseph Marie, comte de Maistre (1753–1821), the Savoyard diplomat and philosopher who became the representative of the King of Sardinia in Russia, and whose most famous work is *Les Soirées de Saint Pétersbourg.* He was extremely hostile to all liberal or democratic thought, and, besides holding the opinions here attributed to him, was a propagandist for the Divine Right of Kings. The young Vigny (at about the time of which he is talking here) seriously flirted with his ideas – clearly they appealed to one side of his complex nature – but by the early 1830s had turned derisively against them. Like the increasingly liberal Abbé Lamennais, in whom he was now much more interested, the events of 1830 – see Book 3 of this work – fired him with ideas of ideal popular liberty. Chapter XXXII of *Stello* is an attack on Maistre and his ethos.

7. *nine sous a day.* 20 sous = 1 franc.

8. *who had made that geometrical plot of ground flourish.* The École Polytechnique, founded in 1794 for engineering, became a military institution in 1804, and was much developed under the Empire, especially in relation to the study and teaching of mathematics, gunnery, ballistics, etc. Perhaps the sallow-faced gunner, Napoleon, is being alluded to.

9. *Laplace's theory of probability* – Pierre Simon, marquis de Laplace (1749–1827), was a famous astronomer (and one-time professor at the École Militaire) who also made important contributions to probability theory.

10. *built by Saint Louis.* 'Every French dynasty provided an icon' – and Louis IX (1215–70) was the Capetian one. He is especially renowned for his holiness, his crusading, and for his creation and administration of a strong royal justice.

11. *Quartermaster-Sergeant Major.* In French, *adjudant.* Not to be confused with a British adjutant who is a commissioned officer, commonly a major. As will become plain, *adjudant* is a warrant officer, a senior non-commissioned rank somewhat like a quartermaster-sergeant or sergeant major in English terms, and is translated accordingly.

12. *mutilated at Marengo and Austerlitz.* These were both Napoleonic victories

against Austria, in 1800 and 1805. They were perhaps the most brilliant and glorious of Napoleon's victories and therefore the most evocative here.

13. *the eternal sun with his* Nec pluribus impar, *and the* Ultima ratio Regum. These phrases are in a rather curious Latin. The first roughly translates as 'We are not inferior to others', which was Louis XIV's personal motto, just as the sun was his emblem; the second as 'The final argument of Kings [or the state]'.

14. *turf raised over the duc d'Enghien.* The death of Louis Antoine Henri de Bourbon, duc d'Enghien (1772–1804), scandalized Europe. His execution was a political crime – very rare then compared with the twentieth century (at least if we except the quasi-legal slaughters of the French Revolution).

As is clear from his name, d'Enghien was related to the French royal house – he was in fact in one (illegitimate, but legitimated) line Louis XIV's great-great-great grandson – and had been the commander of *émigré* armies. But his seizure from Baden by Napoleon's agents in 1804 was a violation of neutral territory, and his trial (for alleged complicity in an assassination plot by Cadoual and Pichegru) summary. His death outraged Europe and no doubt cost Napoleon the potential support of many who might have been tempted to see an emperor as a legitimate replacement for the Bourbons. It was thus the occasion for the celebrated remark of Fouché, Chief of Police, that the deed was worse than a crime – it was a blunder.

15. *entitled:* THE PRISON. This is dated 1821 at Vincennes, and printed in *Poèmes antiques et modernes.* It is a narrative and dialogue in couplets between a dying prisoner and a priest, which is subtitled as of 'the seventeenth century' (and is a little in the manner of Racine). The matter is romantic, philosophical and religious, and one of the ideas to be taken from it is that imprisonment, or servitude, is as much internal as external.

16. *the mountain mists in Ossian.* Ossian was a legendary Gaelic bard and warrior, said to have been converted to Christianity by St Patrick after a three-hundred-year sojourn in the land of eternal youth. Gaelic, or Erse, heroic ballads, lyrics and fragments of prose survive in manuscripts of the second or third century.

What the narrator muses about here are the epic poems woven round some of these by James MacPherson (1736–96). He incorporated the obscure materials into his own extensive imitations concerning the legendary invasion of Ireland from Denmark, and published them as the grand, gloomy, Celtic heroic poems *Fingal* (1762) and *Temora* (1763). MacPherson claimed that his Ossian really was Ossian, as Homer is Homer; and his work was a sensation of the early Romantic movement. But when challenged as to authenticity, notably by Dr Johnson, he could provide no originals. He became a Member of Parliament.

The embarrassment felt by the English reader at the great admiration shown for Ossian, not only by Vigny, but generally on the Continent, and especially by Goethe in *The Sorrows of Young Werther* (1774–87), is an indication of the difficulty of translating poetry into another tongue. Johnson said: 'Sir, a man might write such stuff for ever, if he would *abandon* his mind to it.' Napoleon loved Ossian.

17. *peasant girl that ever Greuze endowed*. Jean Baptiste Greuze (1725–1805) was the most celebrated French genre painter of the eighteenth century.

18. *the Curé*. The French word is retained here because the English 'vicar' or 'parson' has – or rather had – different social overtones.

19. *a gift for Madame*. Madame was the court title for the wife of Monsieur, the King's eldest brother. This was Louise of Savoy (1753–1810). Her husband was the future Louis XVIII.

20. *these words* – Pierre, Pierrette, Pierrerie, Pierrier, Pierrot. In English, in which of course all the punning is lost, these mean: stone (and Peter); Pierrette; jewellery; swivel-gun; clown (and house sparrow).

21. *his name was Michel-Jean Sédaine*. Sédaine (1719–97) was a Parisian poet, librettist and playwright. His work consisted mainly of light comedy such as *Rose and Colas* (1764; see n.26 below). But he also wrote serious comedy, notably *The Philosopher Without Knowing It*. Here he is represented as being at least ten years younger than he would really have been.

22. *I can never forget her*. As will appear, this is a portrait of the princesse de Lamballe (1749–92), the intimate friend of Marie-Antoinette and superintendent of her household, who, having returned from refuge in England in 1791, suffered a particularly vile death during the September Massacres of 1792. Murdered, violated and cut in pieces, her body was paraded round the streets of Paris, her heart torn out and eaten, and her head presented outside the Queen's window on a pike.

The date of this fictional meeting and the subsequent action must be between 1774 (when Marie-Antoinette became Queen) and 1778 (when the first performances of *Irène* were given – see nn.26 and 27 below). So Madame de Lamballe is in her mid-twenties here, and the Queen around twenty.

23. *a little punishment devised by M. de Saint-Germain*. Claude Louis, comte de Saint-Germain, was a general and Louis XVI's Minister of War, 1775–7. He reorganized the French army and introduced Prussian discipline and corporal punishment. His failure with the latter led to his resignation.

24. *Monsigny's Rose*. Pierre Alexandre Monsigny (1729–1817) was a composer of 'fresh and gracious' opera for the court, and collaborator with Sédaine on *Rose et Colas* and other works.

25. *Grétry*. André Ernest Modeste Grétry (1741–1813) was the most celebrated

of eighteenth-century French opera composers. He was also a collaborator with
Sédaine; a protégé of Marie-Antoinette; and a friend of the *philosophes*.

26. *IRÈNE, a new play by M. de VOLTAIRE and of ROSE ET COLAS, by M.
SÉDAINE*. Vigny here takes considerable liberties with dates. Sédaine made his
theatrical début in 1756 – whereas the date of the 84-year-old Voltaire's last
tragedy *Irène*, given a royal welcome in Paris in 1778, is correct for the supposed
action (see next note).

27. *Le Kain* – Henri Louis Cain (1728–78), called Le Kain, was a famous tragic
actor. The date of his death shows that the year (in the story) must in fact be
1778.

28. *There was a little bird . . . As a house.*

> 'Il était un oiseau gris
> Comme une souris,
> Qui, pour loger ses petits,
> Fit un p'tit
> Nid.'

29. *Love me, love me, my little King.* 'Aimez-moi, aimez-moi, mon p'tit roi.'

30. *Oh! draw up your legs, for they can be seen.* 'Ah! r'montez vos jambes, car on
les voit.'

31. *all the Sèvres . . . out of the window.* There is a special point here in that the
manufacture of fine porcelain in France was established under Louis XV's
patronage at Vincennes (1738–45), and only moved to Sèvres in 1756.

32. *My friend Ernest d'Hanache . . . the last Vendée, when he died nobly.* A
legitimist fellow officer of Vigny's in the fifth regiment of Guards, who resigned
from the army in protest at the July revolution of 1830 (see n.2 to Book 3). He
then took part in the insurrection of the duchesse de Berri in the Vendée,
and was killed in combat in June 1832.

The first Vendée (named after that area in France, and from which future
royalist revolts took their name) was in 1793, and was the major internal
military threat to the French Revolution. It was put down with difficulty, and
with an almost genocidal fervour.

33. *the best boy in the world.* An allusion (perhaps via the poet Clément Marot)
to Rabelais's description of Panurge.

34. *M. de Fontanges.* In 1819 de Fontanges was a major in the fifth Regiment
of Footguards; later colonel of the fifty-fifth Foot. He was Vigny's commanding
officer, and something of a family friend.

35. *the duc de Lauzun and the chevalier de Grammont* – The first of these
could, of course, be the duc de Lauzun who appears above as a courtier of
Marie-Antoinette. But it is more likely that he is one of a famous pair. Lauzun

and Grammont were soldiers and courtiers of Louis XIV, and both spent time abroad (in England and Ireland) with the Stuarts. Their fame is for their style and the fineness and grace of their manners – though they also had considerable reputations as libertines. Grammont's posthumous *Mémoires* (1713) about the intrigues at the court of Charles II are notorious.

Memories of Military Grandeur

BOOK 3

1. *candid and humble heroes like Marceau, Desaix and Kléber*. Heroes of the revolutionary armies, all of whom suffered untimely deaths.

François Severin Marceau-Desgraviers (1769–96) took part in the storming of the Bastille as a sergeant, and helped to save Verdun in 1792. He fought against the Vendéens, and, now a general, commanded the right against the Austrians at Fleurus in 1794. 'After a short but brilliant passage of command in the army of the Sambre-et-Meuse . . . 1795–6, he was fatally wounded near Altenkirchen; Kray, his chief opponent, shed tears at his deathbed.'

Louis Charles Antoine Desaix (1768–1800) was a general who, unusually in this company, started his career as an officer in the Royal Army. He protested against the dethronement of the Bourbons and was imprisoned briefly. But he covered himself with glory defending against the Austrians in the Black Forest in 1796–7. In 1799 he conquered Upper Egypt, where he became known as 'the just Sultan'. He was killed at Marengo in 1800, and much and widely regretted.

Jean Baptiste Kléber (1753–1800) from Alsace was at first an Austrian officer, but volunteered for the French revolutionary army in 1792. In the Vendée he was recalled because of his clemency. He commanded the right of the army of the Sambre-et-Meuse at Fleurus, and its left when he was victorious at Altenkirchen. Declining command of the army of the Rhine he went to Egypt with Napoleon (see Book 3, Chapter 4) and was the 'real victor' at Mount Tabor. Left in command there when Napoleon went back to France – in his opinion this was a shabby desertion, and he the victim – he had troubles with the Turko-British treaties, defeated the Turks at Heliopolis and re-took Cairo. There he was assassinated by an Egyptian fanatic. Napoleon, on his deathbed, talked of meeting him in the Elysian Fields.

2. *the month of July 1830*. The revolution of 1830 – also known as the July Days or the Three Days (27–29 July) – was the violent expression of a reaction, at first largely by the Liberal bourgeois deputies led by Thiers, to the rule of Charles X (1757–1836), Louis XVIII's brother and successor since

1824. Under the influence and administration of his minister Polignac – a mystical and driven *Ultra* who had visions of the Virgin Mary – the King had become narrowly autocratic, almost feudal in pretension.

As in the case of many subsequent revolutions the course and upshot of that of 1830 were in very many ways not what had been foreseen. As in 1789, journalists – who were directly threatened by the government – mobilized (and created) popular feeling, especially in Paris. Barricades were erected, idealists fought, and mobs mobbed. On the 28th Marshal Marmont, 'trying to take the offensive against the barricades' with troops who in any case were unenthusiastic about the Bourbons, 'lost the eastern districts and fell back on the Tuileries; on the 29th, with the Louvre surrounded, he gave the order to retreat'. Now alarmed at the mass fervour, and remembering 1789, the Liberal deputies and Thiers intervened, and called in the aged national hero Lafayette to command the bourgeois Municipal Guard (he had commanded the National Guard in 1789). Together they put down the mobs, avoided the possible radicalism of a new Republic and installed the duc d'Orléans, Louis-Philippe, as a constitutional monarch.

This revolution fired, and was fired by, 'young France'. The results of its compromise disgusted many of them, and are part of the subject of some of the very best French fiction – Balzac, Stendhal, Flaubert . . .

It is common and easy to scorn Louis-Philippe – especially since his reign ended in another revolution in 1848 – but Vigny does not seem to have done so.

3. *to seek their lilies*. The *fleur de lys* are, of course, the emblem of Bourbon legitimacy (as in the 'white cockade' of Book 1, Chapter 4). For the Vendée, see n.32 to Book 2.

4. *have conquered new fortresses*. The year 1832, for example, saw a resurgence of French expansionism. There was fighting which was to lead to the conquest of Algeria; the occupation of Ancona against Austrian intervention in Italy; and the seizure of Anvers to protect Belgium from Holland.

5. *the Spanish campaign*. The Congress of Verona had, in the autumn of 1822 – and in face of the opposition of England – authorized Louis XVIII's army to quell the popular uprising in Spain against the absolute power of his Bourbon kinsman, Ferdinand VII. In 1823 100,000 men crossed the Pyrenees under the duc d'Angoulême ('at last the young gallants of the Restoration were to be given the chance to prove that bravery was not the exclusive virtue of the Napoleonic veterans') and the campaign ended with the taking of the Trocadero in Cádiz in August 1823. Vigny himself was ordered on this campaign and enthusiastically awaited adventure, danger and glory. It was one of the dis-

appointments of his life that his battalion was kept on garrison duties at Pau, near the frontier but with no chance of action against the enemy.

6. *never drew his sword . . . hand-to-hand fighting.* A celebrated habit also of General Charles George Gordon – Chinese Gordon – Gordon of Khartoum (1833–85), who, it is pleasant to think, would almost certainly have read this book.

7. *striking tragic poses.* An allusion to the contemporary cult of misanthropic gloom then found so bewitching, and on Vigny's part a typically Romantic anti-Romantic point, of the kind also found in Stendhal. – A dandy in a black coat, alone and apart, yet always very noticeably present with his obscure wound, his contemptuous sex appeal, dark derisive feelings, his past . . . etc. The literary sources are many: Lord Byron (life and works), *Faust, Hamlet*, numerous Gothick hero-villains, *Werther* . . .

8. *I saw the Orders in Council.* The four *ordonnances* of 24 July which dissolved the Chamber, abolished freedom of the press, restricted electoral suffrage and called for new elections on that basis – thus precipitating the revolution. 'At last you are ruling,' said Charles X's daughter-in-law to him, memorably.

9. *like Louis XIV . . . I have been too fond of war.* The King's dying words. This is the place to note that it was a certain Captain Renaud who fought what Napoleon called 'the most beautiful combat of the Egyptian campaign' when his 200 French overcame 600 Mamelukes by sheer courage near Aswan (see *Bonaparte in Egypt* by J. C. Herold, London, 1963). Quite possibly Vigny had absorbed the name.

10. *Charles XII's music – the cannon.* Charles XII, King of Sweden 1682–1718. Peter the Great of Russia's great opponent, and a byword for hectic military passion:

> No joys to him Pacific Scepters yield
> War sounds the trump, he rushes to the field . . .
>
> (Dr Johnson)

Vigny and Captain Renaud would be more familiar with Voltaire's remarks that he 'indulged in no other pleasure than that of making Europe tremble' and that 'he could be induced to do anything in the name of Honour'.

11. *the 30th Floréal, year VI.* 19 May 1798.

12. *I couldn't count them all.* The fleet was vast – about 400 ships. It carried 38,000 soldiers and a host of scientists, antiquarians and orientalists. It was known as the 'left wing of the Army of England'.

13. *at least six leagues.* Since a French league is 2·49 miles this was nearly 15 miles across.

14. *three other frigates.* A frigate was a light, fast warship, not of the line, with

light medium to quite heavy armament (28 guns up to as many as 60), and very superior sail and signals. Frigates could be adventurous, fast-running fighting ships, much loved of young and ambitious captains. They fought other frigates, enforced order on the seas, snapped up enemy transports and merchant ships, corsairs, etc., and acted as scouts for the fleet (as here). In large-scale actions fought strictly to the rules they did not engage with the big two- or three-deck warships – the men-of-war or ships of the line – nor ships of the line with them. Modern frigates have a largely anti-submarine function.

15. *the 24th Prairial.* 14 June; actually the fleet arrived at Valetta on 12 June, but perhaps Vigny is lightly stressing the remoteness of the memory.

16. *the standard of religion slowly lowered itself on Gozo and the fortress of St Elmo.* No doubt a flag carrying the eight-pronged cross of St John Hospitaller. Gozo is the smaller island neighbour – about twelve miles from Valetta as the crow flies.

It was part of Napoleon's general plan for expansion in the East to capture Malta – strategically vital for sea routes in the Mediterranean – from the ancient international chivalric crusading order, the Knights of St John of Jerusalem. They had been there since 1530, and had offered an important scourge and check on Turkish shipping in the surrounding seas, but had become an anachronism. According to Napoleon the Order 'no longer served a purpose; it fell because it had to fall'. He is also recorded as proclaiming at this time: 'My Glory is already threadbare. This little Europe is too small a field. Great celebrity can only be won in the East.' The sober Admiral Collingwood (see below, n.21) thought that the Egyptian expedition was a 'plan which has long been in contemplation in France, for the opening of a trade with India by the Red Sea, and supplying Europe with the produce of the East without the long, circuitous journey around the Cape of Good Hope'.

The island capitulated after only very slight resistance (three French casualties). Had it held out long enough for the English fleet to arrive the Egyptian expedition might well have been destroyed, and history very different. In September 1800 Malta did surrender to the Royal Navy.

17. Orient . . . *vast and still. The Orient* was an enormous triple-decked, 120-gun warship, one of the greatest of its time; cf. the nocturnal impressions of the artist Denon, also on the *Junon*, when ordered to the *Orient* on 27 June: 'It would be difficult to convey an exact idea of what we felt as we approached the inner sanctum of power, dictating its orders amidst 300 sail, in the mystery and silence of the night, with only the moon lighting the spectacle just enough to take it in. We were about 500 of us on deck: one could have heard the buzzing of a fly.' (Quoted in Herold, op. cit.)

18. *Casabianca, the captain . . . and . . . the captain's son.* Casabianca and his son were both lost when the *Orient* blew to pieces a few weeks later (2 August) at the Battle of the Nile in Aboukir Bay. However, for fictional purposes, Vigny saves the boy. See the following chapter.

19. *recessed on to a sharp chin.* Cf. Herold, op. cit.: 'he had the face of an eagle and the hairdo of a spaniel'.

20. *the 18th Brumaire* – The coup against the royalist Directors on 9 November 1799 by which Bonaparte became First Consul.

21. *Sent to France . . . permission.* (In English in the original.) Cuthbert Collingwood, Vice-Admiral and Baron (1758–1810), was Nelson's principal lieutenant. As a very young man he had fought at Bunker Hill against the American rebels. In 1778 he joined Nelson's *Lowestoft*. He was captain of the *Barfleur* at the Glorious First of June in 1794, and did extremely well with the *Excellent* at Cape St Vincent in 1797. He commanded the lee division at Trafalgar and was ennobled for his part in this battle. Consequent on the death of Nelson he proceeded to oversee almost continuous blockades of the French and Spanish coasts (see below), having been given his squadron in 1805.

22. *my child, that you.* The reader may like to note that in the following Colonel Renaud's rather formal manner to his son is both qualified and enforced by the use of *tu*.

23. *the valiant Brueys.* François Paul Brueys d'Aigaïlliers (1753–98) was the French admiral in command of the fleet that took Malta. Proceeding to Egypt, he thought he had achieved a position where he was safe from attack in Aboukir Bay – until Nelson sailed inside and destroyed him on 1–2 August 1798.

24. *you will become a Seid.* Voltaire's coinage for a blind fanatic. In his play *Mahomet*, Séide is a slave of Mahomet's who becomes his first convert.

25. *the 1st Vendemaire, year VII.* 22 September 1798, the French New Year.

26. *the Institute.* Napoleon was a member of the Institute of France, but this is probably the Institute of Egypt, which had been established on 22 August for the propagation of science in Egypt, and for research into every aspect of its natural, historical, industrial and political life. Napoleon had modestly had himself elected as vice-president.

27. *the Pasha's Kehayah, the Emir, the members of the Divan and the Agas.* The Pasha was the representative of the Sultan in Egypt; the Kehayah, his aide-de-camp or usher; the Emir, his commander-in-chief; the Agas, senior officers; and the Divan, the Council.

28. *Abdallah-Menou.* General Jacques Menou, who became Commander-in-Chief in Egypt after Kléber's assassination in 1800. He had married an Egyptian and converted to Islam, probably for political reasons. He was a harsh and enthusiastic colonizer who quickly lost the country to Anglo-Turkish forces.

29. *Chapter 5: An unreported conversation.* General historical considerations in this chapter:

The following interview scene speaks primarily for Vigny's dramatic vision of the inherent possibilities and demands of rampant military dictatorship. Factual accuracy is not an aim; so it is no criticism to remark that neither the historical situation of the Pope's coronation visit to Paris, nor the attitude of the two parties, are strictly in accord with the probable facts, save in some externals – Vigny seems to have collated it with the truly hostile meeting of 1813, with calculated anachronism. Nevertheless its essential truth and its imaginative implications are so considerable that it is useful to recall the background to the Emperor's demands.

Since the earliest medieval times the relations of the Two Swords – the imperial and papal powers – their claims and counter-claims to final supremacy under God, had been at or near the centre of European political history. The conflict was never settled. In every territory and at almost every level of society it found its branch or its mirror in shifting struggles and pacts between secular and ecclesiastical authorities. And although after the rise of nation states (especially France), the succeeding hegemony of the Habsburgs in Spain and central Europe, and the Reformation, the Pope–Emperor confrontation had receded from the forefront of events to an often secondary position, it had never been less than portentous. To speak only of public affairs rather than intimate histories: it had been the reason or the pretext for countless battles, feuds, machinations, intra-Christian crusades, assassinations, etc. – all sorts of death and all sorts of endeavour. Libraries of argument, from the finely intellectual to the grossly abusive, were filled with it.

And, of course, relations with the Church were of the greatest importance to the ruler of Roman Catholic subjects.

The official reconciliation of the up until then revolutionary and regicide French Republic with the Church was enacted in the Concordat of June 1801. Such a reconciliation was strongly opposed by the republican 'ideologue' faction in the country – a continuation of the eighteenth-century rationalist tradition which included many powerful people, including Fouché, an ex-Oratorian priest and celebrated Chief of Police, and Talleyrand, ex-bishop and foreign minister. There was also much powerful anti-clerical feeling, particularly in the army.

Speaking brutally, Napoleon saw religion primarily as a political instrument – and was prepared, like a Roman consul, to be tolerant of any faith which reinforced social order. Of Islam in Egypt (Ali-Bonaparte), and of Judaism – it was he who destroyed the ghettos in Rome and Venice, and in 1808 even tried to convene a pre-diaspora Sanhedrin. As to Christianity, remarks often quoted are: 'In religion I do not see the mystery of the Incarnation, but the mystery of the social order', and 'Society is impossible without inequality, inequality intolerable without a code of morality, and a code of morality unacceptable without religion.'

This Pope was Pius VII (Gregorio Chiaramonti, 1742–1823, Pope from 1800). Thought of initially as a French ally, he consecrated Napoleon as Emperor in 1804 – as here. He had known Napoleon as General Bonaparte during the Italian campaigns, when he was himself only Bishop of Imola. At that time he had been persuaded that co-operation with France would benefit Christianity, and the Church. His election as Pope, just before Marengo, had been opposed by Austria. So Napoleon in Vigny's scene is able to produce uncomfortable truths and insinuations. Later the Pope was imprisoned by him, first in Italy, then in France, from 1809 to 1814. He replied by excommunication, as many previous Popes had to previous Emperors.

With this in mind, we note that among other things in what follows: (a) Napoleon is not merely returning to the claims of Charlemagne who 'revived Rome' from his power base in the Frankish lands of northern Europe in the eighth century, and to the origin of the imperialist ideal asserted in his coronation at Rome in 800. Napoleon wants to go further and show the Pope to be identifiably inferior – and did in fact crown himself. (b) By invoking comparison with Charlemagne he is amusingly predicting his own rule over all Europe – in 1804 he controlled only France and Northern Italy. (c) In his wish for the Pope to move to Paris he is exploding tradition almost to the point of farce (as Pius VII perceives). Quite apart from centuries of tradition, this would be virtually blasphemous to upholders of the Petrine Roman tradition – and perhaps a revival of the dependency on the rulers of France which obtained during the removal of the papacy to Avignon in the fourteenth century.

30. *curtains sewn with bees*. Imperial bees: an emblem in common with – perhaps derived from? – that of the Barberini in Rome, themselves a papal family.

31. *defrocked Oratorian*. Fouché; see n.29 above.

32. *sign away the liberties . . . like Louis XIV*. A reference to the Edict of Nantes, 1682 – which asserted a large measure of independence for the Gallican church – and to its Revocation in 1685.

33. *Secretary of Florence*. Machiavelli, no doubt.

34. *I create my Iliad by my actions, create it day by day*. Alexander the Great is said by Arrian to have slept with the *Iliad* under his pillow.

35. *her lawyer Raguideau who said that I had nothing except my cloak and sword*. Napoleon is said (by Marshal Bourienne, dictating in old age) to have overheard Raguideau's advice through a half-closed door, and then, on the eve of his coronation (i.e. just after this scene), summoned the lawyer, recalled his words,

and shown him the imperial mantle and ceremonial sword ready for the next day.

36. *the camp at Boulogne*. A huge affair – see below – established in 1803 to threaten London.

37. *three aims: to disturb England, to lull Europe, and to concentrate and galvanize the army*. The interpretations of some modern historians are in accord with this. Caligula as well as Caesar had camped on this site.

But, as with the comparable case of Hitler in 1940, others would claim that the intention really to invade across the Channel was much more serious, at least at first. 'Let us be masters of the straits for six hours and we shall be masters of the world,' Napoleon wrote to his admiral, Latouche Tréville – and the 'Army of England' was a very formidable body indeed, renamed in 1805 'the Grand Army'. Oliver Warner (in *Vice-Admiral Lord Collingwood*, 1968) thinks that 'Napoleon was . . . never more in earnest'. (As usual there were fantasies about a tunnel, actually mooted by Napoleon in 1802.)

The flat-bottomed vessels, probably prams, on one of which Renaud sails, were meant as troop-carriers and landing-craft. Large numbers had been built and mustered right down the western coast of France. However, as we see, the English blockade of Brest and Toulon and all adjacent seas was as effective as it was exhausting to the blockaders; the French never became masters of the sea, and the project was finally broken up in August 1805, two months before Trafalgar.

38. *the machine at Marly*. Louis XIV's vast and complicated apparatus for pumping water to Versailles was built in 1685, eight kilometres away at the King's private retreat, the palace of Marly. It was considered to be a wonder of the world. Whether Vigny means by his comparison that its element was water, or that it was near defunct (the palace of Versailles being empty from 1793, and the machine demolished in 1805), or both, is unclear to me.

39. *the* Noyade. 'The Drowner'.

40. *Lord Collingwood*. In history Collingwood was not ennobled quite yet – not until after Trafalgar, 20 October 1805, while Renaud is captured sometime in December 1804.

41 *The frigate*. An obvious slip of Renaud's. The *Victory* is, of course, Nelson's flagship, and one of the most important ships of the line.

42. *mon enfant*. In English – 'my child' – in the original.

43. *the countenance of a Regulus*. Marcus Atilius Regulus was the Roman consul who, in 250 B.C., returned as a hostage to Carthage to suffer a horrible death rather than break his word to his captors.

44. *pauvre garçon*. In English – 'poor boy' – in the original.

45. *Clarissa . . . Lovelace . . . has left it unstained*. This response to *Clarissa*

(1747–8) was indeed so widespread that Richardson says he wrote *Sir Charles Grandison* (1754) – the portrait of the virtuous man – to counter it. The creation of Lovelace, in going beyond the overt intention of the work, is famously comparable to that of Satan in *Paradise Lost*.

46. *Grotius.* The Latin name for Hugues de Groot (1583–1645), the great Dutch military jurist and theorist of diplomatic representation. He was the author of *De Jure Belli et Pacis*, among other important works; he was also a poet.

47. *he constantly exercised his crews.* 'It was Collingwood's belief that if a ship could fire three well-directed broadsides in five minutes, no enemy could resist them, and in the *Dreadnought* he had been able to cut down the time to three minutes and a half' (Oliver Warner, *Trafalgar*, 1959). In the *Excellent* in 1798 he had achieved three broadsides in a minute and a half.

48. *watched over them and for them.* Robert Hay, who served as a seaman in the *Culloden* under Collingwood in 1804, wrote: 'He and his dog Bounce were known to every member of the crew. How attentive he was to the health and comfort and happiness of his crew! A man who could not be happy under him, could have been happy nowhere; a look of displeasure from him was as bad as a dozen at the gangway from another man.'

49. *as often as they pleased.* In French *and* English (in brackets) in the original.

50. *. . . vapouring about my dangers.* This last sentence is almost exactly the wording of a letter from Collingwood to his wife, written from the *Ocean* on 22 May 1806. The previous sentences paraphrase and draw expressions from a letter of 9 March 1808. Vigny had made extensive use of *A Selection from the Public and Private Correspondence of Vice-Admiral Lord Collingwood, interspersed with Memoirs of his Life*, by G. L. Newham Collingwood, London, 1828. 'There are no words to tell what the heart feels in reading the simple phrases of such a hero,' wrote Thackeray a few years after. 'Here is victory and courage, but love sublimer and superior.'

Oliver Warner in *Vice-Admiral Lord Collingwood*, op. cit., says of Vigny's portrait in general: 'In this striking work, although liberties were taken with the facts of Collingwood's career, a true impression of his character and achievement was conveyed by a French writer of distinction.'

51. *Montecucculi.* Raimondo Montecuccoli (1609–80), Count, Prince, Duke of Melfi, was an Italian in the Austrian imperial service who inflicted several notable reverses on the Swedes in the Thirty Years War and afterwards. In 1664 he halted the Turkish advance at Raab with a relatively small force, and was hailed as the saviour of Europe. In 1673 he started a duel with the French under Turenne (see n.11 to Book 1) in southern Germany, the climax of which – in 1675 at Sasbach – Vigny refers to. (But the campaign was resumed against Condé.) He was also a very influential military theorist, and made the famous

remark that 'For war you need three things, 1. Money. 2. Money. 3. Money.'

52. *Kings of the South asking his protection.* This is very likely a reference to the complex dealings that Collingwood, as both military and diplomatic chief, had with the King of the Two Sicilies, the Emperor of Morocco, the Sultan, the Bey of Tunis, and innumerable shifting Turkish beys and pashas in Egypt, in Greece and the Greek Islands, etc. It was all a part of the perpetual and intense jockeying with French power and influence that served to maintain and extend the British grip on the Mediterranean.

53. *French compliments.* In English in the original.

54. *Lord Mulgrave.* First Lord of the Admiralty, who was, peculiarly, an army general. One of his reasons, unknown to Collingwood (or Vigny), for keeping the worn-out admiral at his arduous post was the necessity for preventing the Duke of Clarence – later William IV – from being able to claim it as his royal due.

There is an admirable fictional account of a formidable and dying admiral in the Mediterranean in this period – Admiral Thornton, flagship the *Ocean* – in Patrick O'Brian's *The Ionian Mission* (1981).

55. *mon enfant.* In English – 'my child' – in the original.

56. *Murat, King of Naples.* Joachim Murat (1767–1815) was the son of an innkeeper who became a colonel in the revolutionary armies, and married Napoleon's sister Caroline. He was famous for his courage, dash and tactical brilliance as a cavalry general, though not for his strategic sense. He was made Marshal in 1804, King of Naples in 1808. He was a ruthless suppressor of the revolt against the French in Spain.

57. *the King of Spain.* This was Joseph Bonaparte (1768–1844), Napoleon's elder brother, King of Naples and Sicily 1806–8, and King of Spain 1808–13. He was known as a humane ruler.

58. *Crescentini sang* Les Horaces. Girolamo Crescentini (1766–1846) was a celebrated Italian castrato. He had been choirmaster at Vienna, but came to Paris at Napoleon's request, and affirmed that henceforward he would sing only at the Tuileries for the Emperor. He stayed until 1812.

Les Horaces could be either a lyric tragedy of that name by Guillard (1786), or *Gli Orazii e Curiazii*, which was written for Crescentini by Cimarosa (1796).

59. *braggarts about their crimes.* 'Fanfaron de crimes' was Louis XIV's description of his nephew, the duc d'Orléans.

60. *the Prussian Bülow.* Count Friedrich Wilhelm Bülow von Dennewitz (1755–1815) was prominent in the culminating campaigns against Napoleon. He was at Möckern and Leipzig in 1813, effected the capture of Montmartre later in 1814, and was at Waterloo in 1815.

61. *Macdonald.* Jacques Étienne Joseph Alexandre Macdonald (1765–1840) was a descendant of Scots Jacobite exiles to France and a revolutionary general. After a quiet middle period in his career, spent in Italy, he broke the Austrian centre at Wagram in 1809, and was made a Marshal on the battlefield itself (a unique honour). Later he negotiated Napoleon's abdication.

62. *Woronzoff.* Mikhail Semenovich Vorontsov (1782–1856), Russian Field Marshal. He fought against both the Turks and the French, and commanded at Craonne on 7 March 1814, when Napoleon won one of his brilliant small later battles against the invading allies. He was later chief of the Russian occupation army in France.

63. *Polybius . . . Folard and Vauban.* Polybius (*c.* 205–*c.* 123 B.C.) was a Greek nobleman who, when a hostage in Rome after the conquest of Macedonia in 168, became a close friend of Scipio Aemilianus. He was present at the destruction of Carthage in 146, and helped to obtain favourable terms for the Greek states after the taking of Corinth in the same year. His *History* – in forty books, of which only five survive – sets out to examine why it was that the power of Rome had come to dominate the world he knew.

The Chevalier de Folard (1669–1752), who had fought against the Turks and under Charles XII of Sweden, was the author of *Commentaries* on Polybius, which were much used in military schools.

Sébastien le Prestre de Vauban (1633–1707) was a Marshal of France and probably the world's most celebrated and innovative military engineer. He served under Condé and Turenne, and besides putting a cordon of fortresses around France during 1678–88, he pioneered methods of attack and defence and fortification which both contained and furthered the new uses of artillery. Among his inventions are the socket bayonet and the use of ricochet fire.

64. *28th to 29th.* A mistake, though trifling. In view of the other dates given, and the historical circumstances, it should be 29th to 30th.

65. *his replacement.* Under most systems of conscription – until the modern age of total democratic war – it was acceptable for the better-off to pay for a substitute soldier instead of serving themselves.

66. *the poet . . . deplored his situation in our society.* Notably in *Stello* (1831). This consists of stories in the form of a dialogue (between the representatives of Sentiment and cold Reason) about three unfortunate poets: Gilbert, who starved under the *ancien régime*; Chatterton, who committed suicide under constitutional monarchy; and André Chenier, who was guillotined during the Reign of Terror.

67. *what the altar of the Lesser Fortune was for a Roman soldier.* Such altars are not to be found. John Hayward in a note to Humphrey Hare's *The Military Necessity* (1953) conjectures some confusion with the altar of 'Home bringing Fortune' (Fortuna Redux) which was associated with the military in Rome.

But in any case there were many cults of Fortuna in Roman times, and the purport is clear – that there should be a focal point for military community, consolation and re-dedication.

68. *the progress of invention.* François Germain notes here that such optimistic views were characteristic of French intellectuals of the 1830s, and mentions Lamartine, Victor Hugo, the Saint-Simonians, Ballanche and Tocqueville. I argue that in Vigny's case adherence to them was complicated.

69. *this cross is rarely by their side.* The last three sentences refer to the lavish intellectual and aesthetic reaction against eighteenth-century rationality and Enlightenment which in its specifically Roman Catholic forms in France was led and represented by such figures as Chateaubriand, Lamartine, Maistre, Ballanche, Bonald, Lamennais – and even Vigny himself.

70. *a hundred Belzunces.* François de Belzunce (1671–1755), Bishop of Marseilles, was famous for his Christian heroism during the plague in that city in 1720–21.

71. *active decency.* In French *pudeur virile*, which literally translated – 'manly shame' – seems at once too definite (it carries the contrast with 'womanly' too bluntly, and also has a negative feeling in 'shame' which is quite out of place – the same goes for 'bashfulness', 'modesty', 'discretion', etc.) and too limited for the open and positive direction of the argument.

72. *the utterance of human language.* That the terminology here (*parole . . . mot . . . chose . . . langue*) reminds one of late twentieth-century French linguistics and metaphysics is probably not much more than a function of vocabulary. The impulse of Vigny's austerely hopeful argument is strongly inimical to the self-consciously playful, nihilistic and sceptical drift of the latter. – Though one could argue that they are both attempted answers to the same sorts of question.

73. *the unknown God.* i.e. the true God. – 'Then Paul stood in the midst of Mars' hill, and said, Ye men of Athens, I perceive that in all things you are too superstitious. For as I passed by, and beheld your devotions, I found an altar with this inscription, TO THE UNKNOWN GOD. Whom therefore ye ignorantly worship, him I declare unto you' (Acts 17: 22–3).

74. *reborn Theban Band.* There were two Theban bands, both of them fitting in their varying ways: (1) The much celebrated formation made up of pairs of young citizen soldiers who served under Epaminondas and Pelopidas, and whose bravery was guaranteed by their fighting under the eyes of their lovers. This won the great victories of Leuctra (371 B.C.) and Mantinea (362), but was destroyed by Philip of Macedon at Chaeronea in 338. (2) A third-century A.D. cohort of auxiliaries from the Thebaid led by (St) Maurice, and stationed in Gaul, who are said to have become Christians and refused to persecute their fellow believers or make the sacrifices required by the Roman state. They were first decimated, then massacred.